Murder by the Seashore

Murder by the Seashore

A CALIFORNIA BOOKSHOP MYSTERY

Samara Yew

CROOKED
LANE

NEW YORK

Copyright © 2023 by Samara Yew

Published in the United States by Crooked Lane Books, an imprint of The Quick Brown Fox & Company LLC.

Crooked Lane Books and its logo are trademarks of The Quick Brown Fox & Company LLC.

Library of Congress Catalog-in-Publication data available upon request.

ISBN (hardcover): 978-1-63910-493-2
ISBN (ebook): 978-1-63910-494-9

Cover illustration by Rob Fiore

Printed in the United States.

www.crookedlanebooks.com

Crooked Lane Books
34 West 27th St., 10th Floor
New York, NY 10001

First Edition: October 2023

10 9 8 7 6 5 4 3 2 1

To my dad (Bob Kroeker, because I know he'll be so excited to see his name in a book). Thank you for passing on your love of reading and Southern California to me. Somehow, together, those loves became this book.

Chapter One

The involuntary morning mantra that had been running through my head every day for the past four months began at its usual time, nine thirty AM. It was half an hour before Palm Trees and Page Turners opened for the day, and right as I was getting ready to carefully count the float in the cash register.

I can do this. I can do this. I can do this.

"Scarlett? Are you here? I brought your favorite iced chai latte from the Sunshine Café."

Evelyn Maxwell's cheery voice almost broke my concentration, but I had a few more bills to count. I answered with a quick "I'm here."

Evelyn came over to the register and set the iced latte in front of me. She turned toward the nearest shelf to finish straightening the messy books we hadn't had time to clean up after closing yesterday.

I can do this. I can do this. I can do this.

"Thanks for the iced latte." I closed the cash register drawer and took a delicious sip of the cold drink. "What's the occasion?"

"Sunday," Evelyn said, like it was the most obvious answer in the world.

I raised an eyebrow, hoping to encourage more of a response.

"It's our busiest day. Lots of tourists start their vacations on Sunday, and many locals have the day off. I figured you could use a pick-me-up." She added the last part quickly, and I caught exactly what she meant.

I could use a pick-me-up after what had happened last Sunday. She probably wanted to avoid having to console away another almost meltdown of her employer after such a stressful day at Palm Trees and Page Turners.

Embarrassment swept over me again at the memory of locking the door behind our last customer and turning around to find Evelyn holding a box of tissues, knowing I was about to cry. Our debit machine had crashed in the middle of an afternoon rush right before the receipt printer ran out of ink, and I'd had no idea how to refill it. We'd had to make ugly handwritten receipts for every customer for the rest of the day.

Over the past few months since Connor had left, I'd quickly realized there was more to running a bookshop than simply being a huge bookworm. Though, in my defense, I'd had the perfect solution before we opened for business: I would take care of the literary side, aka the fun side, while Connor took care of the business side with his knowledge and expertise.

Then he left. And now here I was, thrown into a crash course on bookkeeping, inventory, hiring, and payroll, when all I wanted to do was stock the shelves with our beautiful books and organize them by genre and author. I wanted to spend time chatting with customers and helping them find exactly what they were looking for to enrich their time in Oceanside.

"Thanks, Evelyn. I appreciate it."

"You're welcome. I'm sure today will be easier."

Evelyn, my one employee, was as sweet as the latte she'd brought me, though I planned on hiring extra help for the busy summer months ahead. Evelyn had moved here around the same time Connor had broken up with both me and our business, and she'd been my saving grace. Palm and Page, as I called it for short, would've gone under by now if it hadn't been for her motherly encouragement that kept me going every day. She admitted to not having much business sense either but was always willing to try, and we were learning together.

In a few more minutes we would unlock our doors, and already a couple of people had gathered to wait on the sidewalk, including two women who looked to be in their early twenties, probably starting their summer break from university. Sure enough, one of them wore a UCLA T-shirt. They were exactly our target customer, tourists and locals looking for something to read on the Southern California beach right outside the shop.

"Why don't I take the cash register for the first shift and you go back and enjoy the rest of your drink?" Evelyn's dark-brown eyes were warm, and she went to unlock the front doors and greet our customers before I had a chance to reply.

After taking a look around the bookshop to make sure no one needed extra help right away, I went into the back. It consisted of a small office, a washroom, a bit of storage, and a table and two chairs to use for our breaks. The table doubled as a sorting area for our incoming shipments.

The little bell above the front door kept jingling, and Evelyn's friendly greeting rang out over and over again. The store was picking up, so I quickly finished my iced latte and scarfed down a banana. As I headed back into the main part of the store, I gathered what I could of my short, feathery blond hair into a nub of a ponytail. I was all set to assist customers in finding their perfect beach read while Evelyn manned the cash register.

The morning flew by. We swapped back and forth on the register but didn't have time for any task other than helping customers. Tidying the store and office work would have to wait.

Finally, there was a small break in the flow, and I sent Evelyn back to have her lunch.

"Excuse me, where's your romance section?" a woman wearing a sundress and floppy beach hat asked. "That's the perfect genre to read while on vacation, in my opinion."

"I agree." I grinned—these interactions were my favorite moments—and led her toward our romance books, which were right in the middle of the store as the largest section. She was far from my only customer who thought romances were a dreamy escape on vacation.

"Thank you so much. You have a great selection." She eagerly started running a finger along the spines.

I hoped she'd grab more than one.

The rest of the day was more or less the same. Tourists came in, ready to snatch the perfect book, and a few locals as well, who also loved reading on the beach when they had the time. Some were quick to buy a book and go; others took a while to browse and wanted to talk about their favorite genres and authors. I personally loved to read all sorts of books, so I was knowledgeable about anything they asked that was book related.

An hour before closing, the customer traffic slowed as focus shifted to the nighttime dining and entertainment Oceanside offered. Maybe I'd even be able to close early; my feet were killing me. But I often thought that, and there was always that last customer of the day who showed up five minutes before closing.

Sure enough, a woman who looked to be in her early fifties came in right on the 5:55 PM mark.

My eye twitched briefly, but I plastered on a bright smile. "Welcome to Palm Trees and Page Turners."

She gave a quick smile in return before ducking behind the closest bookshelf. She seemed like a grab-and-go customer, at least.

It was less than a minute later when she walked up to the counter with a copy of *Northanger Abbey* by Jane Austen, pinpointing her as a classics fan.

"Did you find everything you were looking for?" I rang up her purchase.

"Yes. Thank you." The woman pushed her grayish-blond bangs out of her eyes and smiled shyly. "You have a lovely store."

"Oh, thank you so much." I didn't even bother keeping the pride out of my voice. I'd overcome a lot to keep Palm and Page open. "I've only been in business a couple of months, but we're already very popular. I love connecting with fellow readers."

"Sounds like a dream job to me." The woman handed me some crumpled bills, a purple-beaded bracelet dangling from her wrist. "I'll stop in again sometime during my vacation."

"Please do. Here's your receipt and book. Thank you for coming."

I walked with her toward the front and said another good-bye at the door, locking it behind her. Whew, another day down. And bonus: no meltdowns today!

"Are we closed?" Evelyn asked from behind a shelf, where she was restocking books.

I could see only the ends of her gray-tinged black curls peeking out.

"Yes! Let's finish up and go home. I'm starving." I headed toward the cash register to count out what we'd made to deposit on my way home.

"What's on the menu for your dinner tonight?"

"Lucia said she was going to pick up a pizza for us. We're going to kick off the week with a movie night." I was always thankful when my roommate came home with takeout. It was a nice break from cooking, though when one of us made dinner, we made enough for us both, so I only cooked during half the week anyway.

"Sounds like a fun night. Steve said he'll cook dinner tonight, though I have no idea what he'll whip up. Always an adventure with that one in the kitchen." Evelyn's mild annoyance betrayed the love and admiration I knew she had for her husband, the newest detective on the Oceanside police force. They truly were best friends. "All I know is it'll be smothered in ketchup."

I laughed with Evelyn before turning back to counting the cash and organizing the receipts for that day. We might even have made it close to our previous daily sales record. I had a feeling that number would only grow as we got further into summer. I was both excited and nervous about my first tourist season as a business owner in Oceanside, or O'side, as I'd learned the locals fondly called it.

Soon we said good-bye and went our separate ways out of the parking lot. After I stopped at the bank, it was a short drive to the townhouse complex where I lived with Lucia Armenta. The sun was setting over the ocean in my rearview mirror as I drove inland, making for a beautiful evening with the gold-and-pink rays dancing across the shallow waves.

I pulled into the driveway of our two-bedroom townhouse beside Lucia's car. Knowing the pizza was already waiting, my stomach rumbled appreciatively. I'd lucked out in the roommate department. We'd quickly become BFFs, despite having met through a ROOM-MATE WANTED ad online a few months ago. Those sometimes had horror stories behind them, but Lucia was great and had a fun sense of humor.

"Mmm, smells good," I said as soon as I unlocked the front door.

Our townhouse had a large living room, kitchen, and half-bath on the first floor, with two bedrooms, another bathroom, and what had been advertised as a den on the second. Currently, the small den was being used for random storage until we settled our debate over what to do with it. I wanted a library/reading nook. Lucia wanted her own mini kickboxing gym. Definitely not two things that could easily share the same space.

"It's all set." Lucia's voice came from our living room.

The pizza box had been placed on the coffee table between two plates and two cups of iced tea. The TV was paused on the opening screen of *Jurassic Park*.

"Really?" I groaned. "This movie again?"

"Hey, you know the rules. The one who picks up the food gets to pick the movie." Lucia grinned wickedly, her brown eyes shining. "And you know how I feel about Spielberg."

"The greatest filmmaker who ever lived," we said at the same time, my monotone completely opposite Lucia's obvious admiration. She was the biggest film buff I'd ever met. I could ask her a question about any movie, and she'd know the answer. If she didn't, she wouldn't be able to concentrate on anything else until she found out what it was.

"I hope you at least got the deluxe pizza." I opened the box and took in a deep breath. "You're the best."

Lucia laughed and patted the blue sectional couch beside her. "Let's get started. I can't wait to find out what happens." She winked at me, and I groaned again at her joke. Like she didn't have this movie memorized.

Sure enough, she started her running commentary the second she pressed start—a continuous dialogue of fun facts about the making of the movie, the actors involved, and the memorable John Williams score. I honestly didn't mind, though; it was almost more entertaining than the movie.

Chapter Two

The early-morning sunlight streamed through the gap in my blinds, shining right in my eyes. I moaned and tossed over to the other side of the bed, mentally kicking myself for forgetting to make sure the blinds had been closed tight. I usually did this at least twice a week.

Shortly after that, my alarm went off, so no more sleep for me. Sitting up, I put my purple-framed glasses on and remembered the ridiculous dream I'd had about dinosaurs chasing me. Lucia had been behind an old-fashioned movie camera trying to capture the whole thing on film. I was momentarily annoyed with her for not trying to save me from the dinosaurs before I shook it off, reminding myself it'd only been a dream. Real-life Lucia would surely save me from rampaging dinosaurs.

I headed downstairs into the kitchen and turned on the coffee-maker. While waiting for my first cup of the day, I stared out the window over the kitchen sink. If I tilted my head and squinted, I could almost make out some distant ocean waves. Almost. But at least our landlord hadn't advertised this place as having an "ocean view," like our poor next-door neighbor's had. Jules Moore brought up every chance she could how she'd been tricked.

"Good morning." Lucia slumped down on a kitchen stool and slowly reached for her favorite Star Wars mug from our mug tree.

"Morning, sleepyhead. You're usually more chipper in the mornings." I poured coffee into my favorite mug—a blue one that read *Just One More Chapter*—and then into her *May the Force Be With You* one.

"I was up way too late going down the Google rabbit trail of *Jurassic Park* facts. I came across this interesting article about the hurricane that hit the filming set."

I turned my back so Lucia couldn't see my eye roll. Of course she'd done that. "Don't you have that company fraud court case starting today?"

"Yes." She yawned. "It's not until this afternoon, though. Maybe no one will notice if I have a quick catnap at my desk this morning."

Lucia was a junior associate at one of the top law firms in Oceanside, and her reputation for being one of the best was quickly growing. She could easily one day be some shark lawyer in a megacity somewhere, but I knew she'd never move far away from the ocean and the small-city feel of Oceanside.

"You better hope no one will notice, especially that Martin Russell."

"He's been out of town lately, thankfully. Not that he'd be able to do anything about it. The case is already mine. But he could send that minion of his to spy on me. What's her name again? Shelly?" Lucia mumbled to herself now, and the reminder of her work nemesis seemed to wake her up as she rose from the counter and headed back to her bedroom with her coffee mug. She and Martin were always in competition over who could get the better cases and clients. And I knew she would rather give up watching her favorite movies than let him beat her at anything.

Lucia slammed dresser drawers and turned the shower on. I grinned at her sudden determination to restart her day as I opened the pantry door to search for something for breakfast. There was only half a box of cereal left, and I made a mental note to go grocery shopping after work. It was my turn to make dinner, after all.

I hadn't even finished my breakfast and coffee when Lucia came back into the kitchen, all dressed and ready for the day, her shiny jet-black hair still damp.

"I'll see you after work." She grabbed a banana from the fruit basket on the counter.

"No breakfast?"

She waved the banana. "I'll get something more on the way. Have a good day."

Alone, I thought about the day ahead. Mondays were usually busy. Not as much as the weekend, but it would still be eight hours on my feet again. I packed a sandwich and apple for lunch, then tossed a candy bar on top. I could use a sugar boost for the afternoon.

I arrived earlier than usual at Palm Trees and Page Turners, since I hadn't gotten my typical breakfast chat time with Lucia. I parked my car in the spot closest to the beach, and the quiet morning waves lapping on the shore seemed to call to me. I headed inside to toss my lunch in the minifridge in the back before going right out for a short morning walk along the beach.

I swapped my regular glasses for my prescription sunglasses and breathed in a deep breath of the salty air. Instinctively, my smile spread, an automatic reaction to my love of the ocean. I'd spent almost my entire life living inland near Phoenix up until about six months ago, when I'd moved to start Palm and Page. But even though I hadn't grown up in a beach town, now I couldn't imagine living anywhere else. The ocean was a part of me. My favorite vacations had always been the ones where my parents would pack our minivan full of beach balls, sand buckets, and water floaties and we'd spend the week at a seaside motel creating sandcastles and chasing the waves.

Murder by the Seashore

A few morning surfers sat among the soft swells, though it didn't look as if they would catch anything big just yet. Only a gentle breeze ruffled the top of the water. If you weren't a surfer, though, it was an absolutely perfect day. The beach was filling up with people staking their claim along the sand, and I set out to weave my way through laid-out towels and sun umbrellas.

My feet sank in the sand, and I wished I'd worn flip-flops instead, but those would be murder to my feet by the end of the day, so comfy sneakers it was. I planned right then to keep an extra pair of flip-flops at work for impromptu beach walks like this one.

A sea gull cawed loudly near my ear, startling me from my daydreaming. My mind had wandered, and I'd started thinking aimlessly about the gorgeous water beside me, completely forgetting about the busy day ahead. I pulled my cell phone out of my pocket to check the time. Nine twenty-five. I spotted the Oceanside Pier ahead and decided to turn around there.

The pier was Oceanside's most famous landmark. Every tourist, and probably every local, had a photo of themselves on the pier. I had to admit it was an elegant, though rustic, structure, with its tall lampposts lining either side of the deck. It was something out of a storybook at night. Very romantic. The memory of my first date with Connor after I'd moved to Oceanside to be near him popped into my head. After dinner, we had wandered down to the end of the pier, where he'd kissed me deeply, surrounded by the ocean.

Now I rolled my eyes. Had he already known he would break my heart a few weeks later? Had he already gotten the job offer and been keeping it quiet? I tried to convince myself I didn't care, but I was lying.

I'd reached the pier and was about to spin on my heel in the sand to head back to Palm and Page when something pale sticking out near the rocks underneath the pier caught my eye.

Was that a . . . hand?

No, it couldn't be. That would be something straight out of one of Lucia's horror movies.

Still, my stomach turned slightly as I inched forward into the shadows, and my palms started to sweat. I tried to convince myself I was being ridiculous, probably working myself up over nothing. It had to be a piece of garbage or driftwood or something.

Ugh. It was a hand.

I was going to be sick.

The hand was attached to an arm, and that arm was attached to a body slammed against the rocks. A woman, from what I could tell, whose light-colored hair was pasted across her face, damp and tangled with seaweed. Her navy-blue capris and yellow top were crumpled and covered in crusty sand.

I screamed and scrambled backward out from the shadows. My arms started flailing, and I was about to take off running down the beach.

My frantic thoughts paused as I realized running was probably not the best course of action for someone who'd innocently stumbled upon a body. I needed to call the police.

I could handle that. I'd call the police, and then I'd freak out.

I came to a stop and plopped down in the sand, unsure if my feet would be steady enough to hold me while I made the 911 call.

"I found a dead woman on the beach. Under the Oceanside Pier," I said into the phone after the 911 operator answered.

The operator asked if I knew who she was or what had happened—which I didn't. He asked if there were any other signs of danger. I didn't think there were, but I twisted my head around. I saw only a pair of elderly women and a young family who'd stopped a few feet away, nervously glancing around but not coming any closer. He then asked me my name—that one I knew.

Murder by the Seashore

Police often patrolled near the beach, so it wasn't long after I'd hung up that sirens sounded nearby. Two police cruisers arrived, followed soon by an ambulance. I jumped up from my spot on the sand and waved frantically at them, just in case they had no idea where the large pier was in the middle of the beach.

Calm down, Scar. The police know what they're doing.

Still, it was like my arms had a mind of their own, and I couldn't seem to stop waving until the police and paramedics stood right in front of me.

"She's under the pier by the rocks. I have no idea who it is." I pointed toward the pier, still in my trying-to-be-helpful-but-actually-being-completely-useless state.

Another police car showed up, though not a typical patrol car this time. An unmarked car with flashing lights on top. I recognized the tall Black man with short hair who stepped out of the driver's side and headed toward us. It was Detective Maxwell, Evelyn's husband. He often dropped her off at Palm and Page when their schedules worked out, so I knew him well.

"Scarlett? What are you doing here?" Detective Maxwell seemed surprised to find me in the middle of a potential crime scene.

His question caught me off guard. I wasn't sure why, but suddenly I had no idea what I was doing there. "Uhhh . . ." I stared blankly while I waited for my mind to jump-start. "I was going for a walk along the beach when I spotted the woman's body under the pier."

"But doesn't your store open soon?" Detective Maxwell checked his watch.

"It does. I arrived early and wanted to stretch my legs before opening."

He gave me a curious look, then walked past me toward the pier. I wasn't sure if I was supposed to follow or not, so I took a few steps in that direction before the officer hanging up the crime scene tape held out a hand to stop me near the edge of the pier.

"Wait here, please, miss. I'm sure the detective will want to take your statement soon."

My what? "Oh, okay."

I wasn't sure if I wanted to watch or not. I was curious who the poor woman was, but the sight of the dead body was still making my stomach turn. I'd barely made it through high school biology without feeling queasy every class, and I had a strict no-gore rule for Lucia when it came to picking movies. There was no way I could handle watching Detective Maxwell examine a dead body.

My woozy stomach won out, and I turned around to look back at the parking lot while the police and paramedics did their work. I swayed back and forth to distract myself but soon realized my mistake as a paramedic rushed over to my side.

"Miss, are you all right? Do you need to sit down?"

"I'm fine." I tried to sound convincing. The attention tended to make my nausea worse, because it didn't give me a chance to forget about it.

"Are you sure? You're somehow both seasick green and white as a ghost." He now sounded more fascinated than concerned.

Luckily, I was saved from having to convince him further when one of his colleagues called him back to the body. Curious, I looked over to see what was going on. From what I could determine, the police were taking photos of the body and the matted hair had been brushed off the woman's face. My nausea was forgotten as I took in her features. I knew that woman from somewhere but couldn't place her.

I must have gasped without realizing it, because Detective Maxwell was suddenly back at my side. "What is it, Scarlett?"

"I might know her."

"Might?"

"Yes. I recognize her but have no idea from where."

He grunted in frustration. "There's no ID, only a hotel key card for the Five Palms Resort and Casino, so if you could try and remember, it'd help us out. Do you know her from around town?"

I shook my head. "I don't think so. At least, I don't think I've seen her more than once."

"A tourist in your store, perhaps?"

That triggered my memory. "Yes! I think she was in yesterday. But we had so many customers come in, they're all blending together." I thought hard about each of the customers I could remember. Had she come in with someone else? No, I thought she'd been by herself. "Oh! I remember. She was our very last customer of the day. She came in right before closing, bought a copy of *Northanger Abbey*, and left."

"That's something to go by, at least. No name?" The detective sounded hopeful.

"No, sorry. I barely spoke with her."

"Do you remember if she paid with cash or a credit card?"

I went over the exchange from last night in my head. "I think she paid with cash, but I'm not positive. I'll double-check my credit receipts from yesterday and let you know for sure."

"Thank you. Is there anything else you can think of that may be helpful?"

I shook my head. "I wish I did know something. Do you think this was an accident, or . . . ?" I was too horrified at the thought to say it out loud.

Detective Maxwell said nothing for a few moments. Then, quietly, "I'll be honest with you—it's hard to say at this point."

I nodded, lost in my own thoughts.

"I'll need you to come to the station later today to give an official statement. And please bring the information about the credit card receipts. There's nothing more I need from you now."

"Am I able to open the bookshop today?"

"I don't see why not, as long as Evelyn can cover for you to come give your statement."

Despite the go-ahead from the police, I was uneasy about opening. It seemed wrong to go about my normal day when someone's life had ended not that far from the store. It wasn't like I knew her or anything, and I'd spoken to her only the one time, but I felt a connection.

"I'll see you later today, Detective." I took one more look around the beach, a chill running down my spine, before heading back toward the bookshop, still debating whether I wanted to open.

Chapter Three

The small crowd gathered outside the store answered my question for me. These people were eager to find their book companion for their vacation, and it was my job to make sure I didn't let them down.

"Hello. Sorry. Pardon me." I worked my way through the crowd to unlock the front door. "Sorry for the delay. Palm Trees and Page Turners will be open in a few minutes."

The sight of Evelyn inside, scurrying around the store and getting it ready for the day, was a balm to my nerves. I didn't feel as much in a fog as I had a few minutes ago. It was a blessing she was trustworthy enough to not only have a key and the alarm code but to get things going if I was running late. She really was the perfect employee.

She stopped dead in her tracks when I entered. "Scarlett! What happened? I heard all the sirens as I pulled into the parking lot, and then your car was here but you weren't. I was so worried. I tried texting and calling, but no answer."

I pulled my phone out of my pocket, having forgotten it was there. I saw several missed messages and calls from Evelyn as well as a bunch from Lucia. Somehow word already seemed to be spreading about the Jane Doe found under the pier.

"Oh, it was awful." I sucked back a sob. Now wasn't the time to cry. We had a business to run, but I had to tell Evelyn what happened. My voice dropped to a whisper, just in case the tourists outside could hear us. I didn't want to scare them out of Oceanside. "There was a dead woman underneath the pier."

Evelyn dropped the stack of books she was carrying, and I winced, hoping no damage had been done.

"Who was it?" Evelyn's horror reflected my own.

I shrugged. "I have no idea of her name or anything, but I think she was in here yesterday. The last customer of the day. Do you remember her?"

Evelyn shook her head. "Not really, no. Was Steve there?" Her voice held a weird sort of intrigue I couldn't decipher. Was she nervous or relieved her husband had been at the crime scene? I did know that she was worried about him. She'd shared that most of his cases at his previous location had gone unsolved and the transfer had been a not-so-subtle demotion. Evelyn's encouragement could keep anyone going, though, so there was a good chance Detective Maxwell would do fine.

I nodded as I headed toward the cash register to open it. "He told me he didn't know yet if it'd been an accident or . . . you know what." I felt like a little kid unable to say the word, but I couldn't. The image of the body was still too raw in my mind.

"Was it obvious what had killed her, or were there signs of a struggle or anything?"

"Not that I could see, but I honestly didn't look too closely. Anyway, we need to open. Thanks for getting the restock and everything done already."

"Of course. I can always handle the store without you. Are you good for me to unlock the doors?" She started to head to the front of the store.

I hurried to finish my task. "Yes. I'm going to quickly give Lucia a call. She left a couple of messages as well."

In the back, I pulled my phone out again and called Lucia. She picked up on the first ring.

"Scarlett! My colleague just got back from the police station and said she'd heard there'd been a murder on the Oceanside Pier this morning. Are you all right? That's close to your store. Did you see anything?"

I almost chuckled at how quickly rumors were spreading. She chatted away, telling me all about the version of events she'd heard instead of waiting to hear what I had to say about what had actually happened.

"I'm fine," I managed to get in. "And it didn't happen *on* the pier but *under* the pier."

Lucia gasped. "So there was a murder."

I realized my mistake. "I didn't say that. But there was a body."

"Wow. Did you see it?"

"I . . . I . . ." Emotion welled up in me again.

"Scar? What's wrong? What exactly happened?"

I took in a deep breath. "I did see the body, because I was the one who found the woman while I walked along the beach this morning."

"Oh no. That sounds awful. How are you doing?"

"All right. A bit shaken. I can't talk much now, though. The store's open, and Evelyn's out there by herself." I could hear the door opening and closing as more customers came in, the jingle of bells tinkling each time. It was setting up to be another busy day.

"Are you sure you're okay to work?" It sounded like Lucia's assessment of the situation was fading back into her original worry over me. "You can close for a day, you know. The bookworms will survive."

"I couldn't do that. What if someone's vacation was ruined because they didn't have the perfect beach read?"

"You put too much pressure on yourself. There are these things nowadays called e-books—have you heard of them? Anyone can instantly download a book onto their phone, and voilà. The perfect beach read."

I groaned. "I'm going to hang up on you if you keep plotting ways to put me out of business. Lots of people still like reading physical books—the feel of the smooth pages between their fingers, the satisfying thump when they close the book at the end. It's magical."

Lucia laughed. "All right, all right. You sound like you're feeling more like yourself. Have a good day. And try not to stumble upon any more dead bodies, okay?"

I humphed in return and ended the call. After stashing my phone away in my purse, I headed back out into the store.

It was busier than I'd assumed. Customers were crowded all around and between the bookshelves and still coming in through the entrance. I was hurrying through the crowd, sure Evelyn would need help at the cash register, when I noticed no one seemed to be buying anything. Evelyn wasn't even at the register. She was talking to a group of people nearby.

"There's nothing to worry about. The police are taking care of everything. Please continue to enjoy your time here," Evelyn said as more and more customers gathered around.

"But I saw the police tape strung up around the pier," one lady said.

"And a body bag," another customer added.

Apparently, no one was actually in the bookshop to shop for a book; they were here out of curiosity over what was happening on the beach.

I wasn't prepared to field questions about potential murders all day. I wanted to talk about fantasy and sci-fi and mystery . . . wait, no. Probably not mystery. But the point was, I didn't want to be talking about anything besides books. At least until I had to go to the police station and give my official statement.

The rush calmed down around lunchtime. Fewer people were in for the gossip, and more were actually looking for something to read. My anxiety began to ease, as I was able to escape into the fictional world with customers and chat about their favorite authors and series.

One man asked for a thriller author I wasn't familiar with, and I headed to check our back stock to see what we had. On the way I bumped into Evelyn, who had a book tucked under her arm.

"Mind if I take my break soon?"

"Sure, just let me check the back for a customer first." I nodded at the book she held. "Did you find something new to read on your break?" We often picked up a book for our break and then paid for it later. Discounts were a great perk of working in a bookshop.

She held the book up. A murder mystery novel.

I groaned. "Really? You too?"

"What do you mean?"

"You're all caught up in the mystery excitement as well?" I eyed the front cover of her book. That crime scene looked way too similar to what I'd witnessed that morning, except there was a hot young police officer crouched over the body. Apparently, not all real-life crime scenes came with a hot young police officer. That would have been a welcome distraction.

"This will be Steve's first murder case here."

"We don't know if it was a murder, though."

Evelyn clicked her tongue. "Well, maybe I can find some sort of direction or clue in this book that will help him out."

So that was it. She wasn't so much interested in the case as in how it would affect her husband's career. If Detective Maxwell could solve a murder like this, if that's what it was, that would do well for his shaky career.

"Well, good luck with that." I went into our back to dig through the books. I wasn't able to find the author the customer had been looking for, but I did bring out some other thriller novels, hoping one would strike his fancy.

After Evelyn was done with her lunch break, I asked if she'd be willing to watch the store while I went to the police station. Only three customers currently browsed through the books, so I was sure she'd be fine. "Please don't hesitate to call about anything, and I'll try to hurry back as fast as possible."

"Don't worry about it. Take your time. Say hello to Steve for me, will you?"

"Of course."

Chapter Four

Outside, the early-afternoon sun blazed down, and sweat immediately began to form along my brow. If I hadn't found a dead body washed up along the shore that morning, I'd be considering ending the day with a quick dip in the ocean. I hoped the creeped-out feeling I got from looking out at the waves would subside soon, and then I'd stash a swimsuit to go along with the flip-flops at the store. I'd be ready for any spontaneous trip to the beach.

The AC in my car took forever to get going. I was almost at the police station by the time I started to feel comfortable, and then it was right back into the heat.

"Hi, I'm here to see Detective Maxwell," I said to the officer at the front desk. "He's expecting me."

"What's your name?"

"Scarlett Gardner."

The officer nodded. "I'll let him know you're here, Miss Gardner. Please have a seat."

I grabbed a seat on a bench nearby and looked around the empty police station. This was my first, and hopefully last, time here. The building was gloomy and drab, with gray walls and fluorescent tube lighting buzzing overhead.

Detective Maxwell stepped out from a hallway and greeted me. "Thank you for coming in, Scarlett. This shouldn't take too long."

"It's no problem. Whatever I can do to help."

He led me back down the hallway he'd come from and into a small room with a table and two chairs.

Uh-oh. This looked exactly like an interrogation room on those cop shows. Was I a suspect?

"Did you have a chance to look through your credit receipts?" Detective Maxwell asked.

I nodded. "I went through them right before coming here, but the time stamp from the last receipt of the day was about an hour before the woman came in. So she paid with cash." I reached into my purse and pulled out an envelope I'd stuffed the receipts in. "Here, you can look through them yourself if you'd like."

The detective reached over and grabbed the envelope. "Thanks. Now, could you please repeat everything you told me this morning— exactly what you were doing and why, when you found the body, as well as seeing the victim yesterday? I'm going to record it."

I launched into the events of both yesterday and this morning, including how I'd thought the hand was a piece of garbage at first and how I'd called 911 as soon as I'd realized it was a dead body. I could tell the detective had hoped something else would trigger in my memory as I went over my story again, but there was nothing. I knew nothing of the woman.

"Thanks, Scarlett." He slid a piece of paper across the table toward me. "Now, could you please write everything down and then sign and date it at the bottom."

I nodded, then took the pen he held out to me and did what he asked. I'd had no idea giving your statement could be so thorough.

Or awkward. Detective Maxwell's eyes never left my paper, as if it were an exam and he were making sure I didn't cheat. When I finished, I asked, "Have you been able to identify the woman yet?"

He shook his head. "Still working on that. But we've got a number of people looking into it, so we should soon have word."

"Still no ruling if it was an accident or not?"

He looked hesitant to say anything.

"I don't mean to pry or gossip. It's just that it happened so close to my bookshop. I want Evelyn and myself to feel safe while we work."

The mention of his wife's name seemed to do the trick, and Detective Maxwell's expression softened. "Well, if it'll put the two of you at ease, so far it's looking like an accidental drowning before her body washed up onshore. We're still waiting for the official report from the coroner, but at this point, I would advise you not to worry too much about this."

"Thank you, Detective Maxwell. Your wife says hello, by the way."

He gave a soft smile. "I say hello back. Thank you again for coming in. I'll walk you out."

He opened the door for me and led me back out toward the entrance. I felt a rush of relief as I realized I couldn't be a suspect if they were letting me go home. Also, if they didn't think there was something mysterious going on, they wouldn't need suspects. Unfortunately, accidental drownings were common when you lived close to the ocean. The tides could suddenly become more dangerous than expected, and there were plenty of party cruises that left from the marinas. Alcohol, nighttime, and rough waves didn't always mix. Though from what little I had known of the woman, she didn't seem like the party type. More like the lounge-on-the-beach-with-a-good-book type.

There was still half the workday left when I got back to Palm Trees and Page Turners, and Evelyn was eager to hear about my trip to the police station. Despite being married to a detective, she'd never personally known anyone who'd had to give their statement to the police before.

"It was fine. Detective Maxwell was very thorough, but I wasn't there too long."

"I sure hope they find the killer soon. I hate thinking there's someone who would do such a thing running around our town."

"Actually, the police think it may have been an accident. I don't think there's much to worry about."

Evelyn looked unconvinced. "Well, still, please make sure you're looking out for yourself and aren't out in the dark alone."

I smiled. "I promise. I have Lucia to defend me, remember?"

Evelyn laughed. Lucia might be a good five inches shorter than my five feet, seven inches, but she was tough. She'd told me about all sorts of martial arts classes she'd taken with her two brothers growing up. I'd never want to find myself against her in a fight.

The rest of the workday finished uneventfully, and after saying good-bye to Evelyn and dropping off the deposit, I headed to the grocery store, brainstorming what I should make for dinner. *Spaghetti! Nah, I made that the other day. Maybe tacos instead.*

I usually did my shopping at a local grocery store near the downtown area of Oceanside, not far from the bookshop. It was a smaller store, but they had the best fresh-fruit selection in town.

"Hi, Scarlett." Carrie Lee, the daughter of the store owner, was behind the first cash register. "I hear your bookshop was the scene of a crime this morning." She waved me over, I surmised in hopes I'd spill all the details.

"No, nothing happened at Palm Trees and Page Turners today." I watched morbid disappointment fill Carrie's deep-brown eyes. "But there was a body found underneath the pier."

"Oh!" The look on her face was a mix of disgust and intrigue. "Who was it?"

I shrugged. "No one knows yet."

"Wow, that's so wild. What's O'side coming to?"

I thought about correcting her and saying it was probably an accident like I'd told Evelyn, but it seemed impossible to correct a rumor that was already out of control. So I settled for "The police are doing an excellent job working on this case."

I hurried to grab a shopping basket and gave Carrie a wave before heading to the produce section to get tomatoes, lettuce, and avocados.

When I finished grabbing my groceries, I was secretly glad to see Carrie's till had the longer lineup, so I used the next one. I didn't know this cashier, and he just made the idle "How are you? Did you find everything you were looking for?" conversation. Nothing about murderers and dead bodies.

Our townhouse was dark when I got home. Lucia must still be working on that fraud case she'd had today. I hoped it had gone well for her and she hadn't been too distracted by what had happened to me. After putting away the groceries, I got busy chopping the veggies and cooking the ground meat for the tacos.

I'd finished plating everything when the front door unlocked and Lucia's shoes smacked against the wall as she enthusiastically kicked them off, something she did at the end of every workday. Moments later, she appeared in the kitchen.

"Okay. I want to hear about everything that happened. And don't leave a thing out." She put her Wonder Woman purse and brown messenger bag on the kitchen island and grabbed a stool, sliding it nice and close to me.

Like that would make any difference in my storytelling in this small space.

"I told you most of what happened this morning already."

"But I want to hear about it all again. We read about bizarre cases of unknown bodies suddenly appearing in the criminology courses I took in university, but I've never known anyone who actually stumbled on one before. It's like something out of a movie." Her eyes gleamed as she said this last sentence. Of course she'd only see the drama and adventure in this.

I gave Lucia another rundown of what had happened. "Oh, I did need to go to the police station to give my statement this afternoon. I don't think I told you that."

"No, but that sounds routine to me. I should've warned you about that when we talked this morning."

I shrugged. "It wasn't a big deal. Detective Maxwell took my statement, and he's a nice guy. It didn't take too long, but I did need to give a lot of detail about what happened yesterday and today."

"Hold on. What do you mean yesterday? I thought you discovered the body this morning. You didn't say anything last night." Lucia sounded accusatory, like I'd been keeping this exciting secret from her as we watched the movie yesterday.

I sighed. "How about I tell you while we eat? It's all ready." I grabbed some dishes and headed toward our kitchen table, not even giving Lucia a chance to protest. I was starving. I needed to stuff some tacos into my mouth before I launched into another story.

Lucia sighed right back at me. "Fine." She grabbed the rest of the food and followed.

After I'd taken a few bites, I told her about how the woman had briefly come into Palm and Page yesterday. "And before you ask, no, I still have no idea who she was."

"Wow. That's interesting. She just seemed like a regular tourist looking for a book?"

I nodded. "She made no mention of criminal activity. Maybe she'd been on one of those party cruises, got drunk, and fell into the ocean." I remembered my earlier thought about her seeming like a lounge-on-the-beach type, but even quiet, bookish people could let their party animal out once in a while, right?

"I guess we'll know more once they do a toxicology report."

"If there was alcohol involved, will that info be released to the public?"

"It'll depend on what her next of kin says. If they can find someone to ID her. But if not, I may have a contact or two who can find out."

I almost laughed at how invested Lucia was in this random mystery. "I don't even know if I care to find out. I feel bad for the poor woman, but it's not like I have a connection to her."

Lucia shrugged. "So, do you want to watch a crime drama after dinner?" She took a big bite out of her taco and looked at me playfully.

"Ha-ha. Nope. I want to read. A rom-com or something. Something that has zero murder or death in it. I want to forget about this morning. I'm already scared I'm going to have nightmares."

Chapter Five

Thankfully, I didn't have nightmares. I slept deeply after being exhausted from the hectic day before. One thing was for sure: it would be a while before I went on a morning walk along the beach alone again.

Lucia and I had a quiet breakfast together, each lost in our own thoughts. I knew her company fraud case was still going on and that it stressed her out. Her interest in Jane Doe was probably more for a distraction than anything else.

We parted ways after breakfast, and I headed to work. Once I arrived in Palm and Page's parking lot, I was careful not to look in the direction of the sandy shore. I didn't want to risk accidentally seeing another body.

Evelyn pulled into the parking lot as I got out of my car, and we walked to the front door together. I dug for my keys in my purse as she leaned against the bookshop sign. I'd had it specially commissioned from a local artisan for our grand opening. It featured two palm trees with a turquoise-and-yellow hammock strung between them. Nestled in the hammock was a woman reading a book. Beneath, in bold, colorful letters, read *Palm Trees and Page Turners Bookshop*.

"How are you feeling today, Scarlett?" Evelyn gave me a gentle smile, like she wasn't sure if she should be tiptoeing around what had happened yesterday or not.

"I'm doing fine. Much better now that I've had some rest."

We stepped inside, and I turned off the alarm and flipped on the lights, breathing in the bookish scent.

"That's good to hear. You might be interested to know they've been able to identify the woman."

"Oh?" I wasn't sure why I was surprised it'd happened so quickly. She'd most likely been on vacation with someone who'd reported her missing. *Her poor family. They must be devastated.* "Who is she?"

Evelyn shook her head. "Steve mentioned it to me this morning. They found someone who knew her, but her name hasn't been released yet."

"Well, this will all be behind us soon, then." I closed my eyes for a moment as what Evelyn had said sank in. The amount of relief it brought caught me off guard. I'd been more caught up over who the woman was than I'd realized. Now I could move on and bring my focus back to running a successful business.

"But if you need to leave again, remember, I can take care of everything here."

My eyes opened, but Evelyn had already turned her back and headed toward the sci-fi section to straighten the books. She'd made a few comments like that over the past few days. I trusted her to handle the store, but it struck me as odd that she felt the need to keep reminding me.

The day started slow, but it still seemed as if every second customer asked something about the woman who'd been found. The intense interest from everyone was frustrating. Why were people coming here to ask? Before leaving the police station yesterday, I'd asked Detective Maxwell if it'd be possible to keep my name out of the media as the one who'd found the body, and he'd agreed.

On my lunch break, I checked the local news online. Almost every report mentioned Palm Trees and Page Turners. That was the problem—not *my* name but my business's. Headlines read things like *Mysterious Body Found Behind Local Bookshop* and *Possible Murder Underneath the Oceanside Pier Near Palm Trees and Page Turners*. Ugh. No wonder all these curious folks were coming in. Some seemed to think a murder had taken place inside the shop. What were they expecting to find? Bloodstains and a chalk outline of the body? Ugh again! Hopefully, the woman's identity being discovered would speed things along and people would forget Palm and Page had anything to do with it.

I tried not to mope about it for the rest of the afternoon, but it got annoying that so few people seemed interested in looking at or buying books. One guy even asked me to take a picture of him outside where the body had supposedly been found. I politely refused, not even bothering to correct him by telling him that the body hadn't been found outside the store, and hurried to look busy so he wouldn't press further.

Hmm, maybe I could turn this around into a new business venture and charge people for photos. Ha!

At the end of the day, as Evelyn and I were closing up, my phone rang, and Lucia's picture popped up on the screen.

"I won!" she screamed into the phone.

"The case?"

"Yes, of course the case. Martin was back in the office today, and you should have seen the look on his face when I got back from the courthouse. Clearly, he didn't think I could do it, but I did."

"That's awesome, Lucia. We should celebrate."

"You read my mind. That's exactly what I was thinking. Do you want to go to Miku Miso for dinner?"

"That sounds great. My treat, okay? You deserve this."

"No argument there," Lucia said, and I chuckled at her confidence.

"Meet you there in about half an hour?"

"See you then."

I ended the call and quickly finished my tasks. Evelyn had overheard and asked me to pass on her congratulations.

"I have no doubt that woman is going to make it big someday. Steve has been a witness for her and always says what a confident lawyer she is."

I smiled. "I'm proud of her."

Miku Miso: Sushi and Grill was our favorite Japanese restaurant, and we often went there to celebrate any little thing. Last month we'd gone because Lucia had finally tracked down a collector's edition of a classic film she loved. I couldn't remember which one, but I'd gladly tagged along for some delicious maki rolls. It wasn't far down the beach from my shop, and normally I would've walked, but I was still freaked out about yesterday and drove the two minutes down the road instead.

Inside, there was a short wait for a table, and I sat on a wooden bench until my name was called. A small fountain in the corner trickled away, and I watched the sushi chefs in the open kitchen slice and dice at an impressive speed. Soon I was ushered to a table for two, where I ordered their specialty green tea while I waited.

It wasn't long before Lucia breezed into the restaurant. She spotted me right away and hurried over, a huge grin on her face.

"Congrats!" I reached over to hug Lucia before she sat down. "I'm so proud of you. And Evelyn says congratulations as well."

Lucia gave a small squeal and tossed her gray blazer on the back of her seat, slightly out of breath. "Thank you!" She poured tea out of the small ceramic teapot and took a sip. "You got the good green tea. Thanks."

"I haven't ordered anything else yet, but I figured we'd have our usual." There were a few house specials we absolutely adored and got every time we came.

Lucia nodded enthusiastically. "I'm so hungry. I might get an extra roll."

"Order anything you want. I'm paying, remember?"

"Hey! What are you two celebrating tonight?" Our friend Hiroki Yoshida came over to take our order.

"You aren't working in the kitchen tonight?" I asked.

Hiroki's grandparents owned the restaurant and were training him to be a top sushi chef. I knew he felt he had a lot to live up to after his grandparents' disappointment over his dad not wanting to take over the family business. Luckily, their grandson was as passionate about their culture's food as they were.

He shook his head, hair falling in his eyes. "We had two servers call in sick tonight and are training two new hires as well, so I'm needed out here to help." He glanced behind him before playfully whispering, "The new hires are slow."

I laughed. "I'm about to post a new summer position at Palm Trees and Page Turners. I'm sure I'll experience something similar, but I'm hoping they catch on quick and work out."

"We're celebrating a huge win for me at work!" Lucia burst out, apparently having been dying to answer Hiroki's original question.

He turned to her. "Excellent! Good job, Lucia."

"Thanks." Lucia was practically giddy with her excitement over her win. It was funny to imagine how serious she was in the courtroom compared to her lighthearted nature the rest of the time.

We placed our order, and Hiroki headed back to the kitchen. My stomach growled; I hoped it wouldn't be too long of a wait.

"So, do you want to tell me about it?" I asked. Lucia loved to give a play-by-play of her wins. Her few losses usually resulted in our watching gloomy movies, with very little chatting during the film.

She did and launched into telling me all about the past two days of courtroom drama. I was caught up in her story, feeling perhaps she'd missed her calling as an actress, as she described how she'd represented the plaintiff who'd discovered his co-CEO was using their software engineering company to commit payroll fraud. Hiroki came back with our food as Lucia finished, her arms thrown up in the air in celebration.

"Careful, Lucia. You'll knock these rolls onto the floor." Hiroki set the food on the table.

"This looks delicious," I said. "Thanks."

"No problem." He placed a Rainbow Roll in front of Lucia. "And this one's on the house, to celebrate your win."

"Thanks, Hiroki. And thank your grandparents for me as well."

"Of course." He smiled before heading to the next table to take their order.

Dinner was delicious, as usual, and afterward we got in our separate cars to meet back at home. I let Lucia pick the movie again to celebrate her win, and she chose *Bridge of Spies* with Tom Hanks. I popped some popcorn before settling onto the couch.

Over two hours later, as the end credits rolled, she turned to me. "I'm curious about something."

Given her tone, my immediate impulse was to make an excuse and head to bed. I was too tired for something serious. "What's that?"

"I was wondering why you drove to Miku Miso when you always walk. It's only a few buildings down the beachfront from you."

I fidgeted with my glasses. "I was scared. And creeped out."

She raised an eyebrow. "Of what?"

"I don't know. I'd have to go under or around the pier if I walked."

Realization and sympathy dawned in her eyes. "I understand, Scar, but I think you'd be sad if you avoided the beach forever. You love the beach. It's the whole reason you opened a business down there, remember?"

"I know, but I need a bit more time. I'll be fine soon."

"All right." She sounded skeptical.

"Please don't worry about me. I'll be all right. I promise. It was a big scare, that's all."

Her expression softened. "I know. I'm sorry for butting in, and I understand that must have been terrifying." She reached over and patted my arm. "What can I do to help?"

"Well, for starters, I think it would help if we didn't talk about it anymore. I feel like I'm reliving it over and over again every time I'm asked to tell the story."

Lucia winced. "Sorry. I won't ask again, promise."

I smiled. "Thanks. I appreciate it. I'd love to be able to move on."

Chapter Six

My regular morning routine was interrupted by a phone call from an unknown number. Lucia looked up from her bowl of Corn Flakes, and I answered her unspoken question with a shrug. I wasn't expecting a phone call. Maybe our neighbor Jules had gotten a new number and needed a quick favor before she dropped her kids off at school. As a single working mom, she was always run off her feet, and Lucia and I tried to help out whenever possible.

I answered my phone, mindlessly stirring my own bowl, hoping the call would be short so my cereal wouldn't turn completely soggy.

"Good morning. Is this Scarlett Gardner?" a grim male voice asked.

"Yes, it is. Who's this?"

"My name is Jeffrey Cooper, from Cooper and Garcia Law, and I represent Lorelai Knight."

My mind drew a blank on all the mentioned names. "I'm sorry. Who?"

Jeffrey sounded equally confused. "She didn't speak with you this past weekend?"

"Did who speak with me this past weekend?"

"Lorelai Knight." He drew out her name.

"Oh. No, I've never heard of or met anyone named that."

Jeffrey was silent for a moment. "Well, this is a bit awkward, isn't it? Are you able to meet me? I'm in Oceanside now. This is a matter that's best to be discussed in person."

"Um, sure. I guess. I'm on my way to work, though. Could it wait until this evening?" Lucia flashed another questioning look, and I shrugged again.

"How about I meet you at your work? Would that be all right? I'd prefer not to wait on this."

"Okay. I own the Palm Trees and Page Turners Bookshop down by the pier. Meet me there in thirty minutes?"

"Thank you very much, Miss Gardner. I'll see you there."

"Okay, who was that?" Lucia finished her last bite of cereal.

One glance down confirmed mine had gone soggy. Gross. "Some guy named Jeffrey Cooper. He said he's Lorelai Knight's lawyer."

Lucia's eyebrows shot up at the mention of his occupation. "Who's Lorelai Knight?"

"I have no idea. Never heard of her. But I'm meeting Jeffrey at Palm and Page soon to sort this all out."

Lucia stood. "All right. I'm coming with you. I don't know what's going on, but you may need a lawyer yourself."

I smiled and stood to pour my bowl down the garbage disposal. I grabbed a yogurt cup from the fridge instead. "You're not my lawyer. You're my roommate."

"Yes, but whoever this Jeffrey is doesn't need to know that."

Thirty minutes later, Lucia and I arrived at Palm and Page. No Evelyn yet, but a tall, wiry man with rust-colored hair in a fancy suit and royal-blue tie leaned against a silver car in the parking lot.

"Scarlett Gardner?" he asked as I approached. "I'm Jeffrey."

"Yes, hi. How are you?"

He shifted his briefcase to his left hand and held out his right. "Pleased to meet you. And who's this?" His bushy eyebrows furrowed as Lucia reached my side.

"Lucia Armenta."

"If you don't mind, this is a personal matter between myself and Miss Gardner."

"And if *you* don't mind, I'm her lawyer." Her gaze never wavered, and I had a feeling I was witnessing her shark lawyer attitude snap into place.

"Why don't we go inside the shop?" I suggested, stepping between the lawyer stare-down. "And I'd prefer Lucia to join us. Thanks." Once inside, I turned off the alarm and turned on the lights. I led them to a small sitting area I'd set up a few weeks ago near the front of the store. It was meant as a place for customers to relax while they looked through the books they considered purchasing. Never had I imagined sitting here with a strange lawyer before the store was even open for the day.

Jeffrey rummaged in his briefcase and pulled out a few pieces of paper. "Here you are, Miss Gardner. This is your copy of Mrs. Knight's will."

My hand shook slightly as I took the paper from him. *What's going on?* I glanced down at it, but it seemed to be a bunch of legal jargon. The only thing I immediately recognized was my name and last week's date. "What's this?"

"Like I said, it's your copy of Mrs. Knight's will. You can keep that, but I'll need signatures on my own copy, if you please." He started to rummage around in his briefcase again.

"Hold on," Lucia said. "My client is not signing anything until you tell us exactly what's going on."

Jeffrey paused and looked up at us. "So you've truly never received any contact from a Lorelai Knight?"

"No. I've never heard or met anyone with that name."

"Well, I'm sure you'll be surprised to learn you are the sole recipient of her fortune, then."

I almost fell off my chair as the impact of his words hit me. Lucia's steady arm reached over to grab mine and keep me upright.

"What are you talking about?" Lucia asked, and I was thankful she at least had a voice. I could barely remember to breathe, much less speak.

"Mrs. Knight contacted me last week to change her will to include only Miss Gardner's name. Well, besides a few charities, that is. She said she was coming down to Oceanside this past weekend to explain everything."

"But why Scarlett?" Lucia asked.

"That I'm not entirely sure. I'd assumed she was of some relation."

I again shook my head and finally found my voice. "No, not that I know of." My thoughts wandered. There was one way . . . but that seemed almost impossible. Hardly anyone knew. "And I definitely didn't meet her this past weekend. I'm confused. If she wants to meet me, she must still be alive, then. So how am I receiving her fortune?"

Jeffrey shook his head, his mouth downturned. "Unfortunately, she's no longer alive. Lorelai was found dead on Monday morning."

I couldn't have possibly heard this Jeffrey guy properly. Or he was making some weird joke. I let out a shaky breath that was part giggle.

Lucia gasped. "That was her?"

Wait. So Lucia believed him? Was he telling the truth? Horrified by my initial reaction of giggling, my hands flew to my mouth. I had no idea how to react to this news.

Jeffrey gave me a stern look, his hazel eyes narrowing behind black-framed glasses. "This is no laughing matter, Miss Gardner."

My face heated. "I'm sorry. I didn't mean to laugh. I'm just in shock. Was Lorelai the woman I found under the Oceanside Pier?"

Now it was Jeffrey's turn to be caught off guard. "You're the one who found her?" His voice had dropped to a whisper.

"Yes," I whispered back. Why were we whispering?

Jeffrey clutched his hand to his chest. "Please tell me it didn't look like she'd suffered."

"I don't think so. It didn't look that way to me, at least, but I honestly have no idea what suffering would've looked like. I mean, I've never seen a dead body before. Well, this one time at my great-aunt's funeral . . ." I was so shaken up that I couldn't seem to stop talking. And I knew I wasn't being very tactful about it. Probably only making the poor man feel worse than he already was.

Sure enough, Jeffrey winced. "She was one of my favorite clients, you see. I'd grown fond of her over the years."

"Had you been representing her long?" Lucia asked.

"My firm has been representing the Knight family and their fortune for decades now. My father represented them, and around the same time Lorelai inherited control of the family fortune, I took over the law firm from my father."

"Could you tell us more about her family?" I asked. "Did someone come to Oceanside to identify her?"

"Not yet—officially, that is. I was actually the one who told the police her identity. Apparently, she hadn't told anyone else she was coming here alone this past weekend from LA. I only knew because of her will change last week. I saw that horrid photo of her on the news Monday evening and called the police station right away."

"But her family's been contacted now?" I asked.

Jeffrey nodded. "Yes. She doesn't have much family left, but I made the phone calls yesterday."

"And her family fortune? Could you tell us more about that, please?"

I was impressed with Lucia's way of questioning Jeffrey without making it sound like we were callous, greedy people only after the money. What inheriting a fortune might mean hadn't even registered yet, but I was also curious to know more about this fascinating stranger who apparently knew me.

"I'm surprised you haven't heard of the Knight family. Knight's Real Estate in LA? They're the leading real estate agents when it comes to buying and selling mansions to movie stars and celebrities."

I shook my head at the same time Lucia nodded enthusiastically. Of course she would know every little detail behind the scenes of movies.

"Oh, there's one more thing, Miss Gardner. Mrs. Knight didn't only leave her money to you but other possessions as well. Did you want to come to LA to take a look, or shall I arrange to have everything sent to your house?"

I rubbed my temples for a moment before answering. "Could I please have a few days to think about it? I need everything to sink in first. And hopefully figure out my connection to Lorelai."

Jeffrey smiled sympathetically. "I can't help you there. Sorry. Until last week, Mrs. Knight had never mentioned you or even a connection to Oceanside, and she darted off before I had the chance to ask. In light of what happened, I regret not asking for more details. Anyway, take all the time you need. I'll be in touch as we continue to get everything organized, but I'm giving you a heads-up: with a fortune like this, it may take a while before everything is officially in your name. But don't worry, it's all legal. Just a lot of crossing the *t*'s and dotting the *i*'s."

"Thank you," I said, and Lucia put an arm around my shoulders, giving me a reassuring squeeze.

"I'll be here for any questions or concerns you have. Scar. And I'll make sure to read all the fine print."

Jeffrey gathered his things and stood, handing me a business card. "Here's my cell number, office number, email, everything. Please don't hesitate to contact me about anything, day or night."

"Thank you," I said again, and Lucia and I both escorted my unexpected guest back outside. I took a peek at the parking lot and noticed Evelyn still hadn't arrived. Strange. She was never late.

I closed the door behind Jeffrey and immediately slammed my back against it, facing Lucia with wide eyes. "What. Was. That?"

Lucia squealed. "You're rich!" She did a little happy dance around the bookshop. "How cool is that?"

I laughed at her enthusiasm but didn't join in the fun. It was a little weird to be profiting off a woman's death. Especially when the woman was someone I didn't even know. "I don't know what to think about it all. I'm not even sure if I want the money."

Lucia paused her happy dance. "Of course you do. Why wouldn't you want it?" She continued before I could explain. "Oh, it's because you haven't heard of the Knight family before. Believe me, they must be loaded. They're real estate royalty in Hollywood. Anyone who is anyone lists and buys with them. And don't worry, they're also well-known for giving lots to charity. It's all honest money. I promise."

"It's not that." I sighed. "I'm overwhelmed, I guess."

Lucia smiled. "We can chat more tonight. I've got to run soon. But it'll all work out, I promise. And I'll do some more digging into both Jeffrey and this Lorelai, if that'll make you feel better."

"Thanks, Lucia."

As Lucia headed out the doorway, she paused and turned back. "So, no idea who this Lorelai actually was, or why she chose you to leave her fortune?"

I started to shake my head and then hesitated. I realized there was something about myself I'd never told Lucia before. Not that it was a big secret; it was just something that had never come up. "I might. But it's too complicated to get into now. I need to talk to Olivia first."

"Good luck with that. See you tonight."

I thought about Lucia's *good luck* comment after she'd left. It wasn't that my sister was difficult to talk to; it was that she was difficult to get in touch with. Olivia was currently living in Sydney, Australia, having been sent by her architecture firm to work on multiple projects. She had no idea when she'd be moving back home, and she loved it that way. Olivia was always looking for the next big adventure.

But there wasn't time to try to catch her now. I struggled to do the math in my head. Two or three AM–ish in Sydney? I'd send her a message later today to set up a time to video chat.

I started the opening tasks around Palm and Page and realized I hadn't even thought about what the money could do for my business. Maybe I shouldn't dismiss the idea of it so easily. I could expand Palm and Page, maybe even attach a little café next to it. Some outdoor patio seating would be charming, with tall beach umbrellas so customers could read in the shade and still enjoy a view of the ocean. Olivia could draw up designs for me.

I was so lost in my daydreams about expanding Palm and Page that I jumped at the loud knock on the front door. Evelyn must have forgotten her key at home.

Instead, I found Detective Maxwell peering in through the glass. There was no warmth in his dark eyes, and his mouth was set in a stern line. Had something happened to Evelyn?

I quickly unlocked the door and welcomed him inside. "Hey, Detective. What are you doing here?"

Murder by the Seashore

"Scarlett." He said my name like he was disappointed in me—a tone I hadn't heard since I was a teenager and my parents used it when I'd snuck out at night. "There's been a new development in the Jane Doe case, and I need you to come to the police station with me."

Chapter Seven

A glint of sunlight through the window bounced off the hand-cuffs clipped to his belt. "Oh . . . okay. Am I under arrest?" I couldn't keep the quiver out of my voice.

"No," he said, but his tone was grim and not reassuring. "But I can't discuss it here with you. You need to come with me."

"All right. Just let me text Evelyn to let her know to open without me and I'll join her in a bit."

Detective Maxwell shook his head. "I'd advise you not to open today. You might not be back for much of the workday." He glanced away for a moment. "I've actually already suggested to Evelyn she should stay home."

What was going on?

Outside, Detective Maxwell opened the car door for me—the back door—and held his arm out, ushering me inside. I dolefully got in, not entirely convinced I was *not* being arrested. As we backed out of the stall, I noticed a few customers were already pulling into the parking lot, including Hiroki. His eyes met mine in surprise as we drove past, and I quickly ducked my head.

Murder by the Seashore

I swear it was almost like Detective Maxwell purposefully drove as slowly as possible down the streets of Oceanside so everyone could get a good look at Scarlett Gardner in the back of a cop car. Ugh. At least it was a ghost car and not a regular patrol car. Maybe they thought we were going out for brunch?

Ha. Nice try at making yourself feel better. Face it, Scar. They all think you're the town criminal now.

When we pulled up to the police station, I wanted to cover my face with my hands as I got out of the back seat. But that would probably make me seem guiltier. I might be embarrassed, but I was certainly not guilty of whatever it was they wanted to accuse me of. But then again, no handcuffs yet. No reading of my rights. That had to be a good sign, right?

Deciding on a compromise, I held my head high as I was escorted into the station, but I didn't make eye contact with anyone. I knew I'd burst into tears if I did, even if it was with a stranger.

I let out a breath when the detective led me into the same interview room I'd been in the other day. Part of me, a large part, had expected to be dumped in a jail cell. Did you still get one phone call, even if you weren't officially under arrest? I knew exactly who I would call—Lucia! Oh, I'd love to see her in action defending me.

"Please, Miss Gardner, have a seat." Detective Maxwell indicated the chair across from him.

So I was Miss Gardner now and not Scarlett? That was a bad sign.

"What's going on? Do you need me to repeat my statement?" That I could handle. I bit my bottom lip.

Detective Maxwell shook his head. "Our Jane Doe has been identified as a Lorelai Knight." He stared closely at me, as if waiting for a reaction. "Does this name mean anything to you?"

My face warmed as I stared back. An hour ago, no, the name had meant nothing to me. But now . . . ah, what should I say? "I . . . uh . . ." was all that came out.

Detective Maxwell sighed, apparently having taken my stumbling response as a full-out confession. "Tell me how you know her."

"I . . . uh . . ."

He pushed a buzzer on the table, one I hadn't noticed before, and asked whoever was on the other end to bring in a glass of water. We didn't say anything until the officer poked her head in and handed him the glass, which he handed to me.

I squeaked out a thanks and took a long sip.

"Feel better?"

I nodded.

"All right. As far as we can tell, Lorelai came to Oceanside by herself, and no one around seemed to know her but you. So, let's start from the beginning. How long had you known her?"

"I didn't actually know her. I only first heard of her this morning before I left for work."

"Then why did she leave you so much money?"

"I honestly don't know. You have to believe me. I'd never heard of her before her lawyer called me earlier today. I was completely surprised this stranger left me her money."

He softened a bit. "All right. Tell me all about this lawyer and exactly what he said, Scarlett."

I relaxed a bit now that I was no longer Miss Gardner and launched into the story of how Jeffrey had assumed Lorelai had spoken with me this past weekend. She hadn't said anything about knowing me or putting me in her will when she'd come to Palm Trees and Page Turners Sunday evening. I told the detective how Jeffrey had explained about Lorelai's family fortune and where it'd come from.

"I don't have anything else to tell you. I'm not under suspicion of killing her, am I?"

Detective Maxwell sighed again and then pushed the buzzer. This time he said, "Bring in the evidence."

My thoughts were in turmoil. What evidence? What did he mean by that?

The same officer who'd brought in the water now handed the detective a plastic zipped bag with what looked to be a glass bottle inside.

"Do you know what this is?" He held it out for me to see but shook his head when I reached out to grab it. Look but don't touch, apparently.

"I've never seen it before."

"The toxicology report of Lorelai's death came back last night. She didn't drown like we'd originally thought. There was poison found in her system."

"Poison?" I whispered.

He nodded. "Which doesn't necessarily mean it was murder. She could have consumed it of her own will, and then it would be ruled a suicide."

I had a strong feeling there was a *but* coming.

"But this bottle, which contained the same type of poison found in her system, was found early this morning near the back of Palm Trees and Page Turners."

"I've never seen that bottle before, I promise! Besides, how do you know for sure it was murder, then? Maybe she took the poison and then went into the ocean?"

"We don't one hundred percent know it was murder, but we believe if it had been suicide, the bottle would be lost in the ocean, or at least not found so far up on the shore."

I was speechless. Was he seriously accusing me of murder based on a poison bottle being found near my shop? "But the last few days have been so busy at work. Anyone could have left it."

"I'm sorry to say, but we have no other suspects at this time."

Other? Other! "So I am a suspect?"

He nodded grimly. "You're our lead suspect at the moment. Where were you early Monday morning between two and eight AM?"

"I—I was at home. Asleep. Lucia can confirm this."

"Can she? Is it possible you left and came back while she was sleeping?"

I could practically hear Lucia's voice in my head telling me to shut up.

Detective Maxwell stood. "I hate to do this, Scarlett, but I have to do my job. Based on a potential murder weapon and a strong motive, we are detaining you under suspicion of the murder of Lorelai Knight. Please stand up and put your hands behind your back."

Chapter Eight

What was happening? Everything was spiraling out of control. Numbly, I stood and did what Detective Maxwell asked, blocking out anything else he was saying. Something about my rights. I'd never understood what people meant when they described events as an out-of-body experience before, but in that instant, I knew that was exactly what I was feeling.

This wasn't happening to me. It couldn't be.

I shivered as the cold metal clamped over my bare wrists and as the full weight of Detective Maxwell's betrayal washed over me. I'd thought we were buddies and he was on my side. But apparently, he'd been planning on arresting me—or detaining me or whatever this was—the entire time.

I was led out of the interview room and down a long hallway. The detective put me inside what looked to be a holding cell, based on all those cop dramas Lucia had made me watch.

Wait.

Lucia!

"Don't I get a phone call?" I nearly shouted as I finally found my voice. "It's my right to get one phone call."

He nodded gruffly before leading me to a scuffed-up phone on the wall, which looked like it belonged in an old-school telephone booth. "All right. Go ahead." He unlocked one of my wrists from the handcuffs.

Thankfully, Lucia's was one of the few phone numbers I had memorized. She'd made me learn it in case of an emergency, which had seemed laughable at the time. I'd asked her what kind of trouble I could get into in Oceanside, and she'd just shrugged.

Well, apparently, murder investigations, for one thing.

"Hello? Lucia Armenta speaking."

"Lucia! It's me. I need help."

"Scar, what are you doing at the police station?" Her professional lawyer voice was replaced with urgent concern.

"What? How did you know?"

"I have this number saved on my phone because clients call me on it. So hearing your voice from *Oceanside Police Station* is freaking me out. What's going on?"

I choked back a sob. "I've been arrested. Or detained. Or whatever it is they called it. I'm in jail!" My voice broke on the last word, and I started to cry. Between angry gulps and fighting back tears, I explained what had happened and about the poison bottle the police had found.

"They can't hold you. They don't have enough evidence right now. I'm on my way. Just stay there."

I almost laughed at her last sentence. Like I had another choice. "Thank you so much, Lucia. Please hurry."

She'd already hung up. Detective Maxwell led me back toward the holding cell, and I wanted to give him a *Just you wait!* look, because I knew Lucia would tear him to shreds, but I didn't have the energy.

I shuffled into the cell and sat down on the nearest bench while the detective locked the door behind me with a loud clank.

"I'm sorry, Scarlett," he said softly before leaving the room.

Then it was just me, the guard, and my terrified thoughts. I was thankful no one else was in the holding cell. I couldn't deal with an actual criminal right now. I drew my legs up onto the metal bench and curled against the wall like the meek, wounded creature I was.

Please get here soon, Lucia.

It wasn't long before I heard shouting down the hall. I recognized that voice. And Lucia was yelling in Spanish, meaning she was really mad. I almost felt sorry for the officers who had to deal with her right now. Almost.

"Scarlett! Are you all right?" she asked the moment she came into the room. She saw me curled up in the corner. "This is unbelievable." She turned to the guard. "You can release her now."

Detective Maxwell caught up to Lucia and gave the guard a go-ahead nod. He unlocked the door, and I sprinted toward my best friend/lawyer and threw my arms around her.

"Thank you. Thank you. Thank you."

"Come on. Let's get out of here." With one last glare at Detective Maxwell, she led me toward the front of the police station and on my way to freedom.

Once we were settled in Lucia's car, I burst into tears before we'd even left the parking lot.

"It was so embarrassing." I sniffed. "I can't believe the police think I had anything to do with Lorelai's murder."

She reached over and patted my arm. "It's going to be all right. They can't bring you in again without any more evidence. And because you didn't do it, there won't be any." She sounded confident. "You did the right thing by calling me."

"I can't believe they detained me." I dug through my purse for a tissue.

"They couldn't have held you for very long anyway, even if you hadn't called me. It's just a scare tactic to toss people in a holding cell while they gather more evidence. It's to try and make you confess sooner."

I shuddered at the thought of being in there longer than the fifteen minutes that I was. "You can confirm I was at home between two and eight on Monday morning, right?"

"Is that when he said the time of death was?"

"Yes. You can confirm, right?"

"I didn't hear or notice you leave the house."

That wasn't as reassuring as I'd hoped her answer would be. "How did the poison end up right outside Palm and Page?"

"I've no idea, but don't worry about it. Trash shows up on the beach all the time. It was probably carried over by the wind or something."

"That had to be pretty strong wind to pick up a glass bottle."

"Scar, don't worry about it. It's a coincidence. Detective Maxwell is smart. He'll realize that."

"You didn't sound like you thought he was very smart when you were yelling at him."

"How did you understand that? You don't speak Spanish."

"Your point was pretty clear." I imitated her shaking her finger, which I hadn't seen but knew she did when she was angry, and we both laughed.

"You seem better. That's good. Do you want me to drop you off at Palm and Page?"

I shook my head. "No thanks. Well, yes. But only to get my car. I need to go home and take a nap. Besides, I'm still too embarrassed to interact with people. Hiroki saw me being hauled off to the police station today. Who knows who else saw? I'm sure the rumors are running wild around Oceanside by now."

"All right. But I need to head back to work after dropping you off. Sorry I can't keep you company at home this afternoon, but I'll take care of dinner. Don't worry about that."

I appreciated the gesture and couldn't remember whose turn it was to cook anyway. I said good-bye once we got to Palm and Page and waved as Lucia drove back to her law firm.

When I got in my car, I realized I hadn't checked my phone all day, as I'd been too distracted from my time in jail. Nervously, I pulled it out of my purse and sat in the driver's seat with the windows rolled down to scroll through the missed messages.

One was from Jeffrey Cooper, saying he had more paperwork for me to sign. Two were from Hiroki, asking if I was all right. Five from Evelyn, apologizing for the "little misunderstanding," as she called it, because she knew there was no way I was capable of murder. She also commented that if anything were to happen to me, she'd be perfectly capable of running Palm and Page, so I shouldn't worry about that. This was an awkward position to be in, having been arrested by my employee's husband. I wondered how Evelyn felt to be caught in the middle.

I texted both Evelyn and Hiroki with very little information, just saying I was fine and on my way home now. I told Evelyn I'd see her on Friday, as Thursday was the one day of the week Palm and Page was closed. I supposed that if I was going to be arrested, Wednesday was the best day to do so, since I'd have the next day off to recover from my terrible experience.

What a sad attempt at looking for a bright side.

I slowed down as I rounded the corner into our townhouse complex, grateful to be home. A moment later, my pulse picked up at the sight of someone sitting on the front step. I couldn't see their face from my angle and weighed whether I should turn around to drive off after everything I'd been through. Who was about to spring earth-shattering news on me now? I got out of my car, slamming the door shut loudly to give them a heads-up that I was home.

I slowly walked closer to the porch as the person looked over. Relief mixed with embarrassment hit me as I realized who it was. "Oh. Hey, Hiroki."

"Scarlett. How are you doing? I was worried about you." He stood and stepped toward me.

"I'm okay. What are you doing here?"

"I thought you could use a friend. I don't mean to stick my nose in your business, but I saw how terrified you looked in Detective Maxwell's car and thought you might need someone to talk to. I headed over as soon as you texted me."

"Thank you. That's very sweet. Would you like to come inside for some iced tea?" I stepped past him to unlock the front door.

"Sure. I can't stay too long, because I have a shift at the restaurant soon."

Inside, I indicated our kitchen stools, inviting him to take a seat while I poured two big glasses of iced tea.

"So how are you doing? Really?"

Hiroki's kind and sincere expression broke me down, and sobs threatened to return. But it also made me want to share everything that'd happened with someone who wasn't directly involved. So I did.

"Wow. What a day for you. Not many people can say they've inherited a fortune and then gotten arrested in the same day. Impressive." He tipped his glass of iced tea at me.

I snorted. "Yeah. Impressive. That's one way to look at it."

"So, no idea who this Lorelai Knight was or why she left you her money."

I again kept my suspicions to myself until I was able to talk to my immediate family about it. "No. Not really."

He let out a low whistle. "That's pretty crazy."

Eager to get the attention off my mysterious benefactor, I asked, "Hey, why were you at Palm and Page this morning, anyway? You haven't been in there for a while."

He shrugged. "I wanted a new book to read and thought I'd check the place out."

"Well, your timing was certainly something." I hung my head in my hands. "I still can't believe you witnessed that."

He chuckled. "It's going to be all right. And I promise I won't tell anyone what I saw."

"Thanks. Though I'm sure news is already spreading around town."

There was a bit of an awkward pause, and then Hiroki cleared his throat. "So, speaking of everything turning out all right, there was something else I wanted to say to you."

One of my eyebrows rose. "Oh?"

"I never said I was sorry for how Connor treated you. And I should have. I should have made sure you were okay after he left you."

"It's fine. It's hardly your fault he was a jerk."

"That's true. But I was friends with both of you, and in a way, I chose his side by not seeing if you needed someone to talk to after he took off. I didn't want to get in the middle of it, but I wish I had." Hiroki and Connor had lived in the same apartment building and had become good friends. Well, Hiroki had been a good friend to Connor.

"He's not talking to you anymore either, is he?" I gave a sympathetic smile.

Hiroki shook his head. "Nope. He's all highbrow now and doesn't have time for his old friends."

Which was sad, considering Connor had grown up in Oceanside. I'd met him while on vacation here with my sister three years ago and had fallen in love with both the town and the surfer boy. We'd done the long-distance thing until I'd finally worked up the courage, and the funds, to relocate and open Palm and Page. My sister had asked me shortly after Connor left if I regretted making such a big change based on where I'd thought things were going with him. I'd answered honestly: no, because I'd come equally for the beach and the love of my new business.

"Well, I'm glad we're still friends." I held out my glass to Hiroki, and he clinked his against mine.

"Friends," he agreed, and smiled.

"I'm glad you stopped by."

"Me too. Though I'm sorry to say I can't stay much longer. I have to get to work soon."

"No problem. Are things going well at the restaurant?"

Hiroki nodded. "I'm still really enjoying it, and my grandparents are thrilled their restaurant will stay in the family. It's something they've worked hard at, and I think they would've been heartbroken if I'd passed on it as well."

"They should be proud. Of both the restaurant and of you."

Hiroki blushed slightly. "Thanks, Scarlett." He put his empty glass on the counter. "Well, I should head off now. You're going to be all right?"

I nodded. "Thanks again."

Hiroki gave me a quick hug before I walked him to the front door.

Chapter Nine

It was almost ten by the time I rolled out of bed on Thursday morning. My mood lifted a bit with the start of a new day.

Lucia and I had had a good chat last night about my current situation, and she had explained some of the legal stuff. Knowing I wasn't going to suddenly be arrested had eased my tension. Detective Maxwell had to believe I'd had no idea who this Lorelai was before she was murdered and there was no way I could have had anything to do with her will being changed to make me her beneficiary.

However, Lucia did advise me not to go out and buy anything too extravagant, such as a new car or an expensive vacation, in case it seemed as if I'd been expecting to come into a large sum of money. I needed to show the police I had as little motive as possible.

Lucia was long gone by the time I'd padded into the kitchen and poured my bowl of Honey Nut Cheerios. While I was eating, I sent a message to Olivia asking if she'd be available to video chat when she woke up.

It wasn't too long before my phone started to vibrate, and I smiled at the photo that popped up—the two of us on vacation in Hawaii sharing a whole pineapple. Delicious.

"Scar!" Despite my sister's energetic greeting, I could see the dark circles under her blue eyes.

"Hey, Liv. I'm surprised you're up. Isn't it, like, super early in the morning there? Are you working on a big project?"

"Early?" She laughed. "Try late. I've been up all night."

"What? How come?"

"It's crunch time. This current project needs to be finished by the end of the weekend or we risk losing major clients."

I would've been super stressed under so much pressure, but Olivia thrived under it. I knew she'd be getting some of her best work done this weekend.

"Good luck with everything. Are you sure you have time to chat?"

She nodded happily, and the whole screen shook as she moved her arm in rhythm with her head. "I need a break anyway. So, tell me everything. What's new with you? We haven't talked in so long."

"Well . . . ," I started, then paused. This was big, and I didn't know how she would react. I didn't want her feeling disappointed I might have found something she'd been missing for so long. And I wasn't referring to the money. "I might have accidentally found my birth mother."

Olivia dropped her phone, and my screen went dark. I could hear her rustling in the background. Her phone must be facedown.

"Liv? Are you still there? Olivia!"

"I'm here. I'm here. Sorry." She picked the phone back up. "Are you sure? When? And what do you mean *accidentally*?"

"Are you okay with this?" I asked cautiously. I was worried she'd be jealous or hurt that I'd possibly found my birth mother when she had been the one who was so eager to look for her own over the years. We'd both been adopted when we were only a few weeks old, Olivia first and then me two years later. And while I was curious about my past and sometimes searched online for answers, Olivia's adventurous spirit demanded to know her story. She'd been aggressively looking for her birth mother since we were teenagers.

"Oh, Scarlett. This is so like you to worry about how I feel. I'm fine. Please, tell me everything."

I could see in her eyes she was not fine, so I proceeded with caution.

I started at the beginning. I told her how a strange woman had been murdered in Oceanside on Monday morning, and then about the unexpected visit from her lawyer, telling me I'd inherited a small fortune from a complete stranger.

"Who else could it be?" I asked. "Why else would a random stranger leave me money in her will unless she was my birth mother?"

Olivia was quiet for a moment, and then she grabbed a tissue from the box behind her and dabbed a tear out of the corner of her eye. "I'm so sorry, Scarlett."

"Sorry? What are you sorry for?"

"That you found, and then lost, your birth mother before you could even properly meet her."

Oh. I hadn't thought of it that way. I'd been too overwhelmed with everything, but now I had even more to process, which I wasn't ready to think about at the moment. "Maybe I'll have a chance to meet my dad, though."

"Maybe. See, I told you doing those ancestry kits could be worth it."

"I'd honestly pushed that to the back of my mind. I didn't want to get my hopes up." I winced at my words when I saw Olivia's face fall. I knew she'd gotten her hopes way up the moment we sent off our DNA samples after she talked me into trying it out on her birthday in February. "Your results could still lead to something one day," I hurried to say. "And I don't even know for sure if that's who this woman was. Can you think of anyone else she could be?"

Olivia shook her head. "Do you have any investors or shareholders in your bookshop?"

"Nope. I got a bank loan."

"Have you asked Mom and Dad about it? Maybe we have long-lost Knight relatives they've never told us about."

"Not yet, but I should." I was due for a chat with my parents anyway. They still lived in Arizona in the house we'd grown up in, and I usually called once or twice a week.

"Do the police know who killed her?"

I was quiet for a minute. "So . . . there's probably one other thing I should tell you." I told her about my trip to the police station the day before and the poison bottle found outside Palm Trees and Page Turners.

"What! Are you serious?" Olivia's phone shook for a moment, as if she'd almost dropped it again.

"I really wish I wasn't."

"I'm coming home. You need me right now."

"No!" I shouted, and Olivia looked surprised. The thought of her missing her project deadline stressed me out more than what was going on in my life. I'd never forgive myself if my sister lost her dream job because of me. "I mean, please don't. You have a job to do. I'm fine. Really."

"You may have found your birth mother, who has now been murdered, and you've been arrested under suspicion of being the one to murder her because the murder weapon was found at your work. Oh, plus the whole becoming-a-billionaire-overnight thing." Olivia threw her one hand up dramatically. "It sounds like you need me. Is there anything else you want to update me on?"

"Well, the billionaire part is an exaggeration. It's not that much money."

Olivia scoffed.

"But you might be right . . . there may be something else I should tell you . . ."

"Scarlett," my sister said, a warning in her tone.

"Well, when Lorelai was murdered, and her body was found under the pier . . ."

"Yes?"

"I may have been the one to find it."

"You're not serious."

Grimly, I nodded.

"What am I going to do with you, little sis?" Olivia sighed.

I shrugged playfully and let out a small laugh. It was all pretty ridiculous when Olivia put everything together like that. "But promise me you'll stay put." I was serious again. "I really want to visit you in Australia someday, and I can't if you've lost your job and have to move back home."

"Fine. I'll stay. But I'm doing this for you and your future travel plans."

"Thanks." I gave her a thumbs-up.

"Promise me you'll keep me updated with all of this. I can be your emotional support sister from afar."

"You've always been my emotional support sister."

Olivia laughed. "I like the sound of that." She tilted her head, and I could practically see the lightbulb go off above her. "So, what are you going to do to clear your name?"

"What do you mean?"

"I mean, how are you going to figure out who actually killed Lorelai? That way, the police will know for sure you had nothing to do with it. What's the plan?"

I shook my head. "That thought literally never even crossed my mind. I'd have no idea what to do."

"Come on. I believe in you. I totally think you can figure this out."

"Oh, I'm not opposed to the idea, now that you've mentioned it." I was lost in thought for a moment. "I just don't know where to start."

Olivia let out a small squeal. "Let's do this! I can help you from here. I'll be like your spirit guide or something. Give you advice."

"All right, Miss Spirit Guide, what should I do first?"

Olivia looked thoughtful as she twirled her curly auburn hair. "How about you return to the scene of the crime? Isn't that what Nancy Drew always did in those mystery books we read as kids? Remember how Mom was so excited to pass down her old books to us? That's the perfect place to start."

"Okay. That's a great idea." I reached over to a basket on the kitchen counter that contained random notepads and pens and grabbed something to write ideas down with. "What else do you think I should do?"

"Hmm. Do you happen to know where in town Lorelai was staying?"

I started to shake my head. "No . . . wait! The police said a hotel key card from the Five Palms Resort and Casino was found on her when she was killed."

"Okay. I think that would also be a great place to check out."

I nodded enthusiastically. "You're right. I'm also going to check around my bookshop, since that's where the poison bottle was found."

"That's a great idea. You can try to find out what type of poison it was and then look into where in town it's sold. Ask the store owner if they remember anyone buying that brand lately."

I stared at my sister for a moment. "You're sure you're an architect? Not a private eye or something? You're really good at this."

Olivia laughed. "Thank you. And no, not a private eye. Though, speaking of being an architect, I should get back to work."

"All right. Thanks for chatting with me and for the advice. I super appreciate it."

"Anytime. And I'm serious about that. Please keep me updated with everything, and maybe there is one other thing you should do."

"What's that?"

"You should find out for sure if this Lorelai Knight was your birth mother."

I nodded. "You're right. It's just doesn't seem real."

"I know. But it could help solve a lot of questions for you. And I don't just mean about the murder."

"I will. Miss you, sis."

"Miss you too. Oh, I forgot to mention. I should be coming home for a bit in the fall if everything is going well."

"Yay! That would be great. Let's do a road trip up the coast."

"Sounds fun." Olivia smiled. "See you. Love you. Bye."

"Love you. Bye!"

I called my parents right after, knowing they were both probably at home enjoying their recent retirement. My dad was spending his new free time working on that novel he'd always wanted to write—some adventure series about a retired accountant who gets caught up in a spy organization. It sounded like he was basing parts of it on his own life. The retired accountant character, at least; not so much the espionage. My creativity-centered mom was finally getting around to clearing out my and Olivia's old bedrooms. I was a little sad my childhood room would probably be home to a craft station or yoga studio or something the next time I visited.

"Hey, Mom. How's it going?"

"Oh, just splendid, honey. We recently booked flights to surprise your sister next month."

A pang of jealousy hit me. I wished I could afford to visit Olivia, both from a money perspective and in terms of the ability to take time off during the summer months. "That's great. You and Dad will have so much fun."

"We're looking at doing a rail tour across the country. And your father is dying to see a show at the Opera House."

"Sounds awesome, Mom. Hey, is Dad around? I want to talk to you both."

"Sure thing, honey." My mom's voice filled with concern. "Is everything all right?"

"Yes, everything's fine. I'll explain when you get Dad."

A moment later, my dad's warm greeting came through the phone. "How's it going, sweet pea?"

I smiled at the nickname he's called me since I was a kid. "I was wondering if we're related to anyone with the last name Knight."

The pause told me that was the furthest thing from what my parents had expected this conversation to be about.

"Um, no," my mom said. "Not anyone that I know of. Anyone on your side, Michael?"

"No, no one. How come you're asking, sweet pea?"

"Well, this woman named Lorelai Knight recently passed away." I decided to keep the whole stumbling-upon-a-murder-victim part to myself. "And she left me a large inheritance."

"Just how large are we talking?" my dad asked.

I told him the amount, and my dad let out a low whistle. "Wow. And you have no idea who this woman is?"

"No. I was hoping you would."

"Sorry, honey. No idea," my mom said.

"Do you think . . ." I paused. "Um, do you think she was my birth mother?"

"We have no idea, sweet pea. We're sorry."

"Everything was handled through an adoption social worker," my mom added. "It was a completely closed case."

"All right. That's what I thought." Disappointment filled me.

"Oceanside isn't that far from Newport Beach," my dad said, referencing the city where I was born. "Right, Grace?"

"About an hour," my mom said. "So maybe there's a chance she was a relative."

I hadn't thought of that. I'd visited Newport only once, but I wondered if being born in a beach town had made the ocean a part of me from the start.

"Sorry we can't be more help, sweet pea."

"It's okay. Thanks anyway."

After our call ended, I spent some time staring at the small list I'd made with Olivia of what to do next. I realized two things.

One: Being tossed in jail was extremely motivating. I was eager to get out there and clear my name.

Two: My new fear of the beach was irrational. Embarrassing, even. I loved the ocean and needed to nip this fear in the bud before it had time to fester.

It was back to the Oceanside Pier for me.

Chapter Ten

I tossed sunscreen, a picnic blanket, my water bottle, a contemporary romance paperback, and the notepad in my turquoise mesh beach bag. I wanted to make the most of my day off as well as do some snooping around the pier. It was the perfect way to multitask.

I parked in the Palm and Page parking lot and looked around the back of the shop. A chill crept down my spine at the eerie thought of a poison bottle having been found so close to my bookshop. I searched for a clue of some sort around the pavement separating the building from the sand. There were two large windows in the back of the shop, giving a direct view of the ocean, and I peeked inside them. Had the murderer spied on me at some point from out here?

All was at peace inside the dark shop. As I continued my search, though I really had no idea what I was looking for, I tried to remember what the bottle had looked like from my brief glance at the police station. Not long enough to read the brand, or even what type of poison it was. I did remember the bottle was made of brown glass with white letters on it. The top also had a screw cap instead of a flip top, so that was at least something to go on.

I paused my search and pulled out the notepad I'd written my task list on. I scribbled down the description of the poison bottle and made a note to Google poisons later.

Hmm, maybe that wasn't such a good idea. Could the police check my search history? Even if I used an incognito search browser? That certainly wouldn't look good for me. I'd have to ask Lucia about that. In the meantime, I'd avoid Googling types of poisons and instead head to the store to browse for matching bottles.

Wait a minute. What type of store would I even go to in order to browse through poisons? Ugh. How could Detective Maxwell seriously believe I was capable of murdering Lorelai? I was completely clueless when it came to criminal activity.

I resumed my search around the back of Palm and Page. I couldn't find anything out of the ordinary, not even a single piece of trash. Suddenly, there were no litterbugs among my customers.

I did a full circle around the building, looking carefully under each rock and behind every plant, ignoring the weird looks passing tourists gave me.

Sighing in disappointment, I gave up and headed down to the beach, swapping out my regular glasses for my prescription sunglasses. The busy late-morning crowd was both a blessing and a curse. Having people around eased my fear of heading back to the pier. Hopefully, there would be safety in numbers if someone suddenly appeared out of nowhere to off me.

But it also meant it was hard to be inconspicuous while searching under and around the pier. I didn't want to draw too much attention to myself.

The yellow-and-black crime scene tape was gone now. Hardly anyone hung out under the pier anyway when there was a big beautiful beach right next door.

I casually headed there, pausing to watch surfers out on the waves. A little boy and girl ran by me, kicking up sand onto my legs as they each tried to be the first to catch a Frisbee. Nearby, a group of college-age girls laughed at something they were watching on a phone screen. I smiled at the life happening around me, before suddenly being hit with a wave of sadness over the fact that Lorelai's had ended so abruptly.

I reached the pier and peeked around the rocks and damp sand. I was sure the police had swept the area well, but it didn't hurt to double-check.

Something yellow, half buried in the sand, caught my eye. I'd actually found something. Maybe Olivia was right and this wouldn't be so hard. It was a clue! It was something that could lead me to the killer and clear my name. It was literally my *Get Out of Jail Free* card. It was . . .

. . . a McDonald's cheeseburger wrapper.

I winced and glanced behind me. At least no one was around to have witnessed my embarrassing failed attempt at playing Nancy Drew. I couldn't believe how excited I'd let myself get over a cheeseburger wrapper.

Shaking off my humiliation, I tried again. But as I searched, a thought hit me. How senseless I'd been. The tide had come and gone a few times since Monday morning, so even if Lorelai or her killer had left some sort of clue behind, it would most likely have been either washed out to sea or buried in the sand. I hadn't even thought to bring a shovel or something with me.

Sighing, I clutched my bag closer and started to head back along the beach. I was so distracted by my disappointment that I didn't see the rock in front of me until I'd launched midair from tripping over it.

"Ouch!" I crashed into the sand, my palms digging into the ground. Something sharp pricked my skin. This was not my day, or week was more like it.

Murder by the Seashore

I pulled my palm toward me to inspect the bleeding and saw something glittering in the sand where my hand had been.

Brushing away the sand, I discovered a silver charm shaped like a palm tree attached to a purple-beaded bracelet. I instantly knew exactly where the bracelet had come from. I'd recognize that signature charm anywhere.

Viviana Diaz was the owner of a thrift shop called Second Chance Treasures, located next to the Sunshine Café. In addition to the used clothing and trinkets she sold there, Viviana sold these beaded bracelets she created. Every single bracelet, no matter the color or pattern, had one of these palm tree charms on it.

Hope swelled in me. Maybe Viviana had sold this bracelet to Lorelai and would have information about her. I shook the rest of the sand off the bracelet and put it in my beach bag.

Part of me wanted to skip the beach day I'd planned and rush right over to Second Chance Treasures. I also wanted to relax a bit—no, I *needed* to relax—after such a stressful few days, but this could potentially be a big clue.

Deciding to compromise with myself, I found a nice spot on the sand away from the pier to spread my picnic blanket out. I could relax and work on investigating at the same time. Plopping down on the blanket, I pulled out my phone to start researching who Lorelai actually was. I had turned off the notifications on my ancestry kit account because I wanted to be able to check any messages on my own time and not be blindsided in the middle of the workday or something. Now I took in a deep breath and then logged into my account.

My heart immediately started to pound at seeing a little number *1* over the notification icon. It had been a few weeks since I'd last logged into my account, and I'd had zero notifications then.

I took in a few more deep breaths and then clicked on the icon.

A message popped up: *Hello, I am hoping you are the Scarlett I've been searching for. I'd love to meet up with you someday soon. Lorelai.*

"That's it?" I said out loud to the waves lapping near my feet. "You want to meet up? Who are you?"

There was no notification that a DNA match had been made, and technically, anyone with an account could send a message to me, so it didn't automatically prove we were related.

Still, it was a very strong suggestion that we were.

I snooped around her profile, but there wasn't much there. It did remind me that she had been a real estate agent in Los Angeles, so that's where I searched next.

The Knight's Real Estate agency wasn't difficult to find; it was the top result when I typed *Lorelai Knight, Real Estate, LA* into the search bar. Lorelai smiled at me from the home page, and I tried to find any part of myself in her.

None of her features particularly looked like mine. I had green eyes, whereas hers were light blue. My blond hair had some red to it, but hers was more of an ash blond turning gray. Mine was straight and hers was curly, but that didn't really mean anything. Maybe she'd had it curled for the picture. I couldn't remember what it'd been styled like when she'd visited Palm and Page, and it'd been tangled and sticking out all over the place when I'd found her on Monday. We both had fair skin, though, and I'd bet she also had needed layers of SPF 50 to enjoy the sun.

I took a screenshot of Lorelai's picture in case I needed to reference it later and continued to explore the website. There were a lot of client testimonials, all anonymous to protect the rich and famous, and a page of their current listings. Turned out Lorelai was the only member of the Knight family actually working at the agency after her in-laws had passed away.

Murder by the Seashore

I let out a low whistle. Some of these houses were pretty sweet, and a hundred times out of my price range. I had a brief thought about Connor and wondered if he'd someday end up living in a house like this if the start-up company he'd left me for did as well as he'd anticipated. Connor had been positive he was on the path toward quick and easy big money, but it was not a path I wanted to follow. Not that I'd ever been offered an invitation.

Shaking thoughts of Connor out of my head, I decided it was time to head to Second Chance Treasures. I packed up my picnic blanket but kept Lorelai's picture on my phone so I could ask around to see if anyone knew her before I left the beach. The police seemed to think she'd come to Oceanside by herself, but it didn't hurt to ask.

"Hi, excuse me," I asked a couple who walked by, hand in hand. "I was wondering if you knew this woman?" I showed them Lorelai's picture, and they both shook their heads before continuing their walk.

I tried again, pausing to ask a family who was having a picnic lunch nearby. They didn't know her either.

I stopped by the lifeguard stand and asked the two guys on duty there, but neither had seen her. Both said they'd keep an eye out for her, and I awkwardly explained the misunderstanding.

"Sadly, this woman was the one who was found dead under the pier on Monday. I was seeing if she had any family or friends around."

"Oh, yeah. I heard about that. Nasty stuff," one of the lifeguards said. "But I don't know anything else about her."

His buddy nodded in agreement. "Yeah, sorry."

Sighing, I asked a few more people before giving up and heading back to my car. So far, it seemed as if no one in Oceanside had actually known Lorelai.

Hopefully, Second Chance Treasures would give me a clue.

Chapter Eleven

As I stepped out of my car at Second Chance Treasures, the scent of bacon and eggs floated over to me from the open back door of the Sunshine Café next to the thrift shop. My stomach rumbled, and my feet started to obey as I took a step toward the café for their all-day breakfast.

"Later." I whispered the promise to myself. I'd grab something to eat after chatting with Viviana.

The bright, cheerful colors of Second Chance Treasures' vintage clothing and random knickknacks greeted me when I walked inside. Viviana was in one corner talking with a customer, and she gave me an acknowledging nod and smile before turning back to the man she was helping. I took the opportunity to look around the shop. I'd been in here only a few times since moving to Oceanside, but it really did live up to its name. I was surprised people had gotten rid of some of the beautiful items that were on display.

I found a little ceramic stack of books with a redheaded girl sitting cross-legged reading on top. It would make the perfect decor for Palm and Page. I'd been meaning to decorate my shop with little trinkets and displays and grabbed a shopping basket to carefully put it in.

Viviana's specialty was the used clothing that took up the majority of the shop, and there were all kinds of fun retro items. I browsed through the tops and brightly patterned sundresses, seeing if anything matched my style and size.

"Hello, Scarlett darling," Viviana's cheerful voice boomed as she came over to me. "How are you doing today?"

"I'm doing well." I smiled back. "How are you?"

She started to nod and then quickly shook her head instead, laughing. "Tired, to tell you the truth. It's sure been busy lately."

"Tell me about it. I've been running off my feet every day this week at Palm and Page. Is this what tourist season is always like?"

"Oh, wait till we hit July. This will feel like nothing."

I groaned. "Yikes. I better get going on hiring more help."

"So, darling, what brings you into Second Chance today? Looking for something special?"

I reached into my bag and pulled out the purple-beaded bracelet from the beach. "I was wondering if this was something you made, and if so, could you please tell me more about it?"

The rings on each of Viviana's fingers sparkled under the bright shop lights as she reached for the bracelet and examined it carefully. Her cheerful, eccentric attitude seemed to shift, and her face clouded over. "Yes. This is something I made and sold quite recently. Why do you ask?"

My heart soared. I was on a roll now with this detective thing. "Well, I'm sure you heard about the murder that happened under the pier the other day."

Viviana nodded, her pink-highlighted raven curls bouncing, but didn't say anything.

"Today I found this in the same spot where the body was. I thought I recognized the palm tree charm and was wondering if you remember who you sold this to."

"Oh, Scarlett. I hope you have nothing to do with that woman. Why are you even looking into this?"

That woman? So Viviana had known Lorelai. "I was the one who found her body, and now I sort of feel like it's something I need to do for her. Find out who killed her, I mean." I thought it best to keep the part about my new inheritance to myself.

Viviana shook her head. "I did know her. Lorelai Knight was her name. It's a shame she was killed, but I have to say, I didn't particularly care for her when she was alive and well."

"Why's that? You seem to be the only one around who knows her. Were you friends?"

Viviana shook her head again. "Heavens, no. Lorelai worked for me a number of years ago. For a very brief time." Her voice dropped to a whisper, even though there was no one within earshot. The only other customers browsed near the back of the store. "She was the worst employee I've *ever* had."

"Really?" Now we were getting somewhere. "What happened?"

She leaned in even closer to me, as if she was ready for a good gossip session, her hair close to tickling my face. "Lorelai was always late to work, always daydreaming about something or other, completely distracted. And then one day she left and never returned. No notice or anything. And to tell you the truth, I think she even stole from me."

"What did she steal?"

"I have no idea. She just seemed the type, you know? Never did anything about it. Maybe I should have, but she wasn't worth my time. I just let it go."

Seemed like a bit of a stretch to me, but I wanted to keep her talking, see what other dirt I could get. "I bet you have good instincts."

"Oh, I do, darling. And I've never hired anyone since. That's why I'm so tired all the time. Anyway, Lorelai suddenly showed up again this past weekend. Out of the blue. Hadn't seen her in over fifteen years, but there she was."

"What did she say?"

"She started off apologizing for disappearing. A family problem was her excuse. Not that I accepted it. Oh, you know what—this is the odd part, and I forgot until now. She asked me about you."

My eyes grew wide. "She did?"

Viviana nodded. "Strange, isn't it? Lorelai asked where you worked."

"Did she say or ask about anything else?"

"No. Just bought that purple bracelet. Probably because she thought I could use her business." Viviana huffed and rolled her eyes. "But I'm doing fine without her pity purchases."

"When did you hear she'd been murdered?"

"Oh, later on Monday. Word travels fast around here. Samantha from next door came running in here that afternoon, spatula in hand as if she'd just ducked out the kitchen door. Screaming the news like the official town crier she thinks she is."

"I still can't believe something like this happened."

"I know! And while everyone was sleeping."

"Well, not everyone."

"What do you mean?"

"Someone had to have been awake to kill her."

Viviana shrugged like it was no big deal. "I guess that's true. But it certainly wasn't me. I was at home all night and even slept in that day."

The front door opened, and another few customers came in. Viviana looked over at them. "If you'll excuse me. I should be getting back to work. It was nice to see you, Scarlett darling. Please come in more often." She squeezed my arm and started heading toward the customers before turning back. "Oh, one more thing. If you're looking to see who murdered Lorelai, you might want to team up with Martin Russell."

Chapter Twelve

I jerked my head back in Viviana's direction. "The lawyer?"

Viviana nodded. "He was in here this morning asking some of the same questions you were. Maybe he's found something else out that could be useful to you. Check with him when you can."

"Thanks for the tip, Viviana."

"Not a problem at all, darling."

I took my time looking around the shop some more but didn't find anything else to claim as my own treasure. I paid for the book ornament, thanked Viviana again for the information, and left.

After dropping off the ornament in my car, I headed to the Sunshine Café, thinking over what I'd learned. So far Viviana was the only person from Oceanside I knew of who had been acquainted with Lorelai. And she wasn't fond of the woman. Could Viviana possibly have been the one to kill Lorelai?

I'd missed the lunch rush, it seemed; the place was quiet in the middle of the afternoon. I looked around for Jules, who worked at the café, but didn't see her.

"Welcome. Please grab any seat you'd like," someone called from the open doorway into the kitchen. I wondered if it was Samantha, the lady Viviana had told me about. She might have more information for me as well. The server dropped off two plates with sandwiches for the older couple seated at a table near me before coming over. Sure enough, her small name tag read *Samantha*, and she pulled a pen and pad of paper out of her apron pocket.

"What can I get you today?" she asked.

I hadn't even had a chance to look at the menu on the table and asked for a glass of orange juice for now. I knew I was going to have some sort of breakfast food but hadn't decided what yet. "Is Jules working today?"

"I think she's still around. Her shift just ended. Do you want me to get her?"

"Sure. She's my neighbor, and I wanted to say hi."

"No problem. I'll be back in a minute to take your order."

"Thanks." I flipped through the menu.

Jules walked over, beaming. "Hey, girl. It's good to see you."

I stood and threw an arm around her in a quick hug. "I feel like I never see you, despite living next door to each other."

"I know!" She nodded, her topknot of box braids bobbing up and down. "I've been working a lot of hours lately because we're short-staffed. And I know it's only going to get busier as tourist season starts."

"Tell me about it."

"I'm glad you stopped by, because there's this wild rumor going around about you, and I'm dying to hear the details." Jules's brown eyes were filled with intensity.

I winced and slumped back down in my seat. "It's not true. I swear I didn't hurt anyone."

"Hurt anyone?" She slid onto the chair across from me. "What are you talking about, girl? I meant I heard you stumbled upon a dead body the other day."

Murder by the Seashore

Relief washed over me. Maybe it wasn't already going around town that the police suspected me of murdering Lorelai. "Oh, right. That. Yes, it's true."

Jules reached over and squeezed my hand. "That's something crazy. You doing okay?"

"Yes. It was terrifying, but I'm fine."

"Now, what do you mean by you didn't hurt anyone?"

I sighed and dropped my voice to a whisper. "The police suspect me of having been the one to murder the woman."

"Yikes! Scarlett, that's awful. You poor thing."

I gave her a sad smile, still feeling a bit sorry for myself.

"Oh, I wish I could chat longer, but I need to get going to pick up the kids from school."

"It's all right. Say hi to them for me. It was nice seeing you."

"You too. I'll bring over chocolate chip cookies tonight as a pick-me-up. You deserve them, hon."

Samantha came back to take my food order as Jules was leaving, and I tried to ask as casually as possible if she'd heard about the murder that'd happened on Monday.

"Of course! Are you new here? The whole town knows." She started yelling toward the kitchen. "Hey, Johnny! Someone is asking about that murder."

My face warmed. I hadn't been expecting this reaction. Soon a tall man with his long hair tied back in a ponytail, wearing a blue apron that matched Samantha's, appeared at her side.

"I heard it was gruesome!" he said. "By the time they found her, she was shriveled up like a piece of dried seaweed and the birds had already started to peck at her." He made a little pecking motion with his hand, and my stomach turned.

"I heard she was on the run from the FBI," Samantha said.

The pair went back and forth with their crazy gossip, none of it remotely true to what had happened, and I couldn't get another question in. But clearly they didn't know anything important, only the most absurd rumors.

"I'll have the eggs Benedict with extra bacon on the side," I interrupted, majorly regretting bringing up the murder after Johnny started describing in vivid detail how a shark had gotten one of the victim's feet.

"No problem. Coming right up." Samantha hadn't bothered writing my order down, and she and Johnny headed back toward the kitchen, still lost in conversation about the murder.

I stared down at the table for a moment, shaking my head in disappointment. Oh well. I was happy to be here for the food.

It wasn't long before Samantha returned with my steaming plate of breakfast for lunch, and my stomach rumbled again as the smell drifted over to me. I was impressed with the generous amount of bacon.

She placed the plate on the table and leaned in close, flipping her honey-colored low ponytail back over her shoulder. "I also heard the poor woman was shot by a sniper who'd been hiding out in one of the lifeguard stands for three days." She walked back to the kitchen without saying another word.

I laughed so hard the couple at the table next to mine looked over with concern, fearing I was losing it. The rumors were getting ridiculous! As if no one would have noticed a sniper hiding for three days in a lifeguard stand. They were tiny huts on stilts with lifeguards going in and out all day. Not exactly the ideal spot to hole up, preparing to murder someone.

My focus returned to the delicious-looking food in front of me, and I took my time savoring each bite while simultaneously trying to decide what to do next. Viviana had also mentioned Martin Russell.

Could he have had anything to do with it? I remembered Lucia saying he'd been out of town earlier this week, so he couldn't have killed Lorelai. But maybe he had a lead on who did and would be willing to share.

That would be my next stop, then: the law firm where Lucia and Martin worked. When Samantha came to clear my plate, I ordered two of their peach iced teas to go and planned on using the sugary drink as a cover to visit Lucia and find out more info about her coworker.

*   *   *

Lucia's law firm, McKenzie, Allen, and Kumar, was located in the heart of Oceanside's small downtown along Pier View Way. I couldn't find parking on the main street, so I left my car in the grocery store parking lot and walked the half block toward the firm. I passed a dentist office, a flower shop, the local library, and a pharmacy on my way.

Hmm, could you get poisons at a pharmacy? Maybe I'd check there sometime.

I paused by the library, mesmerized by a window display promoting their summer reading program. They'd printed dozens of photos of book covers to arrange in the shape of a palm tree. Yes, the saying was *Don't judge a book by its cover*, but some of these looked interesting. I pulled my phone out of my bag and opened the Goodreads app, taking the time to add some of the titles to my *Want to Read* shelf. I might not have much spare time at the moment with getting Palm and Page off the ground and now a murder investigation, but that was the beauty of keeping a TBR—To Be Read—list, one I never seemed to reach the end of. I always had a book to look forward to.

Minutes later I stepped into the chilly air conditioning of the law firm's foyer, and the administrative assistant smiled at me in recognition.

"Hey, you're Lucia's friend, right?" She adjusted her cat-eye glasses.

"Yes, I dropped by to bring her an iced tea." I held up the cup dripping with condensation, feeling the need to prove I had a legitimate reason for being here.

She stepped out from behind the desk with a "Follow me" and led me down a hall lined with small offices.

"Hey, Lucia!" I breezed into her open office and placed the peach iced tea on her desk. "How's it going?"

She looked up from her computer and raised her eyebrows suspiciously at me. "You seem in a much better mood today, considering what happened yesterday. What's up?"

I pulled out one of the chairs across from her desk and sat down. "After talking with my sister this morning, I've made a decision."

"Oh, what's that?" Lucia took a sip of the iced tea. "Wow, this is really good. Thanks."

"No problem." I took a quick sip of my own. Mmm, it was good. "So, the decision I've made is to find Lorelai's killer on my own before the police have a chance to pin it on me again."

Lucia looked like she was about to spit out the sip of iced tea she'd just taken. She swallowed hard while staring at me with wide eyes. "You're doing what?"

"I'm going to find Lorelai's killer," I repeated slowly.

"You can't do that."

"Why not?"

"Because." Lucia paused, seeming to take her time coming up with a good answer. "Well, I don't know. It just seems like something you shouldn't do. It could be dangerous. Besides, where would you start? You know nothing about detective work."

"Actually"—my voice lowered—"I've been following a trail all day, and it's led me here, to Martin Russell."

Lucia gave me another bug-eyed look. "What are you talking about? What trail?"

"A trail of clues." Under my breath, I muttered, "Obviously."

Lucia burst out laughing.

"Why are you laughing at me? It's true." I gave a small pout before repeating what had happened today, from me finding the bracelet with the palm tree charm, which had led me to Second Chance Treasures, to Viviana sending me here to talk to Martin.

Lucia looked impressed now. "Wow. I feel bad for laughing. I'm sorry. It was just you saying things like 'a trail of clues,' like you were Basil Rathbone in the old *Sherlock Holmes* films. I couldn't imagine it."

I huffed at her.

"I'm sorry, Scar. I really am." She gave an apologetic smile. "Forgive me?"

"Fine," I grumbled.

"Now, why don't you tell me more about this? It sounds like you may be onto something."

So I did. I told Lucia about how I'd been adopted but had never known anything about my birth family. I told her my sister had been anxious to find her own with no success, so now I felt guilty that I might have found my birth mother—not that there could be a relationship or anything. I told Lucia about Viviana's grudge against Lorelai, and that Martin had been asking around about Lorelai as well lately, and how I thought he might have discovered something that could help me.

"I was hoping he would share what he knew with me. That's why I came."

"If he's representing someone involved with Lorelai's death, he's not going to talk, but we can try to get something out of him."

"Thanks, Lucia."

"So, Viviana wasn't a fan of Lorelai's? Did she seem suspicious or anything? Antsy when you were talking to her?"

I shook my head. "She had no problem telling me about her past with Lorelai. She didn't sound like she was trying to hide anything."

"Hmm, interesting. Let's go see if Martin's in his office." She stood from the desk and waved for me to follow her out of her office and down the hall. We came to another office with the name *Martin Russell* on the closed door, and Lucia knocked.

"Yes?" a deep voice from inside said.

"Hey, it's Lucia."

An audible sigh followed. "What is it, Armenta? I'm busy with a new case."

Lucia turned to me and rolled her eyes. I wasn't sure when or how this feud between the two of them had started, but it was clear they practically loathed each other. Lucia had tried to explain it to me once, something about Martin stealing one of her cases and making sexist comments about how she'd never be as good a lawyer as he, based on nothing other than that she was a woman. But Lucia had started making *aargh* sounds, unable to actually form a complete sentence in her frustration with Martin, so I didn't catch the whole story.

But from what I'd gathered, Martin didn't like Lucia because he was too prideful to admit she actually was the better lawyer. I majorly owed Lucia one for helping me out. Martin seemed like a complete jerk.

Lucia opened the door to his office, ignoring his protest. "It's your new case I want to talk to you about anyway."

"Hey! You can't barge in like that. And how do you know what— oh, hello. Who's this?" Martin's gaze roamed over me, and he gave a wolfish grin.

I fought the urge to gag.

"This is my client, Scarlett." Lucia jerked her thumb toward me before pulling out the two extra chairs at Martin's desk for us.

Martin gave no indication he recognized my name, so either Lucia had never talked about me at work or he hadn't cared enough to remember anything she said. Probably the latter.

He reached out to shake my hand, and I responded with a quick "Hello." It was probably best to let Lucia do most of the talking for now.

"So, like I said, we'd like to talk to you about your current case."

Martin drew his ice-blue eyes away from me, picking up a pen to play with as if he had no interest in what Lucia had to say. "Why are you wasting my time? Some of us actually have work to do around here."

"I think your case involving the recently deceased Lorelai Knight is connected to my client here."

Martin's stunned look was almost comical. "What—how? How do you know about that case, Armenta? I've kept it under wraps. It's a high-profile case, and I don't need someone sticking her nose where it doesn't belong." He glared at Lucia as he emphasized the word *someone*.

Lucia caught what he implied. "You don't have to worry about me. I don't want your case. Kumar gave me my own special assignment which he didn't trust to anyone else."

Martin's jaw clenched, and he tightened his grip around the pen he held. "What do you want to know, then?"

Lucia leaned in toward Martin and looked him straight in the eye. "Where were you early Monday morning? Like around the time Lorelai was killed?"

Whoa! Where had that come from? Had Lucia straight up implied she was accusing Martin of killing Lorelai? I held my breath waiting for his answer.

"You can't be serious, Armenta. I was coming back from New York on the red-eye. You know that!"

Lucia leaned back and crossed her arms. "Do I?"

"Yes! The whole firm knew I'd flown to New York last week to meet with our colleagues. So if you're implying I had anything to do with Lorelai's death, then you're completely wrong."

"What were you doing asking Viviana at Second Chance Treasures about Lorelai's death, then?" I asked.

Martin looked at me like he'd forgotten I was there, but he seemed more willing to answer my question than Lucia's. His tone softened. "Well, my dear, I was hired by Lorelai's family to represent her estate."

"Oh, but I thought Jeffrey Cooper was doing that."

Martin's mouth gaped. "How do you know Cooper? Wait. Scarlett, right? Are you Scarlett Gardner?"

I nodded. "Yes, I am."

He barked out a laugh. "Cooper might have represented Lorelai, but she wasn't the only member of the Knight family. So don't get too comfortable with that money. It belongs to them, not you."

"Not according to Lorelai's will," I said.

"Cooper's a joke. We'll get that money back. We're plenty motivated."

Ignoring his threat, I asked, "How come her family hired you and not someone closer to where they live? Aren't they in LA?"

"Yes, but they wanted someone where her body was found. They figured she was in O'side because of you, and they wanted a local to keep an eye on things." His eyes glared daggers at me.

"Is her family coming here?"

"Not that I'm aware of. See, there was some dispute in the family when Lorelai gained control of the fortune after her in-laws died. Let's just say family dinners were soon a thing of the past. I don't think anyone cares too much that she's gone, so there's no point being in town. I'm in communication with them every day, though. There's no need to be here in person."

Poor Lorelai. Her family sounds awful.

"Do you have any idea who killed her?" Lucia asked.

Martin started to shake his head and then stopped himself. "I'm not telling you anything. Now, I have to ask you to leave my office. I've got lots to do. But I'm warning you, Miss Gardner. Like I said, money can be a powerful motivator."

"Motivating enough to kill?" I narrowed my eyes.

Martin stood, towering over us. "Get outa here, ladies. I'm not saying another word to either of you."

"Well, aren't you intimidating," Lucia snorted before nudging my arm.

We both got up and headed back toward her office. Lucia shut the door behind us and plopped back in her chair with a frustrated sigh.

"I was hoping there wouldn't be other family members after that money." I groaned as I sat across from her. "I don't want to get into a legal battle with anyone."

"Don't stress about it. Lorelai's will was legally binding. I went over it this morning during a break. They really don't have a case against you. There's a clause about how no one with a criminal record can inherit the money, but that's not you. Besides, you got me and you got Jeffrey. I've done some looking into him, and he has a good track record. He's a respectable lawyer. You're in excellent hands."

I smiled my thanks. "I wonder why Lorelai left the money to me if she has other living relatives? Probably ones who'd actually been involved in her life. Unlike me."

"You heard what Martin said. They had a falling-out at some point."

"That's true. And I appreciate you having my back like this. Martin wasn't very pleasant to talk to. But I should get going soon. I'm sure you have lots of work to get done."

"Before you go, you need to come to the break room and try these delicious cookies one of the paralegals brought in today."

"Yum. And that reminds me. Jules said she's bringing over cookies tonight." I grabbed my half-finished iced tea, and we headed back into the hallway toward the break room at the end of it.

The room was way nicer than the sad table and chairs stuffed in a corner at Palm and Page. There was a kitchen, a large table with six chairs around it, and several cushioned armchairs scattered about. A few people were eating the cookies or making coffee. Lucia grabbed two small ceramic plates out of a cupboard, placed a jumbo cookie on each, and handed me one. We sat down in a pair of armchairs with a low coffee table in between us.

"Mmm, this is good," I said between the cookie crumbs in my mouth. "Can you get the recipe from whoever brought them in?"

Lucia laughed. "Nope. Melina keeps it a secret. People ask every time she brings them in, and she always winks and says it's a family secret she isn't allowed to share."

I laughed with her. "Sounds like something out of a book."

"Or a movie."

We both finished the rest of our jumbo cookies in silence, and after dusting the crumbs off from around my lips, I said, "Martin seemed like a bit of a bust. Do you think he'll ever share what he knows?"

Lucia shook her head. "Client confidentiality, for one thing. Even if he could share, he wouldn't with me. Or with you, knowing who you are."

I made a disappointed hum. "Does he often go to New York like that?"

Lucia nodded. "It's always a nice quiet break around here when he does. But he usually comes back on a Friday, not a Monday like he did this time."

I didn't think too much about Lucia's comment until we brought our plates over to the kitchen and placed them in the dishwasher. One of her other colleagues came over to us.

"Hey, Lucia. Did I overhear you talking about Martin coming back on Monday?" the blond woman asked.

She nodded. "Yeah, how come?"

"I just thought it was strange. I was in a meeting with our colleagues from New York on Friday morning and asked them to pass on some info to Martin if he was still there. They said I'd just missed him and he was on his way to JFK to fly home."

"So Martin did come home on Friday?" Lucia asked.

The woman shrugged. "Sounds like it. It's not a three-day plane journey across the country."

"I wonder why he'd lie about what day he arrived home?"

"Beats me. Anyway, I've got a meeting starting soon. I'll catch you later, Lucia." She nodded at us both in good-bye.

"See you, Jessica." Lucia turned back to me. "Okay, so I definitely think Martin is up to something. Maybe he even killed Lorelai."

"Lucia! Talk about jumping to conclusions." I was shocked for a moment before I thought about it. Martin had made it a point to create an alibi for himself for the time of the murder. "Do you really think he could be capable of something like this?"

"You heard what he said about money being a powerful motivator. Maybe he wasn't only talking about Lorelai's family. Maybe he was talking about himself. He might be in for a big payday with this case," Lucia said. "I've come across some pretty crazy motives like that."

"You mean he teamed up with her family to kill her in exchange for a piece of the inheritance?" I shuddered. Had we been in a room with a murderer just a short while ago? Yikes.

Lucia slowly nodded, as if she was deep in thought. "Okay, I want to help out."

"You are helping out by saying you're my lawyer every time I've gotten into some sort of situation where I've needed one."

"That's true. Which has happened three times this week, I might add." Lucia smirked.

I rolled my eyes. "Trust me. That's three more times than ever in my life before."

"What I was trying to say was—I want to help solve this. I want to figure out who killed Lorelai as well."

I lowered my voice and glanced around the break room to make sure no one was listening. "You're not just hoping it was Martin, are you? So you can get him out of the office?"

"No. I promise. I think we need to figure this out and quickly, before you're blamed again. It'll also help solidify you getting Lorelai's inheritance, so we don't need to worry about someone trying to steal it from you. Also, if it is Martin, he needs to be brought to justice."

"We should also look into Viviana some more."

Lucia nodded. "Agreed. So, am I in?"

"Okay. Deal. I would love your help." I paused for a moment. "But on one condition."

"What's that?"

"No spy, crime, gangster, police, or any other type of movie references."

Lucia laughed. "No promises."

Chapter Thirteen

After Jules had brought over her pick-me-up cookies—definitely delicious enough to rival the ones we'd had at Lucia's work—I suggested we check out the Five Palms Resort and Casino that evening, and Lucia eagerly agreed.

Oceanside, which had once been overlooked by tourists, now boasted a new vibe with the gorgeous beachfront as the main attraction. The beautiful, sprawling hotel catered to tourists from all over the world and was right on the beach. It was a place I could only dream about staying at one day. Aside from the parking lot, the numerous buildings were surrounded by either golden sand or luscious lawn. The main building was home to three restaurants, a ballroom, and the casino. There were a few guest rooms located there as well—mostly fancy suites was the rumor—but the majority of rooms were in the outer buildings dotting the property.

We walked up to the main building, and I took in the gorgeous architecture. The resort's buildings were pale yellow capped with adobe-red roofs. The main entrance was lined with grand archways opening into a courtyard that welcomed guests before they stepped inside the building. The five large palm trees the resort was named for were planted like sentinels between each of the archways. Manicured flora bordered the wandering pathways curving around the property, and tall palm trees swayed in the ocean breeze above us.

I inhaled deeply. Somehow the smell of the ocean was even sweeter here. "Wow. This place is fancy."

"Have you never been here before?" Lucia asked.

"Nope. Just driven by a few times."

"I've had work lunches at the restaurants before with clients. The food is delicious. We should treat ourselves sometime and eat here."

I thought of my nearly empty bank account after putting all my resources into opening Palm Trees and Page Turners. "Maybe just dessert."

We walked through the courtyard and into the lobby of the resort. Stylish armchairs and sofas were scattered around the open space. A string quartet played soft music at one end of the lobby opposite the check-in desk. In the center was a large koi pond with a little bridge crossing to the other side.

"Let's check with the front desk first," I said.

There were two couples in front of us in the check-in line, and I took another look around the lobby while we waited. *Elegant* was the word that immediately came to mind. It had such a classic style to it, almost reminiscent of the golden age of Hollywood.

"I can help you here." The friendly hotel clerk waved us over. "Are you here to check in?"

"Not today," Lucia said.

Like we'd ever be checking in. "We're looking to find some answers about a recent guest of yours."

"All right." Clearly puzzled, the clerk gave us her full attention. "What can I help you with?"

"We understand a Lorelai Knight recently stayed here," I said.

Understanding dawned in the clerk's green eyes, and her demeanor was no longer as friendly. "I'm sorry, but we've been instructed to not talk about the situation with the press." She started to wave the person behind us to step forward. "Next."

"No, wait!" I reached my arms out like I was going to physically stop the guest from stepping forward. Talk about desperate. "We aren't the press. I'm related to Lorelai Knight." Well, only probably, but whatever.

"Oh. Um, well then, I'm sorry for your loss."

"Thank you."

"So, you see," Lucia said. "We have a few personal questions. To help my client here grieve and move forward."

The woman still seemed a bit hesitant.

"Please. We'll be quick," I promised.

"All right," she said, her voice low. "What would you like to know?"

My smile brightened. "So she did stay here, then?"

"Yes. I checked her in myself last Saturday. I remember her because she asked where she could find a bookshop."

I gripped Lucia's arm.

"I found that odd. Most guests want to know about the local restaurants or places to sightsee," the woman continued. "I sent her to this little bookshop right on the beach."

"Yes!" I startled the clerk with my excitement. "That's my shop."

"Oh. You must have seen her, then?"

"No, well, I mean yes. Sorta."

"We were also wondering if Lorelai stayed by herself," Lucia said, saving me from my fumbling.

The clerk nodded. "Yes. She checked in by herself with a reservation for one. And I never saw her with anyone." She frowned slightly. "Not that her stay ended up being very long."

"How long was she planning on staying?" I asked. *Good question, Scar.* I mentally patted myself on the back. I could do this. I could be an investigator.

"She booked a week's stay." The clerk glanced behind us, and I turned to see a growing line.

"One last question." I thought for a moment how I was going to word what I wanted to know. "Did Lorelai seem—I don't know— off? Distracted or anything while she was here?"

"I'm not sure what you mean. She seemed a little anxious, maybe. Like she was trying to mentally prepare herself for something important that was about to happen."

"All right. Thank you so much for your help." I stepped to the side with Lucia. "Now what? That wasn't super helpful."

"How about we check out the restaurants? Maybe she dined at one and one of the waitstaff knows something."

"That's a great idea."

Two of the restaurants, both fine dining, were directly off the lobby: a seafood-and-steak house and a French cuisine restaurant. A third, more casual option, a café and coffee shop, was down the hallway toward the casino.

We stopped by the two fine dining restaurants first, and I pulled up the photo I had of Lorelai on my phone. No one at either location remembered Lorelai dining there. And there was no question as to whether they knew who she was. All the staff of the resort seemed to know the story of their murdered guest.

At the Cove Café and Coffee Shop, we had more luck.

We were going to give the same spiel about me being a grieving relative, but there was no need. The barista was all too eager to share the gossip she'd heard around the resort.

"I'd just missed her, apparently." The young woman's blue eyes shone brightly. "My shift started after she'd left the morning before she was found."

"Do you know if she did or said anything significant while she was here?" I asked.

"Oh, yeah. My coworker told me she was arguing with someone on the phone the entire time she was eating breakfast."

"Do you know what it was about?"

"Something about having cut someone out of her inheritance. It was all so dramatic." She waved her arms around in emphasis, her silver bangles sparkling from the lights above. "And then to think she was murdered the very next day. That's what you call ironic, you know."

"That does sound ironic," Lucia said dryly. "Did she talk about anything else?"

The barista shook her head. "Not that I know of. Man, I wish I'd been working that shift. Then I could say I served a murder victim her last latte!"

I winced at her insensitivity. "Thanks for talking with us."

"No problem. Catch you later."

Lucia sighed as we headed out of the café. "I don't know what I was expecting, but I'd hoped to find out something significant."

"Well, we've confirmed she traveled alone and that she'd cut someone else out of her will. Do you think I replaced whoever that person was?"

"The timing seems to suggest that." Lucia pointed down the hall. "Do you want to check out the casino while we're here?"

"Sure."

I'd never been to a casino before, but I hadn't expected it to be so busy on a Thursday night. I supposed that was an indication of what was to come this summer. We asked at the front about Lorelai, but the man working didn't think she'd been in the casino during her short stay.

"She wasn't here long enough to make use of the casino anyway, even if she was into gambling," I said as we took a quick look around the large space.

"Good point." Lucia suddenly stopped and shuddered.

"What is it?" I looked around to see what the cause of her repulsion was.

"Oh." She looked a bit sheepish. "I heard someone call the name Martin, and it reminded me of you-know-who."

"Martin?" I laughed.

"Yeah, him."

"Do you think he's here?" I looked around again.

Lucia shook her head furiously. "No way. He's totally against gambling. We even had a baby birth date pool for a lawyer at work before she went on maternity leave. And he made a big stink about it. Like, seriously, dude, you can't even make a guess on a baby's birthday? It's just for fun."

"Lame," I agreed, though mostly just to tease Lucia. She found fault with everything Martin did.

Chapter Fourteen

I had mixed feelings about returning to work on Friday morning. Part of me was eager to continue my investigation around Oceanside, but another part wanted a sense of normalcy to return to my upturned life. Fridays were my favorite day of the week, though, because we had a children's story hour in the afternoon.

Evelyn had already beaten me to work, and she was busy tidying up the bookshelves when I came inside.

"Oh, Scarlett. You must have had a traumatic past few days." She rushed over to me to offer a hug, holding my hands afterward to give them a squeeze. "I'm glad you're feeling well enough to come to work. If you ever need to stay home, remember, I can take care of things."

"Thank you. Yes, it's been pretty rough. Hopefully, the police find the real killer soon, and we can put this all behind us."

"Steve's working hard at it. I promise." She clutched my hands to her chest before dropping them. "I vouched for you yesterday. I told him there was no way someone as sweet as you could be mixed up in all of this."

"Thanks, Evelyn." I smiled. "We should get the store ready to open. It's probably going to be another nutty weekend."

"It might not be too crazy, because next weekend is Memorial Day. A lot of families will save their travel for then."

That wasn't super encouraging. Instead of having the frenzy spread out over two weekends, it would all be saved for one. But one day at a time. The mention of Memorial Day looming near also reminded me to get that job application up on our website ASAP. The summer season was here.

*   *   *

Ten o'clock rolled around, and I opened the doors to a small crowd on the sidewalk. Most people had phones and cameras out. It seemed a little strange, but I warmly greeted everyone and ushered them inside. "Welcome to Palm Trees and Page Turners."

I took the first shift at the cash register and had settled in my spot when a guy in his early twenties came over and snapped my photo. The bright flash temporarily blinded me.

"Hey! What was that for?" I held my hands up and took a step back.

He shrugged nonchalantly. "Just wanted to get a photo of the Bookshop Killer."

My jaw dropped. "What—no! You can't—" I sputtered as he walked away. My blood boiled. So I was a tourist attraction now? What was wrong with people?

That's when I realized no one was shopping or looking at books. Everyone was trying to subtly take a photo of me, though no one was quite as daring as the first guy.

"Evelyn, could you please watch the cash register for me?" I struggled to keep my voice steady.

She looked eager to take over as I weaved my way through the obnoxious crowd, all of them trying to get a decent photo of my face. I ducked my head and pulled my hair out of its short ponytail to hide my face—not easy with it barely reaching above my shoulders. Hurrying into the back, I turned on the desktop computer and searched for news about Oceanside. Coming across a local blog, I gripped the mouse and slammed it down as I read the top headline. *Owner of Palm Trees and Page Turners Bookshop Under Suspicion of Murder.*

"Seriously!" This was getting out of hand.

After opening a new Word document, I typed out *No Photos Inside The Store* and blew up the font as big as it could go and still fit on a single page. I took a moment to look for the angriest-looking font possible, but I couldn't find anything to adequately convey my feelings, so I left it as Times New Roman. The poor Enter key took the brunt of my anger as I hit print before closing my eyes in an attempt to calm down, listening to the printer *whir* to life.

I wasn't any calmer as I snatched the paper out of the printer tray and stomped back out into the main part of the bookshop.

A familiar male voice was asking everyone to leave if they weren't interested in purchasing a book, and I stopped dead in my tracks. The majority of the people shuffled out, leaving a few customers behind who turned to the shelves to start browsing.

I was both thankful people were leaving and dreading seeing if who I thought that voice belonged to was actually here. As the crowd parted, I caught a glimpse of the head of shaggy blond hair belonging to the surfer guy I'd once fallen in love with.

"Connor?" I blinked three times, but he wasn't a figment of my imagination. "What are you doing here? I thought you'd be settled in San Francisco by now."

"Scar! So good to see you, love." He came over, attempting to wrap me in a big hug, but I ducked away, letting him awkwardly drop his arms to his side.

"Please just tell me what you're doing here."

"I've made a horrible mistake and came to ask you if you wanted to get back together. Hoping, praying you'd say yes."

My stomach dropped. Those were the words I'd wanted to hear for weeks, and now, suddenly, I didn't. I hated those words. I wanted nothing to do with him now that I'd come to realize what a complete jerk he'd been.

"No."

"No?" Connor blinked, looking genuinely surprised. "That's all you can say is no? I just drove all the way here today, and you didn't even give it a second to think about it."

"I have thought about it. I've thought about it every day since you left." I turned on my heel and stormed away, heading toward the cash register. I yanked open a drawer beneath the counter and dug through the office supplies, looking for Scotch tape.

Attaching pieces of tape to my *No Photos* sign, I marched over to the front of the bookshop and stuck the sign up in the window.

"Scar, please listen to me." Connor followed me around the store like a needy puppy.

"No."

"Please? All I want is a chance to talk things through."

I looked into his pleading blue eyes. Big mistake. My heart melted a bit. Just a little bit.

"Fine." I blew out a sharp breath. "But not here. Not at work. Tonight."

"Okay, I'll take it." Connor grinned. "Dinner at Miku Miso tonight. My treat." And he left before I'd had a chance to give it a second thought.

"I take it that's the boyfriend?" Evelyn asked when I walked back to the cash register. She sounded casual, but I could tell she was dying to know what was going on.

"Ex-boyfriend," I corrected.

"He seems like an interesting piece of work."

"You're telling me. I seriously don't want to hear what he has to say, but I know he'll never leave me alone if I don't."

"So you're going to meet up with him tonight?"

"I need to get this over with. I'll tell him good-bye once and for all, and hopefully, that will be that."

Evelyn gave me a sympathetic smile. "Well, at least he got the people bothering you out of the store. I take back what I said about this weekend not being crazy, though that was a whole different type of crazy."

I looked around at the almost-empty store. "True." Never had I thought an increase in store traffic would result in a decrease in sales. What a depressing thought. "I saw a blog post about how I'm a murder suspect. That's how everyone knows about it."

Evelyn *tsk*ed. "That's awful. I'm sorry to hear you're still a suspect. I certainly hope you aren't arrested again."

The sound that came out of my mouth was half whimper, half disbelieving laugh. "Yeah. I hope that too."

"Palm and Page would be in good hands with me if that happened, though. I don't want you worrying about that."

"I'm sure everything will be okay."

Evelyn looked thoughtful. "I do have some ideas about how I could run this place, though."

A customer interrupted us before I had a chance to ask what she meant. I made a mental note to let her know I was always open to her suggestions. I didn't need to be out of the picture for any changes to happen.

For the rest of the morning, I greeted each person who walked through the entrance with a smile and a "Welcome to Palm Trees and Page Turners," all the while hoping they were actually there for the books and not me, the town's current main point of interest.

"Welcome to Palm Trees and Page Turners," I said to a middle-aged woman who'd entered. "Can I help you find anything?"

"Yes, I was hoping you had something about a murder?" she asked. A little too innocently, I thought.

I wanted to scream and tell her to get lost. My nerves were done for the day. But I kept on a fake smile and asked her to clarify, all ready to lie and say I knew absolutely nothing about the murder that'd happened earlier this week.

"Like mystery books. I was hoping you had murder mysteries to read. Those are my favorites." She glanced around the shelves nearest her.

The tightness in my chest eased, and I quickly turned my head to hide the fire creeping along my cheeks. I'd majorly jumped to conclusions. She was an honest customer. "Sure, right this way." I led her to three tall shelves filled with mystery and crime fiction, and she thanked me.

Evelyn caught my eye, and I thought she perhaps had read my mind and knew I'd been about to lose it. I closed my eyes and took in three deep breaths before looking at my watch.

"I'm going to start getting set up for our story time hour." I headed toward the children's book corner, where we had a colorful area rug spread out. I tidied the shelves and put the small plastic chairs in an open circle. I usually started story time by picking three books to read to the kids before letting them vote on one or two more. Then I handed out bookish-themed coloring and activity pages I'd printed ahead of time.

This week's books were a Berenstain Bears book, a new book about dinosaurs visiting outer space I hadn't heard of before, and the classic *The Tale of Peter Rabbit*.

Two o'clock came and went, and not a single child showed up to participate in story time. I puttered around the shop, helping the odd customer who dropped by, and kept glancing out the front window, feeling a bit like someone who'd been stood up on a date. This was the first story hour since we'd opened that no one had shown up to.

"Where is everyone?" I asked, after Evelyn had finished ringing up a customer.

She started to shrug and then grimaced.

"What? What is it?"

"Er, nothing. I just had a thought . . . but don't worry about it."

I shook my head. "You can't start to say something and not finish it. What are you thinking?"

"Well, you see . . . I was thinking back to when my kids were little. I'm not sure I'd want to bring them to where a murder had happened a few days before."

I threw my hands up in protest. "But it didn't happen here!"

Evelyn smiled gently. "I know that, and you know that. But the majority of Oceanside doesn't seem to know that. Think of it from their perspective."

I did take a minute to think about it, and as much as I hated to admit it, Evelyn might be right. Not that there was anything right about the situation, though. It was so, so wrong.

The bell jingled over the front door, and a young mother with her two kids stepped inside. "Hey, we just got settled into our hotel down the street, and I heard there's supposed to be a children's story time here? We're not too late, I hope?"

I almost let out a relieved giggle, but I didn't want to scare them off. "You're right on time. Story time will take place over here." I led the boy and girl over to the little chairs and invited them to take a seat. Their mother leaned against a nearby bookshelf and read the titles of the various spines. She didn't seem to find it odd they were the only family there.

Story time was the exact distraction I needed, and when we finished, there would be only a few hours left until closing, and then I could go home and—

Nope. I couldn't. I'd already forgotten I had dinner plans with Connor. My anxiety came back in waves.

"It's going to be okay," Evelyn whispered as she passed by on her way to help another customer who'd come in.

I smiled my thanks.

Chapter Fifteen

After story time, the afternoon flew by, and soon I found myself sitting across from Connor at the same table in Miku Miso that Lucia and I had sat at earlier in the week. I was still wearing the denim capris and light-blue-and-white-striped top I'd worn to work, not having bothered to go home and change.

Over Connor's shoulder, I could see Hiroki in the open kitchen. He caught my eye and gave me a questioning look that clearly read, *What are you doing with Connor?* I gave a quick shake of my head, which I hoped he'd interpret as meaning that I'd tell him later as well as that he shouldn't come over to our table. Connor and Hiroki hadn't exactly parted on the best of terms either, and I didn't need more tension.

"So, Scar, tell me how you've been," Connor said a little too pleasantly, and I barked out a laugh.

"Seriously? You want to know how I've been after you abandoned me and our new business we started together?"

He at least had the decency to wince, like he knew deep down he'd been in the wrong. "I'm sorry about that. I really am. But I'm here now and all ready to make things right."

I shook my head. "Nope. You don't get to do that. You don't get to apologize and expect everything to be all right. You broke my heart, and you almost cost me my dream business. It was extremely difficult getting Palm and Page off the ground without your help, but I did it. I don't need you."

"Please, Scar. If you don't want to get back together, that's fine. But I at least need to be your business partner again."

Connor winced again, like he'd realized his slipup. It took me a moment to catch on. He'd said *need to*, not *want to*.

"The start-up business you were a part of," I said slowly. "It tanked, didn't it?"

Connor blushed and took a sip of his water but didn't say anything.

"It tanked, and now you need another job. You thought it'd be easy enough to get your old one back." I was furious now. "I bet you never even wanted to get back together with me, only Palm and Page!"

Connor's blush deepened, and I knew I had him.

"Please, Scar. Let me explain."

"No, Connor. I'm done." I stood and stormed away from the table, feeling like a heroine in a dramatic novel. I kept my head held high and didn't look back, proud of myself for showing such confidence.

I was complete jelly on the inside and my palms were sweating, but Connor didn't need to know that.

I stepped outside the restaurant and took in a deep breath of the salty sea air, which instantly calmed my racing heart. The smell of the ocean had always been a balm to me. As I walked toward my car, I heard the front door of Miku Miso open and slam shut, followed by a "Scarlett!"

I sped up my pace, hoping I'd reach my car in time and theatrically drive off, leaving Connor behind. Maybe my tires would even spin out dirt at him or something. That'd be great. I chuckled as I pictured it.

But before my vision had a chance to come true, Connor caught up with me and grabbed my arm. I yanked it away, causing him to stumble back a step. That would have to do instead of leaving him in my dust.

"Don't touch me!"

"Sorry, sorry." He held his hands up.

"What do you want, Connor?"

"I want to talk. I want a chance." His tone was incredibly whiny, like a child's. I had no idea how I'd fallen in love with him once.

"No."

"Listen, you're right. The company I was working for turned out to be a bust. I'm broke, Scar. I need help."

"I can't help you."

"Yes, you can." His voice dropped to a whisper. "I've heard you've come into some money recently."

My jaw dropped. "How . . . how did you hear that? Not that I'm saying it's true or anything." *Nice recovery, Scarlett.*

"A buddy of mine down at the police station. You remember Jake Adelstein, right? He's the one who told me."

"He shouldn't have." I'd met Jake only once or twice, and all I remembered of him was that he never seemed to stop talking. Loved the sound of his own voice.

Connor held up his hands again. "You're right. And that's on him. But now I know, and I was wondering if, by chance, you might be able to lend me a little something. I promise I'll pay you back. Just enough for me to get back on my feet."

I was silent for a moment, glaring daggers at him. "You know, Connor? I think it's a little suspicious you happen to be back the week there's a murder which resulted in me inheriting the poor woman's money."

Now it was Connor's turn to look angry. "You're not saying I had anything to do with the murder, are you?"

I shrugged. "It's a little too convenient. You needed money, maybe you somehow found out I was in Lorelai's will, and then you killed her."

"Scarlett!" Connor's shout caused a few people walking from their cars to turn toward us. He lowered his voice and stepped closer to me. "I cannot believe you would say something like that. I didn't even know the lady."

I simply shrugged again.

"Listen, I promise you I had nothing to do with it, but if you want to hear what I think, I think you better take a closer look at that new employee of yours."

Now it was my turn to be completely caught off guard. "Evelyn?"

Connor nodded. "She was asking me weird questions at Palm and Page today before I saw you."

I bristled at his casual use of my bookshop's nickname. He didn't have a right to be so cozy with it. "What kind of weird questions?"

"What I knew about the murder. If I'd been contacted by the police about it. That sort of thing. Maybe she had something to do with it and was trying to see if anyone's onto her."

"No way. That's the most ridiculous thing I've ever heard. I refuse to believe she'd do something like that."

"But you'd believe I'd do something like that?"

I ignored his question, mostly because I didn't have an answer for him. I didn't know Connor anymore. He'd completely changed from the man I'd fallen in love with. "All I know is your buddy Jake needs to start keeping his mouth shut." I brushed past him. "I need to go."

I expected him to try to physically stop me again and was thankful he didn't.

"So this is it, then?"

Sighing, I turned back around. "I don't want to be mad at you anymore, but I don't want anything to do with you either."

"Yeah, but—argh! Scar, you just don't understand." Connor stormed off back to the restaurant and called out over his shoulder, "Fine. Whatever."

Real mature. I let out a long breath, letting myself hope for a moment that it was over. Maybe he would leave me alone and I'd never see him again. But knowing how persistent Connor could be, the only way that'd happen would be if he left Oceanside again. The city definitely wasn't big enough for both of us.

After getting in my car, I took a few moments to breathe. What a big mistake it'd been to say yes to dinner with Connor. The entire evening had been an absolute disaster. I cringed, remembering the way I'd behaved in the restaurant. I'd have to apologize to Hiroki's grandparents for causing a scene.

I drove home and called out a quick greeting to Lucia, who I could hear watching a movie in the living room. I headed straight for my room and changed into a pair of pajama shorts and a top. It was a little chilly in the house from the AC, so I threw on an old red hoodie before joining Lucia on the couch.

"Hey, how was your day?" She scooted over to make room for me.

"Awful." I shoved my hand in the bowl of popcorn she held.

"Awful? What do you mean?" She grabbed the remote and hit pause on her movie, turning to give me her full attention.

"Connor's back in town." I groaned as I said his name.

"What? Why?"

"He needs money and heard about my new inheritance."

Lucia stared at me for a moment. "Okay, that's definitely something right out of a movie. He's like the villain in a bad rom-com. I can't believe he had the nerve to ask you after what he did. You said no, right?"

I glared at her. "Of course I did. First, he wanted to get back together with me, then he wanted to work at Palm and Page again, and then finally I got it out of him that he's really after the money. I said no to all three."

"How did he even hear about your inheritance?"

"He apparently has a blabbermouth of a friend at the police station."

Lucia clicked her tongue. "That's not right."

"I know." I stuffed another handful of popcorn into my mouth. "Hey, I want you to listen to a theory of mine and tell me if it's too out-there or not."

"All right."

I told her about how I thought maybe Connor had orchestrated Lorelai's death so I'd receive her money and then he could convince me to give him the money.

"I don't know," Lucia said, after I'd finished. "It sounds a little too far-fetched to me. I have no idea what Connor's connection to Lorelai is."

"I don't either, but we should try and figure it out. It seems too coincidental to me that he happens to come to town this week."

"How about first I'll ask about his friend at the police station. What's his name?"

"Jake Adelstein."

"Adelstein. Okay. I'll ask around and see if he really is a blabbermouth. Maybe he did mention something to Connor after the murder and that's when he came into town. Then we could assume Connor had nothing to do with it."

"Okay," I said, though a small, terrible part of me would love to see Connor behind bars.

"Was dinner at least good?"

On cue, my stomach grumbled, and I grabbed more popcorn to shove in my mouth. Lucia laughed and handed me the bowl.

"Thanks." I smiled sheepishly at her.

"I'll heat you up some of my leftover dinner. It's just boring pasta. Nothing fancy."

"Thanks. You're the best."

"And don't I know it."

I stood to follow her to continue our conversation in the kitchen, but I didn't make it far before our doorbell rang.

I groaned. "I sure hope that isn't Connor."

"If it is, we're filing a restraining order against him," Lucia said. "That guy is unbelievable."

Chapter Sixteen

I was fuming by the time I'd reached the door. How dare Connor show his face after what he'd done?

Yanking the door open with all my might, I was ready to yell at him to get out of Oceanside already.

I sucked in a deep breath. "I can't believe you would—Oh, hi, Hiroki."

Hiroki stood there looking bewildered at my anger toward him. He shyly held up a white bag that looked to be full of sushi takeout. "Everything okay, Scarlett?"

"Yes. I'm so sorry. I thought you were someone else. Please come in." I stepped aside and let him into our house.

"Connor?" he asked.

"What?"

"Did you think I was Connor?"

"Oh. Yes, I did. How did you know?"

Hiroki shrugged. "Lucky guess. Well, that and the fact you were just at the restaurant yelling at him. I wasn't sure how many different people you like to yell at in one night."

I had to laugh. "Only one. So don't worry. I've hit my quota for the day. How come you stopped by?"

"In between all that yelling, I noticed you hadn't eaten anything and thought you might be hungry. My shift is over for the night."

"I'm starving, to be honest. Thank you. That's so kind of you."

"No problem."

Lucia rounded the corner. "So? Do we need to head down to the police—Oh, hi, Hiroki."

Hiroki and I burst out laughing at Lucia's reaction being the exact same as mine was a minute ago.

"Hiroki brought dinner," I said, in answer to Lucia's confused look.

He held up the bag. "Want some, Lucia? I brought plenty for all of us."

"Yum! That sounds better than pasta. I'll put the leftovers back in the fridge."

We followed Lucia into the kitchen and set out the sushi spread on the kitchen table. Lucia came over with a stack of plates, and Hiroki divided out the disposable chopsticks and a few napkins. I opened the four takeout containers and took a look at the different colorful rolls inside. Hiroki had outdone himself. It looked delicious, and I doubted we'd be able to finish it all.

"Do you want to talk about why Connor's in town?" Hiroki asked, after we'd had a few bites. "You don't have to, but please know I'm here for you if you want to talk. He didn't contact me at all about returning."

I smiled at him and thought back to our conversation from the other day, where he'd told me he regretted not having been there for me the first time Connor broke my heart. "You know that woman who was murdered on Monday?"

Hiroki blinked, chopsticks paused in midair. This was clearly not the direction he'd expected the conversation to go. "What about it? You don't think Connor had anything to do with it, do you?"

"Well—" I started, only to be interrupted by Lucia.

"She doesn't! We have absolutely no proof of that."

"Okay, hold on. That wasn't even what I was getting at in the first place. We'll come back to that." I ignored Lucia's evil eye and quickly moved on. "What I was going to say was remember how Lorelai left me her inheritance? Well, Connor has gotten wind of it and now wants some of the money."

"Wow. That's crazy," Hiroki said. "That's a sleazy move after he broke things off."

"Yeah, so I'm not surprised he didn't contact you. Unless you also happened to randomly inherit a large sum of money."

"Nope. Can't say that I have." He playfully shook his head. "Have you figured out why she left you her money yet?"

"Possibly. I'm not entirely sure. That's part of the mystery, but there's a chance she's my birth mother." I grabbed a few more sushi rolls to put on my plate.

"Your birth mother?"

Poor Hiroki. I was feeling a little bad he couldn't keep up with this conversation. It was just so crazy, as he'd said. I told him my story and how both my sister and I had been adopted from two different birth families.

"I don't know how long ago she found me. She came into Palm and Page the night before she died and didn't say one word about it. Just bought a book and left."

"Maybe she was nervous," Hiroki said.

"Nervous?"

"Maybe she wanted to say something but wasn't sure what to say. It must have been a big moment for her as well. Finally seeing the daughter she'd given up after thirty years."

"Twenty-eight," I quickly corrected him, not sure why I was a little offended that he thought I was older. That was the furthest thing from the issue here. "But you could be right. I honestly hadn't thought about that."

"That's sad," Lucia said. "She was probably planning on coming back once she'd worked up the nerve but never had the chance."

"She did say something about dropping by again." My heart hurt at the thought. Just because I hadn't gotten my hopes up about finding her didn't mean she'd felt the same, and now we'd never have the chance to properly meet. Lucia was right; it was sad.

A fat tear rolled down my cheek, and I hastily brushed it away, but not before Lucia saw and wordlessly nudged the box of tissues on the table toward me.

Hiroki started collecting the empty containers. I'd been wrong; we had finished it all. Apparently, detective work and yelling at one's ex-boyfriend could create a big appetite.

"I should get going," he said. "Thanks for sharing your story, Scarlett. Let me know if I can do anything to help."

"Sushi always helps." I smiled at him. "Thanks for dropping by. Again. I super appreciate it."

"Yes, thanks, Hiroki. You can stop by with sushi anytime," Lucia said.

"No problem. See you both later." He dumped the containers in the trash can and let himself out the front door.

I turned back to Lucia. "So, Connor said something else pretty bizarre to me tonight."

Lucia rolled her eyes as she started to collect the plates. "What else did the Slime King say?"

I snickered at her nickname for him. He really was the king of slime. "He said to take a closer look at Evelyn because she was asking him weird questions when he was in the store. Thought she maybe had something to do with Lorelai's murder."

Lucia paused, her hand hovering above my plate. "What? There's no way. That doesn't even make sense."

"I know. I know that doesn't sound like her at all, but she's been making all sorts of weird comments lately about running the store herself. What if she wants me out of the picture so she can take over?"

Lucia shook her head. "No way. I don't believe it."

I sank my face into my hands. "I don't know what to believe right now. Connor's gotten in my head. But what if?"

"I don't know, Scar. Is Evelyn really that desperate to run Palm and Page? Couldn't she just start her own business?"

I shrugged and stood to help tidy the kitchen. "Starting a business from scratch is a lot of work. Trust me. I know."

"Okay, so let me get this straight. You think Evelyn, sweet, motherly Evelyn, murdered Lorelai so she could run a bookshop?"

"No. Yes. Maybe. Anything is possible."

"Scarlett, think it through. Her husband is the lead detective on the case. And do you really think she'd risk spending the rest of her life in jail?"

"Not if she's trying to frame me. I'd be the one in jail then."

"Okay, fine. Just for kicks, let's entertain this idea." Lucia started pacing around our small kitchen, her hands waving widely, emphasizing every word. "You think Evelyn is framing you for murder so she can run Palm and Page while you're rotting away in jail?"

I winced. "K, well, you don't need to be so graphic, but yes. Maybe."

"I thought Evelyn liked you, though. Have you done anything to offend her?"

"No. Nothing." I was a little offended myself at the thought of my trusted employee trying to get me tossed in jail. "We've gotten along well the entire time she's worked at Palm and Page."

"No arguments over wages? Working hours? Nothing?"

I shook my head at each suggestion. "She hasn't complained about anything, and I know it's getting to be too busy for just the two of us to handle, but I told her I plan on hiring more help."

"Does she seem to be enjoying her job?"

"Yes, of course. She's always cheerful and seems to genuinely like helping our customers. But as you said, if she wanted her own book-shop, she could start one. Yes, it's a lot of work, but it's probably less work than framing your boss for murder." I let out a laugh in disbe-lief over such a ridiculous thought and turned on the tap to rinse the plates. After loading them in the dishwasher, I turned around and leaned against the counter, watching Lucia continue her pacing. "But she has made those comments lately about taking over Palm and Page if something happened to me."

"Something like you being in jail for murder?"

"I thought her comments were a little odd. Premeditative, almost. And sometimes it seems like she'd like to be in charge. Not exactly bossy, but opinionated."

"Okay, we'll come back to motive later. Let's talk about opportu-nity. She could've easily left the poison bottle outside the bookshop to frame you." Lucia paused. "But how would she know it wouldn't lead to her?"

"Maybe Evelyn made sure she had an alibi for the time of the mur-der. Maybe she snuck out of her house in the middle of the night to kill Lorelai and snuck back in. Her husband would've never known she'd left, and that would be the perfect alibi—to have the lead detective on the case think you were sleeping in the same bed the entire night."

Lucia pointed at me. "That's good. Detective Maxwell would never suspect his own wife. Especially if Lorelai was a complete stranger to them. Wait, was she a complete stranger?"

"I'm not sure."

"Didn't you say Lorelai was the last customer of the day?"

I nodded.

"Maybe the time of death was off and she'd been murdered ear-lier. Maybe Evelyn followed Lorelai after work and killed her before going home. Lorelai had the misfortune of being at the wrong place at the wrong time."

"So you think Evelyn just picked a random easy target?"

"Exactly."

My head was foggy, trying to sort through so many thoughts. But the thought screaming at me the loudest was how terrifying it was that I might've accidentally hired a murderer.

Chapter Seventeen

The next morning at the breakfast table, with a clearer head and a fresh start to the day, I didn't quite agree with Last Night Scarlett.

Lucia stumbled into the kitchen. "Morning." She yawned.

"Hey. So, I was thinking about something . . ."

"You think Evelyn murdering a stranger is completely bonkers?"

"Yes, how did you guess?" I poured coffee into my mug, breathing in the strong smell.

"Because I feel the same way." Lucia put her head in her hands. "I'm so embarrassed we let our imaginations run wild."

"Me too. I can't believe we thought Evelyn could be capable of something like that. She's the sweetest lady I know. Besides, how would my inheritance fit into everything if Lorelai was a complete stranger to Evelyn? That would've been a huge coincidence."

"That's a good point."

"I blame Connor for all this," I said. "Or the ridiculous amount of sushi we ate. Viviana's still on my radar, though."

Lucia nodded. "I think she or Martin are the most likely suspects at this point."

"Mm-hmm." I took a sip of my coffee. "Anyway, what are you going to do with your day off?"

"Jules and I are heading out in half an hour or so with the kids to the farmers' market."

"That sounds nice. That's one thing I miss about not working Saturdays—being able to do all the fun local things that take place on weekends. No one seems to plan anything for Thursdays." I briefly considered switching the hours at the shop, but weekends were too good for business to pass up, especially in the summer.

"I'll bring you back something yummy," Lucia promised. "The Simply Scones booth always has a fun new flavor. Would you like some of those?"

"Sure, that'd be great. And can you pick up some jam to go with them?"

We finished getting ready, me for my busy day at work and Lucia for her fun day of sampling food from local vendors and restocking our kitchen with delicious treats.

The doorbell rang while Lucia was still brushing her teeth, so I opened it for her and greeted Jules.

"Hey, girl!" Our neighbor gave me a quick hug. "How's it going?"

Some of my worries slipped away. Jules's energy was contagious, and she always brought a smile to our house.

"Honestly, I'm a bit jealous of your trip to the farmers' market with Lucia."

"Come with us! Ditch work and join us. You're not needed at your own store, right?" Jules winked.

"Ha. I wish." I looked behind her. "Where are your kids?"

"Already loaded up in the car." Jules pointed to the minivan in the driveway next to ours and waved at her three kids in the back seat. Liam, Anthony, and Jade, all of elementary school age, waved back. "Just waiting for slowpoke Aunt Lucia."

I laughed. "She should be here soon. She's just brushing her teeth."

A look of concern came over Jules's face. "How have you been doing with the whole murder-suspect thing?" she asked quietly, as if she thought her kids might hear.

"Not that great. I know the police haven't found who the real killer is, so I'm still a suspect. I've actually been trying to find out who it was myself."

"Really? How's that going?"

I shrugged. "One step forward. Two steps back."

"I'm here. I'm here." Lucia came bounding down the hall. "Hold on."

"The kids are eager to see you. Hurry up. Jade made you something special in her art class, but act surprised when you get it. I wasn't supposed to tell you."

Lucia practiced her surprised face. "Like this?"

Jules and I both laughed.

"Yes! That's perfect," Jules said. "Now, come on. Put those cute pink shoes of yours on and let's get going."

I closed the door behind them, listening to their carefree laughter.

*   *   *

Cautiously, I greeted Evelyn, who'd pulled up seconds after me, in the parking lot of Palm and Page, and she followed me toward the bookshop's front door. I was ninety-nine percent positive Evelyn wasn't a murderer, but something bothered me about the whole thing, and I couldn't quite put my finger on it. Besides, being extra vigilant wouldn't hurt.

Nervously, I stepped aside and pretended to dig around in my purse for my store keys, letting her walk ahead of me.

"Here. I have mine handy." Evelyn dangled the keys in front of her. "I've got it."

Throughout the day, I continued to be on alert around Evelyn. I overanalyzed every comment she made, searching for any clue or hidden confession in her words. She was nothing but her sweet self the entire day, giving my nervousness at being around her no validation. The conflicting feelings made me clumsy and jumpy.

"What's up with you today, Scarlett?" Evelyn asked, after I'd dropped a book for the fourth time that morning. Poor things. "Are you still upset over what Connor said?"

That he alluded to you being a killer? Yes. "That's part of it. Let's just say dinner didn't go well last night."

"I'm sorry to hear that. I hope he doesn't bother you anymore, even though he seemed pretty determined to get his job back. Do you want me to talk to Steve about it?"

I shook my head. "No. Thank you, though. I'm hoping he leaves Oceanside soon." The last thing I needed right now was to get the police more involved in my life.

"Do you know how long he's staying in town?" Evelyn started moving toward the cash register, where a customer had approached to have her purchases rung up.

"Nope, he didn't say."

Evelyn turned to give the customer her full attention, and I watched the interaction. She smiled and asked the customer if she had found everything all right. Evelyn laughed at something the woman said and processed the transaction quickly and efficiently, giving the customer a wholehearted good-bye.

There was no way someone like Evelyn could be diabolical enough to not only commit murder but then turn around and frame someone else, especially someone like me, who she was supposedly fond of.

No, it wasn't possible. Lucia and I had let our imaginations get away from us yesterday. I cringed at the thought of how quick we'd been to think we had it all figured out. I almost felt like I owed Evelyn an apology, but there was no way I wanted her to know I'd suspected her. It would ruin our relationship, both at work and outside it.

The bell above the door jingled as another customer came into the shop. "Welcome to Palm Trees and Page Turners."

"Hello." The young woman smiled, pushing her sunglasses onto her head. "I hear this is the place to find the perfect book to read on the beach."

"It is! I can guarantee I can help you find something. What sort of genres do you like?"

The woman looked thoughtful. "All sorts, really. Though I'm not the biggest fan of nonfiction."

"Don't worry. The majority of what we carry is fiction. I find people tend to be looking for an escape from reality while at the beach and not wanting to learn about something."

"How about a fantasy novel? I've always liked books with princesses and wizards and all sorts of magic."

"Follow me." I led her around the corner of a nearby bookshelf and pointed out the start of our fantasy section. "I have it organized by middle grade, young adult, and adult throughout this area, and then in order of author's last name."

"Oh, this is perfect. I'm sure I'll find something." She started to head down the aisle toward the adult section. "I think I'll even grab more than one. I'm here all summer."

"Wow. That sounds like a nice long vacation."

"It is, though I want to look for part-time work while I'm here. I'm starting nursing school in the fall and want some extra in my savings. It took me a while to settle on a career choice, so now that I have, I want to give school all I've got. This summer will be half work and half holiday for me."

Having Palm and Page be a part of such a unique trip to Oceanside for someone was exactly why I'd wanted to open the bookshop. "I'm actually looking for part-time help for the bookshop."

"Oh, that sounds perfect for me."

"The job posting isn't up yet, but I hope to get to it soon. Keep an eye out for it on our website."

"I will. Thank you so much."

I wished the woman the best in picking out some novels and told her I'd meet her at the cash register when she was ready.

"Thank you. You've been very helpful."

"No problem. Let me know if you need anything else."

I was busy with another customer when the woman wanted to check out, so Evelyn helped her. Afterward, I sent Evelyn on her lunch break.

As I watched Evelyn retreating toward the back, I wondered again if she even had a mean bone in her body. Ugh, something wasn't sitting right, and I couldn't quite completely dismiss her from my limited suspect list. I still wavered back and forth. Most of the time she was so nice, but then sometimes the odd comments she made about taking over had me wondering what her true intentions were.

Finally, as we were closing for the day, I gathered up the nerve to ask Evelyn a few questions that might give me a hint as to whether or not she'd been involved in Lorelai's murder.

"How's your husband's case going?" I asked as casually as I could while I counted out the cash for the day.

Evelyn stopped dusting and sighed. "It's okay," she said, and I could tell she was trying to sound positive about it.

"Any new leads?"

"Not that I'm aware of, but he doesn't talk about his work much at home. I'm sure he'll figure out everything soon."

"I heard this is the first murder case in this part of Oceanside in years. I hope he doesn't feel too in over his head to have been assigned it."

"Steve's doing just fine," Evelyn said briskly.

Okay. That did seem strange to me. Evelyn was always open with me, but it was clear she didn't want to talk about this. Something was up, and I needed to push a little further.

"Did he tell you about the murder right away? I mean, I'm sure he could have used the support."

She shook her head. "No, he didn't tell me about it until he came home that evening, even after I texted him when you told me he'd been at the scene. He must have been very busy getting right to work."

"And to think he left for the day having no idea what it would hold. Did you see him that morning?"

"Of course. I got up early to make him breakfast before his shift. We always eat any meal together that we can when our shifts line up." She started walking toward the back. "I'm going to work on sorting through our stock in the back for the rest of the afternoon. Let me know when you're done."

"All right." I thought about the conversation. I hated to admit it, but I did have a feeling Evelyn was hiding something. If her breakfast story was true, then she would most likely have been home when Lorelai was murdered, so she couldn't have done it.

But how did I know she was telling the truth? No one else had witnessed it, and it would be weird to ask Detective Maxwell if she'd been at home that morning. He might toss me back in that cold holding cell for suggesting his wife was a killer. I'd have to talk this over with Lucia later and get her take on it. Also, I was due for another update with Olivia; maybe she had new suggestions for me as well.

Which reminded me, I'd never gotten around to following up on the poison lead by checking which stores sold poison in brown glass bottles.

I headed toward the back after finishing up my tasks. I was about to call out to Evelyn to say I was ready to leave when I heard a loud sniff.

Was Evelyn crying? I hid by the door to listen to her. Another sniff followed by a muffled sob. Yep, definitely crying.

Was she crying out of guilt for murdering Lorelai? Or fear that I was onto her?

I quietly backed up a few steps, then walked loudly toward the back, hoping to give her enough time to wipe away the tears. If she was crying because she'd had something to do with Lorelai's death, I wasn't ready to deal with that yet.

When I entered the back room for the second time, the sniffling had stopped.

"Are you ready to leave?" I asked cheerfully.

"Yes. Just one moment," Evelyn said quickly, followed by the sound of her blowing her nose.

I concentrated on a book spine next to me, not ready to make eye contact with Evelyn. My chest tightened with guilt for choosing not to acknowledge her tears, but something was off about the way she'd been acting, and I was nervous about any confessions she might make.

We left Palm and Page and quickly said our good-byes, each promising to get a good night's sleep before our usual crazy Sunday coming up.

I thought I recognized someone on the beach nearby as I headed toward my car. It was one of the customers who'd been in earlier that day, the woman who liked fantasy books. I gave her a quick wave in greeting when she turned her head toward me, and she responded by waving me over to her spot on the sand. She was reading in a beach chair, catching the last bit of light before dusk settled over the Pacific Ocean.

"I wanted to say thank-you again for having such an amazing shop." She pointed to the open book in her lap. "I enjoyed my afternoon reading."

"That's great to hear. Did you spend the whole day on the beach?"

She nodded. "I grabbed lunch from a taco truck down by the pier and relaxed the entire day."

"Guac 'n' Roll? They have the best carnitas tacos."

"Yes! That's exactly what I had. It was delicious. I'm Autumn, by the way."

"Scarlett." I reached out to shake her hand. "I'm sure I'll see you around lots if you're planning on spending the majority of your time at the beach. And I look forward to seeing your application for the job."

Autumn, whose cinnamon-colored hair matched her name, nodded enthusiastically. "For sure."

"Well, I should leave you to your book. See you later."

"Bye. Have a good evening."

I headed back to my car, slightly envious of Autumn's day. It sounded absolutely perfect, lounging on the beach, reading, and eating tacos. I made a promise to myself to take a day and do exactly that once I solved who'd murdered Lorelai and got this whole mess cleaned up, including clearing my innocent name.

Maybe Lucia and I could have a mini day at the beach sometime soon, just an evening or something. I made a mental note to suggest that when I saw her.

I stopped in at the pharmacy on my way home. It was only open for another ten minutes, so I didn't have much time to look for something poisonous that came in a brown bottle. I was greeted when I came into the store, and I headed past the bandages and vitamins toward the medicines in the back.

As I stared at the various medications, I realized I didn't know if Lorelai had been poisoned by liquid or a pill. Hmm. I took a look at both. There was cough syrup in a brown glass bottle, though it looked quite a bit smaller than the one Detective Maxwell had shown me. Could the answer be that simple? An overdose of cough syrup could cause severe sedation, making drowning very possible; mixed with alcohol, it could be fatal. I wasn't sure if that would be considered a poison, though.

"Excuse me?" I asked a passing pharmacist.

"Yes?"

"Does this come in a larger size?" I held up the bottle of cough syrup.

She shook her head. "No, sorry. That's the largest there is."

"Just at your pharmacy or in general?"

"In general. At least for public retail. A hospital or health clinic might be able to order it in larger quantities."

"All right. Thank you very much. You've been really helpful."

"No problem," she said. "Please let me know if I can help you with anything else."

Yes. Where can I find a poison that comes in a large bottle, one that will kill a woman? "No, that's everything. Thanks."

I looked around more but couldn't find any more brown glass bottles.

Chapter Eighteen

"I'm still leaning toward no on Evelyn being the killer," Lucia said while I finished serving the chicken stir-fry I'd made for dinner that night with the fresh vegetables Lucia had bought at the farmers' market.

"What made you think of that?" We'd been pretty quiet in the kitchen while I cooked, and she washed the breakfast dishes we'd never gotten around to during the day.

"I was thinking about the farmers' market today with Jules and the new apron she bought from one of the craft booths."

"Uh-huh." I had no idea where she was going with this.

"There was this adorable yellow-and-white-striped picnic blanket I was thinking of getting but ultimately decided against, since we already have so many picnic and beach blankets."

"Not sure where you're going with this." I grabbed cutlery from the drawer.

"And then I thought about how one of those beach blankets is that nice teal-and-purple one Evelyn gave you for your birthday in January, even though she'd only been your employee for, what? A few days?"

I nodded. I'd hired Evelyn about a week before my birthday, right after Connor left. Another point proving Connor to be a loser: he'd dumped me so close to my birthday. "That was nice of her. It's one of my favorite beach blankets."

"That's exactly my point."

"What is? The beach blanket?"

"No. That Evelyn is really nice. Why would she buy you a birthday present when she had no obligation to, then turn around and frame you for murder four months later?"

Lucia had a point, but something was still bugging me. I didn't want to believe it—I really didn't want to believe it—but I had a gut feeling Evelyn was involved somehow. She might not have been the one to murder Lorelai, but maybe she was connected to whoever did.

"Hey, speaking of beach blankets." I remembered my idea from earlier. "Do you want to spend an evening at the beach sometime? We live so close but rarely go together."

"Sure." My roommate beamed. "Sounds like fun. Does tomorrow work? It looks like I'm going to have to work lots of late evenings this upcoming week, so it might be my only chance to relax for a while."

"Perfect for me. Do you want to meet me there around six thirty after the shop closes?"

"Sounds good."

* * *

During my lunch break the next day, I was scrolling through Instagram under the hashtag *#bookstagram* when I came across something called A Blind Date With a Book. Intrigued, I read about the concept and instantly fell in love with the idea. I looked at dozens of photos featuring people purchasing books all wrapped up in brown paper and tied with a string. Each book was simply labeled with a few key words, such as the genre, instead of the title and author. Readers would have no idea which book they were going to read until they opened it.

We could easily do this at Palm and Page. I would head to the small craft store downtown for rolls of large brown paper as soon as I had the chance. Already I was picturing which books I would wrap and the words I could use to describe the story without giving too much away. I knew we had a couple copies of *Confessions of a Shopaholic* by Sophie Kinsella in the romance section. I could include words like *rom-com*, *book to film*, and *London*. Or for *Becoming* by Michelle Obama, words like *memoir* and *empowering*. I grabbed a scrap piece of paper from the table and started scribbling down my ideas.

"Hey, Evelyn?" I looked around for her when I went out to the main part of the shop after I'd finished eating. I was too excited about sharing my new idea to worry about being suspicious around her. "Have you heard of something called A Blind Date With a Book?"

She looked over from the books she'd been reshelving between helping customers. "No. What's that, dear?"

I gave her an explanation of the concept. "We could totally do that, and I think customers would get a kick out of it."

"Oh, that's a cute idea."

"I'll set aside some of the books I'm thinking of and then pick up brown paper tomorrow. I'm thinking of clearing off one of the shelves close to the front so we can really feature these books."

Evelyn smiled. "I'll think of suggestions for books as well. Customers will love this."

*   *   *

Lucia was leaning against her car parked next to mine when I locked up Palm and Page.

"See you, Evelyn," I said.

Evelyn waved as she got into her car and drove away.

Evelyn hadn't done anything suspicious today, so I still wasn't sure where she landed on my list. Probably near the bottom, since her potential motive was so weak. Connor was at the top, but maybe I needed to admit to myself that it was mostly because I was still mad at him for ambushing me the other day. Viviana and Martin were somewhere in between.

"How's it going?" Lucia asked.

"So good. I came up with a fun new bookish project at work. I can't wait to tell you all about it. Plus I'm majorly looking forward to the beach."

"Me too. I packed us a picnic dinner. Nothing fancy, just whatever was around the kitchen."

"That sounds fine. Thank you. I hadn't even thought about dinner."

"Walk, lounge, or dinner first?" she asked.

"Lounge while eating dinner? I'm hungry now that you've mentioned food. Then we can walk when it's starting to get dark." The pier and immediate surrounding beach were lit up once the sun set so people could still enjoy it well into the evening.

Lucia laughed. "Sure." She opened her trunk and pulled out a brown wicker picnic basket. It usually sat at the back of our shoe closet, so I was glad to see it finally enjoying the daylight.

I opened my car and grabbed my beach bag, which had been left there since the other day. No sunscreen was needed this late in the evening, but I was glad the blanket was still there. We spread it out near the water, right above the lapping waves, and Lucia opened the basket. Inside were sandwiches, fruit, and a bag of chips. I plopped down on the blanket beside her and fluffed out my mint-green sundress around me.

"This looks great." I pulled out a sandwich and took a bite.

"The only thing missing is something to drink. I figured we could grab something from the snack stand after. I've heard they've extended their hours now that it's the beginning of summer."

I nodded, my mouth full.

We ate our picnic while I told Lucia about the Blind Date With a Book project I was planning. She came up with a few suggestions as well, though all the titles had a pattern of being books that had been turned into movies. And knowing Lucia, her key words were probably based on the films, as she wouldn't have read the books.

Around us, families and couples gathered their things after a day at the beach, and we spent time people watching. The calm evening was turning windy, but it was still warm enough that we didn't need hoodies or jackets.

The sun started to set over the water as we finished our dinner. Lucia grabbed her phone out of her purse and took photos. "This is gorgeous!"

I watched the pink and orange streaks dance across the sky. A few sea gulls flew past, making it a picture-perfect moment. I took a few photos myself and sent them to Olivia. She might get the perfect sunrises in Sydney, but nothing could beat our California sunsets.

I added a few heart emojis and typed *Miss you* as a caption to the photos. I hoped she'd made her weekend deadline, though I would've been very surprised if she hadn't. Olivia was the hardest-working person I'd ever met.

After the sun had dipped below the horizon, Lucia suggested we head over to the snack stand to get our drinks.

"Sure, sounds good." I stood after her, and we gathered our picnic stuff.

We strolled toward the snack stand, which was designed to look like a classic surfers' shop with an awning made of large, dried palm leaves and old surfboards stuck in the sand out front. One surfboard was painted with chalkboard paint and had the menu written on it. Nearby were a dozen picnic tables with bright-orange umbrellas scattered around the patio and colored lights strung up above. It always seemed like a fiesta at the snack stand.

We were almost there when Lucia stopped in her tracks and made a disgusted sound.

"What's wrong?" I asked. "Did you stub your toe on something?" I looked down but could only see sand. No rocks, beach toys, or other culprits.

"No, look." Lucia pointed toward the snack stand, where a couple had just left with drinks and a large platter of nachos. "Martin Russell."

"Oh, ugh." I made the same sound Lucia had made in solidarity. "Well, at least he and his date are heading away from us."

"That's true. I don't think he saw us." Lucia took another step toward the snack stand. "I don't think I could stand hearing his sexist, demeaning remarks outside the office. During work hours is bad enough."

"I feel sorry for his date." I brushed my hair out of my face as the wind started to pick up.

We reached the snack stand and each ordered a strawberry lemonade.

"Do you want to walk along the pier?" Lucia asked.

I took a long, contemplating sip of my lemonade. "I guess so. Sure." The pier had always been my favorite place to go for walks, and I no longer wanted to be hesitant to do so after Lorelai's murder. It was time to face my fear and take back my source of serenity.

Though I'll admit I did hurry past the spot where I'd found Lorelai, slowing down once we were safely farther along the pier.

If Lucia had noticed my change of pace, she didn't comment on it. She started to tell me about the newest case she'd received and about her upcoming holiday to visit family in Mexico in a few weeks. It'd been a couple of years since she'd seen them, and she looked forward to it. I'd miss her around our house for the two weeks she'd be gone but was happy she'd found the time to go.

I took the last sip of my lemonade, and Lucia reached out to grab my cup. "I was about to toss mine. I'll meet you back here." She headed back toward the trash can at the beginning of the pier. Apparently, Lucia had noticed my change of pace there and was allowing me to be a scaredy-cat for a little longer by making sure I didn't walk past the murder spot more times than necessary.

Night had completely fallen by now, and I noticed my little spot on the pier seemed darker than everywhere else. Looking up, I realized the light above was burned out, so I took a few steps toward a better-lit area, trying to tie my hair back in the wind as I walked.

Something—or someone—slammed into my back, and I stumbled forward, catching myself on the railing of the pier.

"Hey! Watch out." I started to turn around to see who had bumped into me so violently but instead was met by a pair of hands reaching out from the darkness. I was shoved hard before I could see who they belonged to.

My top half went over the railing, quickly followed by my legs and feet, which floundered in the air as I gracelessly crashed into the choppy ocean below.

Chapter Nineteen

I'd barely been able to let out a scream before being engulfed by the inky-black Pacific Ocean. Tumbling around beneath the waves, I frantically tried to find my bearings and get my head above the water. I kicked against the pressure of the water, my lungs urging me to find oxygen ASAP.

At last, I broke through the rough surface and gulped down a breath of precious air. Bobbing in the water, I wiped my tangled, wet hair out of my face and tried to figure out what had happened and how far from shore I was. One minute I'd been standing on the pier, minding my own business, and the next I was in the ocean. I gazed up to where a few people stared down at me. The burned-out light was a ways down the pier, showing how far I'd drifted in such a short time.

"Are you all right?" someone called.

I nodded, which only caused my head to fall beneath a wave again. "I—I think so." I did a quick assessment of myself; my limbs were shaky, but there wasn't any pain. No injuries, just shock.

"Can you swim?" someone else called down. "You won't be able to get back up on the pier here. You'll have to swim to shore." The woman wildly waved her whole arm in the direction of the beach, like she was trying to land a plane.

"Yes. I can swim."

"Okay. We're calling an ambulance for you just in case."

"I'm fine. Really." I grimaced and started to swim as quickly as I could toward the shore. The last thing I needed right now was more attention.

Lucia's face peered down at me. "Scarlett! What are you doing down there?"

I fumed. She made it sound like I'd had a choice in the matter. "Someone pushed me!"

Lucia looked around at the people on the pier like she was trying to figure out who'd done it. I highly doubted whoever had pushed me would've stuck around.

"Just meet me back at the beach." I continued my swim, the skirt of my sundress heavy around my legs, making it hard to kick. I was exhausted once I'd reached the shore and eagerly accepted Lucia's warm hug. I noticed she had my beach bag and purse in her hand, which luckily hadn't fallen into the water with me.

"Are you all right?" she asked. "What happened?"

"I'm fine. Honest. Just shaken up." Sirens approached from a distance. I groaned. Someone had actually called an ambulance. A large piece of seaweed was tangled around my leg, and I struggled to peel it off. Frustrated, I straightened and left part of the seaweed stuck to me. I needed a shower, not medical attention.

Lucia indicated the bags in her hands. "Isn't it strange that whoever pushed you didn't grab your stuff? So it wasn't some sort of weird mugging."

I stared at her. "You're right."

"Do you think it was an accident?"

I shook my head furiously. "No way. Someone pushed me with both hands. It wasn't like they bumped into me by accident or anything. This was definitely deliberate."

The ambulance pulled into the closest parking lot, and two paramedics ran out, carrying their equipment.

"Over here!" Lucia waved them over, even jumping up and down.

"Lucia!"

"What? I think you need to be checked over anyway, despite feeling okay. You never know."

I sighed. She did have a point. But then I saw someone else hurrying down the beach after the paramedics. I sucked in a sharp breath. It was Detective Maxwell.

"What's he doing here?"

She shrugged. "His job? This was an assault, Scarlett. That's a crime."

"Not something major enough to demand a homicide detective."

"Were you the one who fell off the pier, miss?" the first paramedic asked, once they'd reached us.

Obviously. I'm the only one here soaking wet and covered in seaweed, looking more like the crazed sea witch than the little mermaid. "Yes."

"Any injuries or pain?" The second paramedic opened her red first-aid bag.

"I don't think so—" I started, before being interrupted by Detective Maxwell.

"Scarlett! What happened?" His accusatory tone filled me with guilt at first, despite there being no reason for me to feel that way. And that only increased my irritation.

"Someone shoved me off the pier," I said as calmly as I could. Even though the wind remained warm, a chill started to settle in me, and I shivered.

One of the paramedics grabbed a thick black blanket and tossed it over my shoulders. "Why don't you sit in the back of the ambulance? I think the adrenaline is starting to wear off. That's why you're shaking."

"I don't want to go to the hospital," I said, my voice a slight whine. "I want to go home."

"How about we assess you at the ambulance first, and then we can decide whether or not you'll need to go to the hospital," the paramedic said with a gentle smile. "You're looking okay to me, but we need to be sure."

"All right," I said quietly, and they led me to the parking lot.

Lucia, still holding my bags and hers, followed behind me, and Detective Maxwell followed her. Apparently, he still had more questions for me.

"Scarlett?" an astonished voice said from my right. "What happened to you?"

I turned to see Hiroki with a group of his friends setting up to play nighttime beach volleyball under the floodlights near the nets.

Could this evening get any worse? I was thoroughly embarrassed now.

"I'm fine," I tried to assure him, keeping my eyes on the ground. I didn't sound convincing even to myself. "I just fell in the water, but I'm not hurt or anything."

"Are you sure?" he asked in a tight voice. I looked up, and he raised an eyebrow, clearly not believing me, as I was currently trailing after two paramedics on the way to an ambulance with a police officer following behind. "Did Connor do this?"

I shook my head. "No . . . I don't think so, at least. I didn't see who pushed me."

"You were pushed?" He jerked his head in the direction of the ocean as if looking for the culprit. "That's not okay."

I sighed and hung my head again. Worst evening at the beach ever. Out of the corner of my eye, I saw Lucia give him a subtle but firm shake of her head. He got the hint and didn't probe further.

His tone softened. "Let me know if you need anything, okay? I'll talk to you later." Hiroki waved good-bye, still looking concerned, and turned back to his friends and volleyball game.

Once we'd reached the ambulance, I sat in the back. I didn't want to admit it, but the paramedics had been right to suggest this. Being off my feet and away from the curious stares of everyone began to ease the hard knot of tension inside me.

Until Detective Maxwell started pressing me with question after question.

"Could you please describe what happened tonight, Scarlett?" he asked as one of the paramedics took my blood pressure.

"I was standing on the pier, waiting for Lucia to return from throwing out some garbage, when someone pushed me into the water."

"That's all you can tell me?"

I nodded. "That's all I know. It was too dark to see anyone, and I was in the water before I could even process what'd happened."

"But there are lights along the pier." He narrowed his eyes, his voice gruff.

"Not where I was standing. The light above me was burned out."

The look on the detective's face made it easy to read his thoughts. How convenient it was that I'd happened to be standing in the one dark spot along the pier. Thankfully, he didn't ask further questions on the topic.

"Did you see anyone around you recognized before you got to that spot?"

"No." I thought for a moment. "Wait . . . I mean yes. I did see someone."

"And who was that?"

"Martin Russell. He's a lawyer who works with Lucia."

Lucia made a small scoff.

Detective Maxwell nodded. "Yes, I know who Martin is. Isn't he working on a case against you being Lorelai's heir?"

I willed my face to remain neutral. "He is."

"Are you sure you saw him tonight?"

"Yes, of course I'm sure. He was at the snack stand getting nachos. I'm pretty sure he was on a date." Why was Detective Maxwell asking me if I was sure? Did he think I was lying? Did he think I was trying to throw Martin under the bus to get him to stop representing Lorelai's family? "I have no idea if Martin was the one who pushed me. I just saw him at the beach not long before it happened. That's the truth."

"You're all clear to go, Miss Gardner," one of the paramedics said. "Get into dry clothes as soon as possible, and get plenty of rest."

"Thank you so much." I hopped down from the ambulance. "Are you all done as well, Detective? I'd like to get home."

"Yes, that's everything."

"I have a question for you, if you don't mind," I said.

He gave me a funny look but then waved his hand, as if he was welcoming me to go ahead.

"How come you came tonight? This wasn't a homicide."

"As soon as I heard something had happened at the Oceanside Pier, I hurried down here. I thought it might have to do with Lorelai's murder. Imagine my surprise to find *you* here, I might add."

My face warmed. "I promise I don't know who did this or why. I don't even know if I was the intended target or happened to be in the wrong place at the wrong time."

"Unless it's a case of mistaken identity or you majorly overcharged a customer for one of your books today, I think this could very well have to do with Lorelai's murder. And given your involvement with the case, I think you were the intended target."

Lucia stepped in to my rescue. "If that's all, Detective, I think it's time my client went home to rest, as per the paramedic's orders, from this terrifying experience."

He looked like he was about to argue but instead said, "All right. I'll be in touch if I need anything else."

"Thank you," I whispered to Lucia. "He doesn't seem to like me very much."

"Let's get you home. Are you okay to drive?"

We started walking back to the Palm and Page parking lot. I nodded. "Yes, I'll be okay."

"Do you think someone was trying to do more than hurt you?" She ran a hand through her long hair, glancing at me.

"What do you mean?"

"Do you think someone was, you know, trying to kill you?"

"What? Why would someone do that?" The thought sickened me.

"Maybe someone figured out you're trying to find who killed Lorelai and wanted you out of the picture."

"Or wanted me out of the picture to make their way to the inheritance." I shuddered.

Lucia nodded. "That's possible as well."

I gave it some thought. I didn't at all feel like I was close to figuring out who the killer was, but maybe I was doing good enough of a job to spook them. Or someone was very determined to get that inheritance. Either way, it was a terrifying thought.

At our cars, I reached into my beach bag and pulled the blanket out. I spread it across the driver's seat and tossed my other items in the back.

Murder by the Seashore

"I can't believe this all happened." I shook my head, giving a disbelieving laugh.

"It'll be all right. I'll see you at home." Lucia gave me another quick hug and then got into her car.

Chapter Twenty

I was a complete zombie at work all Monday morning. Every time Evelyn tried to get my attention, she'd have to ask two or three times before I finally realized she was talking to me. I lost count of how many bookshelves I bumped into by accident. It was like some of the ocean water had gotten into my brain and my thoughts were swimming around aimlessly.

Over and over I went through who could possibly have murdered Lorelai and who could have pushed me into the ocean. Had my tumble just been meant to scare me, or was it attempted murder, as Lucia had suggested? I shuddered at the thought.

There was Evelyn, who had a possible motive to be mixed up in all this—a bizarre motive, but it was still something. There was also Connor, who'd mysteriously shown up in town a few days after the murder. He also had a motive, since he seemed to think he'd benefit from Lorelai's inheritance. Had he always been completely bonkers and I'd just never noticed? However, Connor claimed he hadn't been in Oceanside on the day of Lorelai's murder. Viviana Diaz was still on my radar as well, simply because she was the only person in town who actually seemed to have known Lorelai.

And then there was Martin. Martin could potentially be in for a big payday if he was able to succeed in getting Lorelai's will overturned. And he'd have a very rich family in his debt. That seemed like something he'd appreciate. Martin had also been around at the beach right before I was shoved into the water. Could the woman he'd been with possibly have something to do with this? Perhaps she hadn't been a date but was actually a member of the Knight family. I wanted to investigate her as well, but I had no idea where to start. I could barely remember what she'd looked like. She'd had . . . hair?

I groaned out loud as I organized the messy bookshelves around the store.

"Are you all right?" Evelyn asked, after finishing ringing through a customer. "And are you sure you don't want to take today off after what happened last night? I'll be fine by myself."

Evelyn had told me the version of events she'd heard first thing this morning before I'd had a chance to share my own story. She'd learned parts of it from her husband and parts from her neighbor, who'd apparently been on the pier. It'd been mostly correct, though I hadn't been submerged for a full two minutes after falling in the water, nor had a handsome paramedic jumped in to save me like my knight in shining armor. I'd saved myself, thank you very much. And I thought my story was plenty dramatic without all this embellishment going around. It made everything even more embarrassing.

"Yes, I'm fine. Just a little, ah, stiff." I winced at my small lie, not wanting to admit my groan was mostly about my lack of success in finding the murderer. Though it wasn't completely untrue; I was pretty sore from yesterday's catastrophe. I rubbed my right shoulder for good measure as my mind wandered back to my suspects.

I needed to start crossing people off my list, and soon, before I was tossed into the ocean again to sleep with the fishes.

My next plan was to talk with Olivia again. Hopefully, she'd have an idea for me of what to do. She deserved an update anyway.

I messaged her on my break, and we arranged for a time to chat tomorrow evening my time.

The day dragged on. I rang up purchases on automatic pilot and had to triple-count a poor customer's change because I'd completely zoned out the first two times.

It wasn't until around two in the afternoon that I remembered my Blind Date With a Book project from the day before. Thinking about wrapping and labeling the books perked me up.

"Hey, Evelyn? Do you mind if I quickly run to the craft store? I forgot to buy the brown packaging paper."

"Of course. I can't wait to see how they turn out."

It didn't take long to find the brown paper in the small, locally owned craft store, and even though I wished I could browse through the aisles of colorful paints, beautiful stationery, and silky ribbons, I was on a time crunch. I grabbed two rolls of paper and made a bee-line to the checkout.

"Hey, Scarlett!" An overly cheerful voice intercepted me. "How are you doing after your dip in the ocean last night?"

I turned to find Carrie Lee from the grocery store holding a shopping basket full of yarn. "How did you hear about that?"

"Hear?" She chuckled softly. "I didn't have to hear. I saw the whole thing."

"You were at the pier?"

I was momentarily confused by her dreamy sigh until she said, "I was on the most romantic date of my life. Even the ruckus you caused didn't ruin the evening."

Rude. "I'm glad to hear."

Carrie didn't seem to pick up on my sarcasm. "After dating so many idiots, it's been nice to be with someone so smart. I could listen to lawyer talk all night."

Whoa. There was no way. It'd be too big of a coincidence, but then again, how many lawyers had been on dates at the Oceanside Pier last night? "I'm sorry, who did you say you were on a date with last night?"

"Oh, I don't think I said. His name's Martin, and he's a lawyer." She repeated his occupation with admiration.

"And you were on the pier when I fell in?"

"Well, not quite on the pier, but on the beach. We totally saw you swim and climb out of the ocean like the creature from the black lagoon, though. Wow. All the crazy stuff seems to happen to you."

Hmm. So either it wasn't Martin who'd pushed me, or he'd booked it off the pier pretty quick. "How long have you two been dating?"

"Just over five months now, and it's been wonderful." Carrie twirled the end of her silky black ponytail around a finger. "He's so busy with work but always makes time for me. Like last night, he had to briefly meet a client at the beach, but then his entire focus was on me for the rest of the night."

"Well, I'm glad you're happy."

She beamed a big smile again. "Anyway, I'm delighted to hear you're doing okay. I need to go pick out a few more colors for the scarf I'm knitting for Martin, so I'll see you around."

I couldn't help but stare at her already full basket. Just how colorful was this scarf going to be? "I should get going as well. It was nice bumping into you."

When I got back to Palm and Page, there were only a few customers in the shop, which gave Evelyn and me time to wrap the books we'd set aside at the cash register counter. I grabbed a black Sharpie pen and labeled the books with four or five key words.

"Oh, what's this?" a woman asked as I finished up the last one.

"It's called A Blind Date With a Book." Her comment made me realize I needed to make a sign for the bookshelf explaining the concept. "You pick a book based on knowing only a few key words about the story. No title, cover, author, or anything."

"I love that idea." She reached over to sort through the books on the counter. "*Romance, 1920s, New York City, Enemies to Lovers.* Wow, this sounds exactly like my type of book date. I'll take it!"

I laughed at her enthusiasm—exactly the reaction I'd hoped for. "I hope it's love at first page."

* * *

"Good night," I said to Evelyn in the parking lot after setting the alarm and locking the door that evening. "See you in the morning."

"Are you ready for the scavenger hunt tomorrow?"

I stared blankly at her. "Uh, the what?"

"The scavenger hunt. Didn't you remember it's happening tomorrow afternoon?" A cloud of worry drifted onto Evelyn's face, like she was actually afraid I was losing it.

"Oh, sure. Of course, I remember," I lied, not wanting to admit I'd no idea what she was talking about.

Clearly, Evelyn didn't believe a word I was saying. "The one the community center is hosting." She pursed her lips, eyebrows raised.

Right! The community center was hosting a different activity every day this week to kick off summer. Tomorrow's was a beachwide photo scavenger hunt, and we'd been asked a few weeks ago if Palm Trees and Page Turners wanted to be on the list of locations. At the time, I'd thought it'd be great for getting potential customers through the door and eagerly said yes. We'd been encouraged to put out snacks and water for participants, and I'd been ready to go all out.

Oops. I'd completely forgotten about it until now, with the murder taking up the majority of my brain space and the Blind Date With a Book project taking up the rest. I'd have to make a quick stop at a bakery tomorrow for goodies.

"Yes, I'll have everything ready. Thank you for reminding me."

"Bring snacks people can easily grab and go. Like cookies or granola bars." Looking pleased we wouldn't be a failure of a stop for the photo scavenger hunt, Evelyn got in her car and waved as she drove off.

Whew. Now I could deposit today's earnings and go home.

Lucia's car pulled into our driveway ahead of mine, and I helped her carry in grocery bags from her trunk.

"Was there a sale or something?" I pulled out six bags of potato chips from the last grocery bag.

"Yes." Lucia's eyes gleamed. "Two for one. I thought they'd make the perfect brainstorming snack."

"Brainstorming? About what?"

"About who shoved you in the ocean, of course." Lucia started chopping an onion for tonight's dinner, chicken curry with rice and naan bread. "It must've been Martin."

"And you're not just saying that because he's your evil archnemesis?"

"No. I'm saying that because he lied about being on a flight when Lorelai was murdered and he was at the beach last night. Plus he's working for Lorelai's family to get the money back."

"Maybe. What a sleazy thing for the guy to do, though." I stepped back and leaned against the entrance to the living room, trying to avoid any burning tears from the onion. Apparently, it didn't faze Lucia at all, as she continued to chop away.

Lucia shrugged. "Martin's a sleazy guy. He gives the rest of the lawyers at our firm a bad name. I'm honestly surprised one of the managing partners hasn't fired him yet. I have a suspicion he has an in or something with one of them. Why else would anyone have hired him?"

"You really think that?"

"Maybe. Anyway, he was all worked up over something today at work. I don't know what. He was yelling at someone on the phone and then went running out of the office this afternoon and didn't return."

"Strange," I said. "I did learn something else about Martin today."

"What's that?"

"His date last night was Carrie who works at the grocery store."

"Whoa, how'd you learn that?"

I explained about my trip to the craft store.

"I mean, Carrie's a little excitable, but I don't think she'd kill anyone." Lucia dumped the onion pieces into a hot pan.

"I agree."

We were both quiet for a few moments, and my thoughts wandered down a different path. "Speaking of lawyers. What about Jeffrey?"

"Lorelai's lawyer?"

"Yeah. Maybe it was him."

"What would his motivation have been, though? It sounded like Lorelai was one of his best clients, and he seemed very loyal to her."

"Hmm, you're right." I frowned. "Never mind."

"Hey, don't give up. It was a good thought. We'll figure it out."

Thinking of Jeffrey reminded me I still needed to get back to him about Lorelai's possessions. While Lucia finished making the chicken curry, I sent him an email about having everything sent over at his convenience. I had no time to make the drive to LA to pick it up.

Lucia was right about one thing: the potato chips were a great brainstorming snack after dinner, though we came nowhere close to eating all six bags, nor did we narrow down our suspects.

We headed to bed shortly after, and I slept deeply from all the excitement from the past few days.

Murder by the Seashore

Thump.

I startled in the pitch-blackness of my room, willing my fuzzy brain to make sense of what I'd heard. The loud thump sounded like it'd come from outside our house, near the driveway, but I wasn't entirely sure I hadn't imagined it.

Thump.

That one was distinguishable and even louder than the first. I sat up in bed and scrambled to find my phone and turn the screen on. One AM.

Lucia's bedroom door opened, confirming I hadn't dreamed the two loud sounds, and I raced out into the hall to investigate.

"That wasn't from in the house, was it?" Lucia asked.

I rubbed my sleepy eyes under my glasses. "No. I think it came from outside. Maybe it was one of our neighbors."

"Okay. Let's check."

We hurried to our front entrance, and Lucia opened the door. She took one step outside onto the porch in her bare feet and started screaming.

Chapter
Twenty-One

A crumpled body lay on the front porch at our feet, a small pool of blood starting to form beneath the figure's head.

I joined Lucia in the screaming.

"Who is it?" Lucia asked between hitched breaths, a hand to her chest.

"I don't know." Racing back inside and upstairs to my bedroom, I grabbed my phone from the nightstand. I hurried to punch in 911 as I headed back to our porch.

Lucia was peering closer at the body, and a few neighbors had started to gather near our porch. Jules was among them, her arms wrapped tight around herself, and she looked as if she was saying a prayer.

"Oh, Scarlett," Lucia whispered. "I think it might be Martin."

I was in the middle of speaking with the 911 operator and didn't think I'd heard Lucia correctly. I couldn't concentrate on both conversations, so I finished giving the operator our address. He replied that the police and an ambulance would be there soon.

"Sorry," I said, after the call ended. "Did you say it's Martin?"

Lucia nodded. "I think so, but I'm not positive." The body was facedown. "It's hard to tell, but it looks like his frame and his hair. Well, despite the blood."

The dark pool of blood was now drying on the back of his head, and it blended in with his brown hair, the sight causing my stomach to turn. But Lucia was right. From what little I could tell, it did look like Martin. He even wore a suit similar to the one he'd worn the other day when I visited their law firm.

"What happened?" Jules came closer to us, her big brown eyes full of fear. "Do you know this man?"

"Possibly," Lucia said. "Though I have no idea what happened. I was just woken up by two loud thumps."

"I heard that too. I was scared Anthony had fallen out of bed, so I got up to check on him. Then I heard you two screaming your heads off and came outside," She stared at the body. "This is awful. I can't believe something like this would happen in our little complex."

Emergency sirens grew louder and louder, and I was thankful they'd arrived so quickly. At least then we could find out the identity of the man. Lucia and I stepped back from the body and let the police officers do their work. Detective Maxwell wasn't among them, and I hoped he had the night off. A dead body found on my own front porch wouldn't do well for proving my innocence.

"Scarlett? What happened?" a male voice that had joined the small crowd called out.

I groaned. No way. "Connor, what are you doing here?"

He stepped forward, his steps a little wobbly, like he'd been drinking. "I was on my way to talk to you. I need you to listen to what I have to say. Please, Scar. You're my only hope."

Yep, definitely had been drinking. He always got more dramatic than usual even after only a few drinks. "It's the middle of the night,

Connor. I was asleep until this happened, so I wouldn't have wanted to talk to you anyway."

"But I need you to understand what I'm going through. It's so horrible." Connor was on the verge of begging now.

I noticed my neighbors all looking back and forth between Connor and me, like the dead body was the show opener and now Connor's melodramatic pleading was the second act. We'd be the center of town gossip for days.

"Connor, listen to me," I hissed. "Now is not the time or place to have this discussion." I wasn't sure how much more of him I could take when an officer interrupted our little exchange.

"Miss? Are you one of the residents here?"

I nodded, noticing other officers started to put yellow crime scene tape around our porch and keep the small crowd back.

"Can I ask you a few questions?"

"Sure." I turned my back so I wasn't looking at Connor and the crowd anymore, then told the officer what little I knew of what had happened. They'd turned the body over after taking photos of the scene, and it was Martin. A wave of nausea hit me again at my having personally known the victim, and I had to look away. "I have no idea why he was at our house at one in the morning," I said in answer to the officer's next question. "He's a colleague of my roommate's, but she doesn't know why he was here either."

"When was the last time you saw Martin Russell?" the officer asked, and I squirmed under his intense gaze.

"Saw or spoke to? Because I saw him at the beach yesterday, or two days ago now, I guess. On Sunday evening, I mean. But that was from a distance, and I didn't speak to him. I did talk to him at his office last week on Thursday afternoon. I brought Lucia a peach iced tea."

"And what was the conversation about?" The officer thankfully didn't comment on my nervous rambling about unimportant details.

"I recently received an inheritance from someone, and Martin was the lawyer representing another party involved." I couldn't believe this was my life. I didn't even know how to explain everything. "It's really messy. See, a family member of Lorelai's—that's the person who died and left me the money—wants the money for themselves. Martin was trying to get it back for them, even though legally it belongs to me."

"And do you know who this family member is?"

I shook my head. "No. I don't even know if it's a single person or multiple people. Like I said, it's all very messy."

"All right. Do you have any idea who might have killed Martin?"

I looked back out into the crowd, and my gaze fell on Connor still swaying about on his feet. Had he really just come to talk about his money problems? "No, I don't."

The officer followed my gaze. "Are you sure about that?"

"Yes, I'm sure." I didn't like Connor, but I wasn't about to incriminate him for a murder before I knew more. Though between his desperation for my inheritance and now his showing up at the same time Martin was found dead, he was definitely my number-one suspect.

"All right. Thank you for your time." The officer nodded before making a beeline toward Connor, pulling him aside to chat.

Oops.

But my curiosity got the better of me, and I strained to hear their conversation. Connor insisted he had no idea who that man was. He'd never met anyone named Martin Russell or used legal services from McKenzie, Allen, and Kumar. Connor turned pale and took a step back from the officer.

"I saw someone!" His voice rose. "I saw someone running down the sidewalk away from here before I arrived. It was probably who killed that guy."

I couldn't tell if he was telling the truth or making something up to throw attention off himself, but still, I listened.

"Was it a man or a woman?" the officer calmly asked.

"Uhh . . . a woman?" Connor sounded extremely unsure. Probably a lie, then.

"Can you describe her?"

"It was too dark to see much, but I think her hair was black. And she was running."

The officer didn't seem convinced of Connor's story. He asked Connor if he had a safe place to sleep for the night and sober up. When Connor gave the name of the motel he was staying at, the Surf Side Inn, the officer said they'd make sure he got there safe.

Another car pulled up, and my heart dropped at the sight of Detective Maxwell getting out of it.

"Detective," the officer who'd been talking to Connor said by way of greeting.

Detective Maxwell sort of gruffed at him, making it obvious he'd been woken up and called in when Martin's body was found.

"Why are you here, Miss Gardner?" He stared at me with cold, dark eyes.

"I live here." That hadn't come out as confidently as I would've liked. Someone brushed against my side, and I turned to find Lucia, all set to jump in and defend me if needed.

"Do you know what happened?" He pointed to Martin's body still lying on our front porch, waiting to be examined.

I repeated what I'd already told the other officer, and Lucia chimed in with her story as well. She had no idea why Martin would visit in the middle of the night either, but she did tell Detective Maxwell about how peculiar Martin had acted at work that day.

"I have a gut feeling it had to do with Lorelai's death," she said.

"Have you had any arguments with Martin recently, Miss Gardner?" Detective Maxwell asked.

"No. We talked at his law firm last week about the inheritance, but it wasn't an argument."

"Would you say you had a grievance against him, then, if he represented a client who also wanted Lorelai's money?"

"No!" I took a step back. "I mean, I wasn't worried about losing the money."

"And what do you mean by that? Did you do something to ensure you wouldn't lose the money?" He glanced at Martin's body.

I wiped my sweaty palms on my yellow pajama pants. "No. I didn't do anything. I meant, Jeffrey Cooper's a good lawyer, and I don't think there's a loophole or anything for Martin's client to get the money. Not that I even care so much about the inheritance—" I cut off at Detective Maxwell's raised eyebrow. I needed to get my rambling under control.

"Any more questions, Detective?" Lucia asked, arms crossed.

Before he could answer, an officer waved him over, pointing at what looked like a brick on the ground. The detective nodded at us sharply before going to work examining the body. We hadn't been told to do anything in particular, and there was no way I could fall back asleep knowing what was going on outside, so Lucia and I leaned against the porch railings and watched.

Well, Lucia watched. The shock began to wear off, but I still felt a little queasy from looking at another dead body. Instead, I gazed out at the crowd of onlookers, wondering if the murderer stood there right now.

Connor had been escorted back to his motel with instructions to sleep it off and not bother me again while drunk, and Jules had gone home as well.

I didn't really know anyone else still gathered. I recognized a few of the faces from our passing each other around the complex, but there was no one with any connection to Lorelai or Martin that I knew of.

A familiar car pulled up to join the crowd, catching me by surprise.

"Scarlett? Are you here?" Evelyn looked around the scene.

I slowly waved at her, my head tilted in confusion.

"Evelyn? What are you doing here?" Detective Maxwell asked before I had the chance.

"When you got the call about the murder, I overheard the address and recognized it as Scarlett's. I had to come and make sure she was all right. I was worried."

"That's nice of you," I said. "I'm fine."

Evelyn stepped closer to us, coming into full view beneath our porch lights. I had the funny thought that if Connor's witness story was true, the description would match Evelyn. She had black hair. But then again, so did thousands of people in Oceanside. Viviana Diaz included. Though, if I remembered correctly, hers had streaks of pink hair dye.

I shook my head, as if to get rid of the thought, but everything kept coming back to Evelyn.

She joined Lucia and me as we stood watch, putting a comforting arm around each of us. The police finished what they were doing, and the body was taken away. We were told to get some rest tonight and then come down to the station first thing in the morning to give our statements.

Nervousness gnawed at my stomach. This would be my third time at the police station in just over a week, and I wasn't looking forward to it.

Murder by the Seashore

After the police and Evelyn had left and it was just Lucia and me, she said, as if she could read my thoughts, "Don't worry. They won't be putting you in a holding cell again. I'll make sure of it."

I started to smile but ended up stifling a yawn. "Thanks. I'm still nervous about going, though."

"I know, but try and get some sleep anyway."

I trudged to my room and fell right into bed. It didn't take me as long as I feared to fall asleep, but my dreams were full of running away from tidal waves and chasing Connor down the beach, courtrooms filled entirely with sand, and long rides in police cars that went nowhere.

Chapter Twenty-Two

I woke completely exhausted from my dreams around six and tried to fall back asleep for another hour but wasn't able to. I couldn't stop thinking about the night before. Martin Russell found dead on our front porch? How bizarre. Part of me wondered if I'd dreamed it.

But when I went down to our kitchen after getting dressed and Lucia immediately asked if I was ready to face the police again, I knew I hadn't.

"No," I mumbled, and Lucia chuckled.

"I know it's not ideal, but like I promised, no more holding cells. It'll be similar to the first time you went after finding Lorelai's body. The police need you to make an official statement, and that's it."

"Promise?"

Lucia gave a dramatic bow, hand over heart. "I promise. We'll head over when you're ready."

My stomach wasn't settled, so I went with plain buttered toast and a glass of water for breakfast.

"No coffee today?" Lucia asked when I sat at the kitchen table beside her.

"Nope. I don't think my stomach can handle anything richer than water."

"You won't be so nervous after this is over. We can pick up something on the way back. Maybe at the Sunshine Café?"

I thought of the breakfast food I'd had there last week. At the time, it was delicious. Now my stomach turned. "Let's talk about something else. How's your family doing? Have you spoken to them recently?"

"I have, but I haven't told them anything about what's been going on in Oceanside lately. They'd want me to come right home."

"My parents would as well. I've only told them about the inheritance but not about the murder. Now murders." I blew out a breath. "I'll wait until the killers are behind bars before I tell them the whole story."

Lucia drove us to the police station, where Detective Maxwell took my statement and another officer took Lucia's in a separate room. I squirmed under his intense gaze the entire time but was relieved he didn't ask me any more leading questions about being Martin's killer. I could still read suspicion in his eyes, though.

I gave both an oral and a written statement of what had happened. Detective Maxwell didn't give any clues as to whether they were close to finding out who'd killed either Lorelai or Martin, or even if they thought it was the same person who'd killed them both. It made me nervous that I could still be at the top of his suspect list.

"Ready?" Lucia asked when we were back at the entrance of the police station.

"Yes, let's get out of here."

"That wasn't too bad, though, right?"

I gave her a side-eye. "I guess not. But I hope that's the last time I need to come here."

"I hope so too. Did you want to get something to eat?"

I shook my head and then remembered the community center scavenger hunt happening this afternoon. "Actually, I need to stop by a bakery before work. Do you mind?"

"Of course not."

Piece of Cake was an adorable little bakery located a few blocks from the beach. The pink awning over the patio seating reminded me of cupcake frosting, and I wondered if that'd been done on purpose. I'd been here only a few times before, but when the delicious smell of freshly baked cookies and muffins hit me as we walked inside, I made a promise to myself to come more often.

"Mmm." I smiled at Lucia. "Okay. You were right. I'm hungry now that the police station is behind me."

"Yeah, I'm definitely getting second breakfast."

I ordered a blueberry cream cheese muffin and an Earl Grey tea for myself as well as four dozen assorted cookies for the scavenger hunt. We sat outside with our goodies to quickly eat before heading to work.

"The sun feels wonderful." I sat back in my chair and tilted my face up to catch some rays. "I wish we could stay all morning."

"I know. Me too." Lucia stood and tossed her empty coffee cup into a nearby trash can. "But come on. I'll drop you off at work."

Evelyn was already inside Palm and Page when I got there. She rushed over and gave me a motherly hug as soon as I crossed the threshold into the store. "Oh, Scarlett! Last night must have been awful for you. I can't believe you found two bodies only one week apart."

I hadn't thought about that. Mondays really were the worst day of the week. "I'm okay. I gave my statement to the police this morning, so I'm glad that's over."

"I bet. Oh, you can't imagine how I felt when I heard your address come over the police call for Steve. I thought you were the one who'd been murdered!" She shook her head fiercely.

"Do you often wake up to police calls for him?"

Murder by the Seashore

"No, I've trained myself to sleep through them. But last night I was out late with friends and hadn't actually fallen asleep yet when he got the call. I'd just crawled into bed."

"Wow. At one AM? Are you turning into a party animal, Evelyn?" I teased, though part of me went on high alert. What had she been doing out and about in the middle of the night?

She laughed. "No, no parties. My friends and I went to the movies. We saw the last show and then grabbed dessert afterward."

"I didn't know there were any restaurants open that late."

"Oh, many extend their hours in the summer for the increase of traffic during tourist season."

"I'll have to check out some of them." I would've never, ever pegged Evelyn as a night owl. Rarely did she mention evening plans, and she always came to work so chipper in the mornings.

"I do hope that's the last murder around here. I don't think any of us can take it anymore," Evelyn said.

"I know. And I wonder if the two were connected."

Evelyn shrugged and turned her back toward me to start straightening up a bookshelf. "I have no idea. I never met either of them."

"You didn't happen to see anything odd last night around town, did you? If you were out during the night."

"You know what? Now that you've mentioned it, there was something a little odd."

"What's that?" I took a step closer to her.

"You know that Viviana lady who owns the Second Chance thrift shop?"

"Yes?"

"Well, I did see her running around in the dark."

"Really? I wonder why."

Evelyn shrugged. "No idea. Though she was headed in the direction of your neighborhood when I saw her."

"What time was that?" My heart sped up.

Evelyn seemed thoughtful for a moment. "Probably around eleven. It was on my way back from the movie theater."

So too early to match the time Martin was murdered. Still, it did seem suspicious. I tucked that bit of information away for later. I'd have to pay Viviana another visit.

"Was she running away or toward something?"

Evelyn shrugged again. "Neither, I think. She was just . . . running. It was kind of funny."

I hesitated before asking, "You know what else is funny?" It was hard to see her reaction with her back turned.

"What's that, dear?"

"Someone mentioned to me they thought you might've been involved with Lorelai's death."

Evelyn stumbled forward into the bookshelf. "Oh." Her voice shook. "Is that so?"

"I said no way. You're the nicest person I know."

"Well, thank you for sticking up for me. I'd hate for any nasty rumor to start spreading. Now, I think I'll go sort through our stock in the back. I've already counted out the opening day's float for you."

I raised an eyebrow as I watched Evelyn scurry to the back.

Chapter
Twenty-Three

During my lunch break, I did a quick Google search of various restaurants around Oceanside. Evelyn had been telling the truth about at least one thing: some had extended their hours for summer. That didn't automatically clear her name, though.

The first team for the photo scavenger hunt arrived soon after I stepped back into the main part of the bookshop. The teams could be made up of two to six people, and this first team was a family of four.

"Okay, the instructions say to each grab your favorite book and make a face like you're reading it for the first time." The mom enthusiastically read from the crumpled sheet of paper she held. "They'll never know if it's actually your favorite or not, so just grab something."

Her two sons, who both looked to be in their preteen years, groaned.

"Mom, you're way too into this," the taller one said. "I still can't believe you're making us do this on vacation."

"Yeah," his brother chimed in. "I want to learn how to surf."

"Later, later." Their mom waved them off. "Now, grab a book. It's Dad's turn to take the photo."

I glanced over at Evelyn, and we shared an amused look. The parents totally reminded me of my own: an overly competitive mother and a father who lovingly went along with her schemes.

I hid my grin as I turned back to watch the family, stifling a laugh when one of the boys grabbed the nearest book, only to make a disgusted face at seeing the regency romance cover and shove it back.

Finally, all three of them had a book and made excited faces like they were discovering the story for the first time, as per mom's orders. The dad snapped a photo, and they started to head back out the doorway.

"Wait," I said. "Would you like some cookies?" I waved them over to the small snack table I'd set up.

"Yes, please!" The two boys bounded over, and each shoved a cookie in his mouth.

The mom shot me an evil death glare.

"It's okay, honey. We're already so far ahead of everyone else." The dad tried to soothe her. "The kids need a snack."

"I want that grand prize! It includes a spa day certificate, and three meal vouchers for all of us, and a free surfing lesson." She said the last part quietly, like it was going to be a surprise for her sons if they won. I thought it was sweet she wasn't actually as insanely intense as she appeared; she was doing it for her kids.

After the family left, things started to pick up. At one point, there were seven teams in Palm and Page, all trying to take photos with their favorite books. It seemed like everyone had the same idea the first family had—no one would actually know if the book was their true favorite or not, so they grabbed whatever. The store was going to be a complete mess at the end of the day, but I didn't mind.

It was fun seeing tourists and locals having such a great time, and everyone was so caught up in the challenge that no one took photos of me like people were doing the other day. It completely took my mind off the murders.

But I didn't have the extra time to spend tidying the messy bookshelves after we'd closed, so it would have to wait until the next day. I was eager for the video chat I'd set up with my sister. Olivia was going to be shocked to hear what had happened since we last talked.

First, I decided to stop by the grocery store to see if Carrie was working and pay my respects. I might not have been a fan of Martin, but she'd been head over heels about him.

Carrie wasn't at any of the cash registers when I arrived, so I asked a cashier if she was working that evening.

"Oh, sure. She's doing inventory in the back," the kind woman said. "I'll page her for you."

A few moments later, a tear-stained Carrie appeared. "Hi, Scarlett. What are you doing here?"

I offered her a quick hug, which she awkwardly accepted. "I wanted to check in. I'm so sorry for your loss. I wasn't sure if you'd be working today."

Carrie sighed and indicated for me to follow her to a quiet corner of the store. "We're too busy for me to stay home, especially with my dad visiting my grandmother in Korea this week. But thankfully, I can hide in the back and not be bothered by customers."

"Is there anything I can do for you?"

"That's sweet of you to offer, but I can't think of anything." She paused for a moment. "Though I guess you could tell me if it's true or not . . ."

"Is what true?"

"That Martin was found on your front porch."

I nodded, biting my lower lip. "Yes, my roommate and I found him in the middle of the night."

Her face fell. "That's what I heard. Were you two . . . you know? You can tell me. I want to know the truth."

"I'm not sure what you mean." I wasn't certain if it was just the grief, but Carrie seemed to be having a hard time forming her words.

Carrie stared at her feet and spoke so quietly I almost didn't hear her. "Were you and Martin having an affair?"

The thought was so ridiculous, I had to bite back a laugh. "No, of course not. What makes you think that?"

"Well, why else would he be at your house in the middle of the night?"

She had me there. "Unfortunately, I don't have an answer for you, but I promise we weren't having an affair. Martin was a colleague of my roommate, so he might have been there for a work thing."

"That makes sense, I guess." Carrie's posture relaxed.

I gave her a small smile. "I'm sure you must miss him a lot."

"I still can't believe he's gone. The weekend before this one, we even talked about looking at engagement rings."

"That must have been a special phone call."

Her eyebrows drew together. "Phone call? What do you mean?"

"Oh, my roommate said he was in New York that weekend, so I just assumed it'd been a phone call."

Carrie shook her head. "Martin wasn't in New York. He was with me at the Five Palms Resort. We spent the whole weekend there."

That was one mystery confirmed. Martin *had* lied about when he came home. "What were you doing there?"

"Mostly spending time at the casino. A little staycation, you know?"

I almost nodded in understanding but then remembered something Lucia had said when we were at the resort. "But Martin hated gambling."

Carrie laughed. "Martin? No, he definitely didn't hate it. To be honest, I started to worry he was becoming an addict and was thinking about talking to him about it."

Something about that made sense. It was like Martin needed to have this facade of being the perfect guy; he must have been embarrassed about his love of the casino. But if he'd been at the resort and casino the entire weekend, it also meant he hadn't been the one to murder Lorelai.

"Anyway, I should get back to work, but thanks for stopping by, Scarlett."

"No problem. Take care."

Lucia had texted me earlier to say she was working late, so I grabbed some frozen dinners before heading home for a quick meal. I didn't have time to cook with two murders to solve.

Thirty minutes later, I slid onto my seat at the kitchen table with a steaming plate of broccoli cheese bake, starting up my laptop as I did.

"Hey, sis!" Olivia's smiling face appeared on the screen. "How's it going?"

I swallowed the bite of broccoli I had in my mouth before answering. "So much has been going on. Oceanside is out of control."

"What? What happened?"

"Another body was found last night."

Olivia gasped. "Oh no. Who was it? And where?"

"A local lawyer named Martin Russell." I paused as the scene of finding his body replayed in my mind. "And he was found on our front porch."

Olivia gasped again, even louder. I hoped she wasn't getting light-headed.

"That's awful, Scar. Are you okay?"

I nodded. "I'm fine, and Lucia is fine. It was terrifying, though. We woke up in the middle of the night to two loud thump sounds."

"Yikes. Wait, two? Was there someone else?"

"No, I think one was the sound of someone hitting him on the back of the head, and the second was Martin falling to the ground." The police had found a brick covered in blood lying in our sad, dried-up flower bed next to the door. They thought that was what had been used as the murder weapon. I wasn't quite ready to share that level of gruesome detail with Olivia yet. Talking about it might make me lose my dinner.

"Yikes," Olivia said again. "I'm so sorry that happened to you. And be careful. Whoever killed Martin might've been after you."

That thought had crossed my mind, and it was terrifying. I gave a grim smile. "Thanks."

"Do you know why this Martin was murdered? Or what he was doing on your front porch when he was?"

"I don't know why he was on our front porch, but I think his death has something to do with Lorelai's murder. He was the lawyer representing members of her family trying to get the inheritance back."

"Interesting. But his murder wouldn't benefit them. It would benefit you."

My heart sank. I hadn't even thought of that. The police could very well think I was the one who did it, and I'd never get off their suspect list. "You have to help me, Liv. I need to solve this as quickly as possible so the police don't arrest me again. And so people stop treating me like I did it. Palm and Page could suffer because of this." I told her of the blog posts calling me a murder suspect and of the customers taking photos of me. "Any ideas of what to do?"

My sister looked concerned. "Is there anyone you suspect? Why don't you tell me about them first?"

I nodded. "Okay. Well, there's Connor—"

"Wait, stop! Hold on. Connor's back?" Olivia's lips curled, and she made a fake gagging sound.

I grimaced. "Yeah, and it isn't pretty. He showed up after hearing I was supposed to receive the inheritance and begged me for some of the money. And he was even there last night when Martin was found. At one in the morning."

"Wow. You really think Connor is capable of murder?"

"I don't know," I admitted. "He's turned into a pretty sleazy guy."

"Well, to be honest, he wasn't that great to begin with. You seemed happy, so I didn't want to tell you." Regret filled her face. "I wish I had, though, after he dumped you so cruelly."

"Apparently, the start-up company he was working for fell through. He's desperate for money now."

"Don't give him any, Scar. Stay away from him. Especially if you think there's even a slight chance he's the murderer."

"I'll keep my distance."

"Okay, good. Now tell me, who else is on your suspect list?"

I'd gotten so caught up in talking with Olivia that I'd forgotten to eat my dinner. I pushed the cold plate aside and continued. "You know Evelyn, my employee?"

"Yes. I thought you really liked her."

"Well, I do, but she's been acting suspicious lately. She was also there last night, though she didn't arrive till later. She claimed she'd overheard the call her husband had received—he's the detective assigned to the case—and was coming to check on me."

"Why is that suspicious?"

"She also said that before that she'd been out late to the movies with friends. And Evelyn doesn't seem like the late-night-movie type of person."

Olivia frowned. "What would her motive be, though?"

I told her about Evelyn's comments about taking over Palm and Page.

"How does her killing Lorelai get her your bookshop?"

"I think she might be trying to frame me. There was a bottle of poison found near Palm and Page, remember? Oh, speaking of which, do you know of any type of poison that comes in a glass brown bottle?"

Olivia shook her head. "Sorry, I don't know my poisons that well," she said with slight sarcasm. "So you really think Evelyn might be trying to frame you?"

I sighed. "No, but I think she has something to do with all this. Maybe she wasn't the one to kill Lorelai, but—" I thought of something. Something awful but totally plausible. "What if she and Connor are working together?"

"Whoa. Where did that idea come from?"

"What if Evelyn isn't the only one who wants to take over? What if Connor wants to as well? He was asking for his job back. They could be working together to get me out of the picture."

"That's crazy talk."

I agreed it was crazy talk, especially since Connor had been the one to put me on Evelyn's trail, but it would totally be like him to turn on her to protect himself.

No, it couldn't have been Evelyn. I'd flip-flopped too much on this and needed to officially cross her off my suspect list. I must have imagined my odd sense about her. She was too sweet to be involved in a murder.

"So, any other suspects?" Olivia asked.

"One more. Do you remember that cute thrift shop I took you to when you visited in the winter? The one called Second Chance Treasures?"

"Vaguely."

"The owner—her name is Viviana—is the only person around who seems to have known who Lorelai was. Anyway, Viviana was also seen running around town in the middle of the night by Evelyn yesterday."

"How did she know Lorelai?"

"Apparently, Lorelai worked at her store a long time ago but suddenly disappeared without giving any notice. Viviana also thinks Lorelai might have stolen from her."

"Did she report Lorelai to the police?" Olivia asked.

I shook my head. "Nope. She said she never did anything about it."

"That does seem a little strange."

"I agree. Any idea of what to do next?"

Olivia rocked her head from side to side and looked lost in thought for a moment. "I think you should talk to all three again and see if any of them has a connection to Martin. Even if it's something small."

"That's a good thought."

"Maybe Lucia can help. You said Martin was a lawyer, right? Did she know him through her work?"

I nodded. "They work—well, worked—at the same firm, actually."

"Oh, perfect. Start there."

"Thanks, Liv. I wish you were here."

Olivia smiled. "Me too. And again, be careful around Connor. Out of the people you mentioned, I think he might be the killer."

"I will. I promise." I held my pinkie up to the screen in an indication of the pinkie promises we used to make as kids. "Did you get your major project done over the weekend?"

Olivia beamed. "I did. I even had time to get ahead on a new project."

"My sister, the workaholic." I grinned. "Don't forget to try and find time to relax. You're in a foreign country. Get out and see some sights."

"I will, I will," Olivia promised.

Olivia told me more about the project she was now working on before we said our good-byes. I was reheating my dinner when Lucia came home.

"I learned something interesting at work today," Lucia sing-songed when she came into the kitchen. "Something that'll definitely be of interest to you."

I looked up from my dinner. "What's that?"

She dumped her messenger bag and purse on the floor and grabbed the seat across from me. "You remember my colleague Jessica? The one who mentioned Martin had come back early?"

I nodded.

"She's been assigned to take over Martin's cases."

My mouth twitched. "Even the one with Lorelai's family?"

Lucia nodded excitedly, and I felt a little betrayed she was so enthusiastic her coworker would be working against me. I'd secretly, and seemingly stupidly, hoped that with Martin's death, Lorelai's family would drop the case. Apparently, that wasn't how things worked in the lawyer world.

"You don't have to look so happy about it."

"But now I have more information." Lucia smirked. "This might even give us the edge we need to get ahead."

"What are you talking about? What did you learn?"

"A name."

"What do you mean, a name? A name of what?"

"A name of the family member who hired Martin." Lucia waved her hands around in the air, emphasizing each word. "He represented someone named Isla Knight."

Chapter
Twenty-Four

"Isla Knight? I've never heard of her. But same last name, so they must be related. That's a great lead, Lucia."

"I know." She gave me a smug grin.

"What else did you learn? Do you know where she lives or anything?"

Lucia shook her head. "Jessica wasn't able to tell me anything else, just a name. But it's enough for us to start doing our own digging."

"Okay, great. Let's start now."

Lucia reached into her messenger bag and pulled out her laptop. "I'm hoping even a basic Google search will bring us something. The Knights are a pretty well-known family."

We hunched over the computer, clicking through pages about the Knights. There wasn't a single reference to anyone named Isla. Even articles with family photos that listed every person in the caption had no mention of an Isla.

I blew out a long breath. "This is so weird. And frustrating. Does she even exist?"

"She has to," Lucia said. "Maybe she's a little camera shy. Let's check some social media accounts."

We did. We spent an hour on the computer, clicking through pages and pages of social media profiles. There was an Isla Knight who lived in the United Kingdom, but she looked to be about twelve years old. I highly doubted she'd been the one to hire Martin. Another Isla Knight in Germany, but she also looked too young. There were a couple of Elsa Knights and Ida Knights, but no Isla.

"Is she a ghost?" I whispered.

"I have no idea. I'm usually pretty good at creeping people online, but I don't know where to look next." Lucia pouted for a moment before turning off the laptop. "Let's take a break. Maybe an idea will come to us later."

"Maybe." I sighed. How had people even found anyone before the internet? "So, Jessica can't tell us anything?"

Lucia shook her head. "Nope. It would risk both our jobs to betray the trust of a client. I can't do that. Sorry, Scar."

"Don't apologize. I understand. It's just frustrating. Do you think this Isla is our murderer?"

Lucia shrugged. "It's possible."

We were both lost in thought for a few moments. Thinking about Martin's cases reminded me of something. "Hey, so I dropped by the grocery store to see Carrie today."

"How's she doing?"

I shook my head. "Not so good. She really misses Martin."

To her credit, Lucia didn't make any sassy comments.

"It sounded like they were quite serious. Serious enough to spend a weekend together at the Five Palms Resort. The weekend Lorelai was murdered, in fact."

Lucia caught on quickly. "So he did lie about being out of town that weekend, but that means he still had an alibi for when Lorelai was murdered. Why wouldn't he tell us the truth?"

"Maybe because they spent the entire time at the casino gambling, and he was embarrassed about it."

Understanding dawned on Lucia's face. "I knew it. I knew he had to have some sort of vice. No way was he as perfect as he tried to appear."

"That must have actually been Martin who you heard when we were there last week."

Lucia nodded. "It would be easy for us to verify Carrie's story by going to the casino and asking around. Sounds like Martin might have been there often."

With plans to head back to the Five Palms Resort and Casino soon, we resumed our search for Isla Knight, though nothing else showed up. Our empty search only brought about a headache, one that didn't ease by the time I went to bed. We were so close, yet still so far. There was this amazing clue sitting right in our laps, but we had no idea what to do with it.

* * *

Palm Trees and Page Turners was super busy the next day. I wouldn't have been surprised if the bell above the door flew off its hook after swinging back and forth all morning. A few weeks ago, I'd have been relishing in the business we were getting. I'd have felt like I had succeeded in being a small-business owner.

But now I was anxious. In my head, I questioned every single customer who walked through our front doorway. *Hey, you. Are you actually here for a book? Or are you hoping to get a glimpse of a murder suspect?*

I always convinced myself it was the latter, smiling nicely to customers' faces but glaring daggers at their backs. I was positive each sale was only a pity sale or a sale for people to tell their friends they'd bought a book from a store that'd been a crime scene. Tourists still seemed to think this was the case, not realizing it'd happened at the Oceanside Pier down the beach.

The pressure was on to solve this case, for my sanity alone.

"Are you all right, Scarlett?" Evelyn asked, after she got back from her lunch break. "You seem a little tense today."

I shook my head as if to clear my foggy, bitter thoughts. My headache from the night before had come back. "I'm all right. Just still stressed over everything that's been happening."

"Why don't you go out for lunch today? I can watch the store," she suggested.

Again with the comments about watching the store. But a grilled cheese sandwich and fries from the Sunshine Café would hit the spot right now. Besides, there was a lull in customers now, as people were probably out for lunch themselves. "You'd be okay with that?"

"Yes, yes. I'll be fine. And then afterward, why don't you get around to posting that summer help position? We'll need the extra set of hands around if this business keeps up."

One of us at least was being positive about the increase in business. Perhaps Evelyn hadn't noticed that hardly anyone had actually bought anything after coming into the shop. Or maybe she was covering her bases for when I was tossed in jail after her frame job.

Okay, wow, enough of those thoughts; Evelyn was off my suspect list. I needed to eat, because I was beginning to get hangry.

"That's a good idea. I'll do that. Thanks, Evelyn."

I grabbed my purse from the back and took one last look around the store before leaving. Traffic was still low, so I was sure Evelyn would be okay.

My assumption about everyone being out to lunch proved correct. When I got to the Sunshine Café, there was a line out the door to put a name down for a table or order takeout. I'd have to do the latter and eat back at Palm and Page or even on the way home, depending on how slow they were.

I got in line and pulled out my phone to post on the Palm and Page social media accounts, distracting myself from the sun beating down.

"Hey, it's the Palm Trees and Page Turners lady, right?" a cheerful voice said behind me.

I inwardly groaned. Was I not safe anywhere? Hopefully, they didn't want a photo or something. If they did, I was heading back to Palm and Page on an empty stomach. Everyone would just have to deal with my grumpy mood then.

I turned around to see who it was and recognized Autumn. "Oh, hey. How's your summer going?"

"It's going well for the most part, but I keep hearing these crazy rumors about what's been going on around town."

Uh-oh. Here it comes.

"I've heard there have been two murders recently. One was at your bookshop." Autumn's blue eyes widened. "Is that true?"

I quickly shook my head and raised my voice, hoping anyone listening to our conversation who thought the same thing would finally get the message. "No, it wasn't. I promise. It happened underneath the pier on the beach."

"Oh." Autumn smiled. "That's good. I love your shop and would hate to be too scared to return."

"Palm Trees and Page Turners is perfectly safe." My voice shook slightly. I hoped to convince her, but by Autumn's worried look, I was scared I'd done the opposite. She probably thought I was a little nuts. I tried to speak calmly. "There's nothing to fear about my bookshop. And I know the police are working as hard as they can to catch the murderer soon and put them behind bars."

"That's a relief. I want to enjoy the rest of my time here in peace. And I'm still interested in that position, if it's available."

"It is, though I haven't put the posting up. I will tonight or tomorrow. I promise."

Autumn's smile turned into a thin line. "Did you hear the second murder happened at someone's house?"

I pursed my lips, unsure of what to say. "Umm . . . ," I started awkwardly.

Autumn gasped. "It wasn't in your house, was it?"

"Well, not *in* my house, no." I noticed people were staring at us now, so I lowered my voice. "Technically, it was outside my house."

"Oh no! What happened?"

I gave Autumn a brief synopsis, leaving out Martin's name and the possible connection to the first murder. I didn't need to scare the poor girl any more than she already was. Autumn deserved to enjoy her summer in peace.

"Wow," she said, after I'd finished my story. "I sure hope the killer is caught soon. Maybe I should leave town. This is getting scary."

"I'm sure you'll be okay. You haven't noticed anything suspicious around, have you?" I tried to sound casual.

She gave me an odd look. "Is your coworker investigating or something?"

That was not at all the response I'd been expecting. "My what?"

"Your coworker. I came into your bookshop yesterday to grab a new book, and your coworker asked me some weird questions. That was one of them. If I'd noticed anything suspicious around town, I mean."

"Evelyn asked you that?"

Autumn shrugged. "I didn't catch her name."

What was Evelyn doing asking our customers strange questions like that? Had I crossed her off my list too soon? "I don't remember you coming in yesterday."

"I came around this time. Maybe you were on your lunch?"

"Yes, that's probably it. I'm sorry I missed you."

We'd finally made it inside the Sunshine Café, and I savored the cool air for a moment before taking a look at the menu. I already knew I wanted a grilled cheese sandwich and fries, but I wanted to see if there was anything else to add. "What are you getting?" I asked Autumn.

"Anything you recommend?"

"You can't go wrong with their all-day breakfast menu. Though today I'm getting a grilled cheese. All their sandwiches are pretty good, actually."

"It all sounds great. For some reason, greasy food always tastes better when you're on vacation."

I laughed. "It's been a long time since I've been able to go on one, so I'll take your word for it."

Jules was working the takeout till when I got to the front of the line. Her slightly grumpy face broke into a wide grin when she saw me. "Hey, girl!"

"Hey. What are you doing out front? Aren't you a cook?"

She rolled her eyes. "Well, I did go to culinary school, so I prefer chef. But none of that matters to our new manager." She made air quotes around the last two words.

"Oh? What's going on?"

Jules leaned in closer. "Samantha got a promotion and is going on a power trip. She's trying to do everything in the kitchen herself, leaving those of us who actually know what we're doing to work the tills and take orders."

"That sucks. I'm sorry."

"If I didn't need to hire a sitter for my kids for summer break coming up, I'd be looking for a new job. Maybe in the fall I will."

"Let's keep those orders coming in, Ms. Moore." Samantha's head poked through the pass-through window.

Jules discreetly rolled her eyes again. "Anyway, what can I get you, Scarlett?"

I placed my order for my sandwich, fries, and an iced chai latte before stepping to the side while Autumn ordered a turkey club sandwich and paid. We chatted a bit more while we waited for our food to be ready. I gave Jules a quick good-bye wave as we stepped back out into the heat.

"I'll see you later, okay? Please don't hesitate to come into Palm and Page at any time." I patted Autumn's arm as we parted ways in the parking lot. "It's totally safe."

"Sure thing." She smiled. "It might be my favorite store in the world."

"Aw, that's so sweet. Next book is half off on me, okay?"

She beamed at that, and I was happy to have made a fellow bookworm's day.

I chowed down on my sandwich and fries in the car on the way back to work and was pleasantly surprised Palm Trees and Page Turners wasn't too busy when I got there, so I could take a few extra minutes to finish my lunch in the back. As I cleaned up my trash and finished my iced chai latte, my cell phone rang.

"Hello?"

"Scarlett Gardner? It's Jeffrey Cooper, Lorelai's lawyer."

"Oh, hi. What can I do for you?"

"Well, I'm at your house, actually. I hoped you'd be at home this afternoon, but no one seems to be here." He sounded slightly annoyed.

"No, I'm at work. Was I expecting you?"

"No," he said after a beat. "But this is important."

"Is it something that can be handled over the phone?"

"No. I have Lorelai's possessions for you, and I don't want to leave them out in the open. Plus there's something I need to give you in person."

I sighed. "Does it need to be right now?"

"Well, I did drive all the way from my office in Los Angeles," he hinted, sounding more annoyed than before. "And if Lorelai hadn't been such a close client, I wouldn't be taking the time to do this."

"I thought you were having everything shipped."

"Like I said, I need to see you in person."

I opened the back room door a crack and peeked out into the main part of the store. I could see only a customer or two wandering the bookshelves, and Evelyn was helping one at the cash register. There was no line. Everyone must still be out for lunch or spending the afternoon on the beach. "Okay. Give me a few minutes, and I'll meet you at my house."

Now that Jeffrey had gotten his way, his friendly tone returned. "Thank you, Scarlett. I appreciate it. See you soon."

I waited for Evelyn to be done with her customer before pulling her aside. "I'm so sorry. I have to go home and deal with something that's come up."

"Is everything okay?" Evelyn's brow furrowed in concern.

"I think so, but it's sorta urgent. I feel bad leaving you again."

"Don't worry about it. I planned on you being busy this afternoon anyway, with that help-wanted ad."

Right. I'd completely forgotten about that again. At the rate this was going, summer would be over by the time I hired our summer help. "I'll do that this evening at home. You're sure you'll be okay here? I'll try and come back as soon as I can, but I have no idea how long this will take."

"Go. It's totally fine. I hope everything's okay."

"I'll make sure to call you if I think I'm going to be there a while."

Evelyn looked like she was about to say something else, but a customer came up to the cash register to make a purchase. "I'll see you later."

Chapter
Twenty-Five

O n the drive home, I thought about what Jeffrey could possibly have besides Lorelai's possessions that was so urgent for me to see. If it was some sort of paperwork, that could have been sent electronically. No need to come here to show me.

A new neighbor must be moving in, because a driveway in our complex was filled with cardboard boxes.

Wait, no. That was our driveway.

I pulled in as best I could but ended up parking at an angle to get off the road. Hopefully, Lucia wouldn't be home anytime soon, since there was no room for her to park.

There were more boxes piled on our front porch, and at the sound of my car, Jeffrey's head popped up from behind them.

"What's all this?" I got out of my car and headed toward the front porch.

"Lorelai's stuff."

"What do you mean?" I gazed around the driveway in astonishment. There had to be more than fifty boxes of various sizes piled up.

"Like I told you, I had all of Lorelai's things boxed up from her house and office for you. You're the owner of all this now." Jeffrey had a gleam in his eye, like he was glad all this junk—er, Lorelai's earthly treasures—was someone else's problem now.

"I had no idea it would be this much stuff." I took another uncertain look around. I'd assumed it would be a couple of family heirlooms and important documents. "What am I supposed to do with all this?"

He gave a slight laugh. "I don't know. Whatever you want."

"But there's no room in our townhouse for all of it."

Jeffrey shrugged. "Feel free to go through everything and toss or donate what you like. I won't be offended. And here, this is also for you." He handed me a black jewelry box tied with a red ribbon. A small white envelope was tucked under the ribbon with my first name written in beautiful cursive.

"What's this?"

"I closed out Lorelai's safe deposit box today, and this was the only thing inside, along with a note addressed to me with instructions to bring it to you as soon as possible if she never got the chance."

I untied the delicate ribbon and opened the jewelry box, letting out a small gasp. Inside was a gorgeous pendant necklace with a scarlet jewel in the center. "It's beautiful." And definitely not something that could have been sent via email. Next, I opened the envelope and read the short note to myself.

A scarlet for our Scarlett. I hope to be able to give this to you in person one day.

"This is mine?" I'd never owned something so beautiful before.

"It's got your name on it," Jeffrey lamely pointed out. "And don't forget all this other stuff is yours as well."

Ha. Like I could.

"Here, I'll help you bring it inside."

* * *

One and a half sweaty hours later, I finally hauled the last of the boxes inside. I'd texted Evelyn to let her know I wouldn't be able to return to work and to close the store without me. Jeffrey had helped bring in about three boxes before he got a phone call to return to the office, so with an apologetic wave, he left me on my own.

I stood huffing and puffing as I looked around the living room at the boxes piled seven high. They completely blocked the large bay window we had in the front, but at least we could use our driveway again.

I filled a glass with cold water and downed it before heading back out to repark my car. Lucia was just pulling up.

"Why's your car so crooked?" She raised an eyebrow at me.

"You'll see once you get inside. But hang on a moment, and I'll straighten it out."

"What do you mean, I'll see inside? What could be inside the house that would affect your terrible parking outside the house?"

"Hold on. I'll show you."

Lucia looked like she had a dozen more questions but thankfully kept her mouth shut as I reparked my car. There was no way I could easily explain what had happened. She'd have to see it.

"Okay, Scarlett. What's going on?"

"Jeffrey Cooper stopped by earlier," I said as we were about to step inside. "And he left me a little gift."

Inside, I swept my arm out to the living room, letting Lucia take it all in.

"Where did our window go?"

I laughed. "You should have seen the boxes spread out all over our driveway earlier. That's why I was parked so crooked. There was hardly any space."

Lucia walked over to the boxes. "What is all this stuff?"

"It's Lorelai's. Jeffrey had it boxed up and brought it over, since it's technically mine now."

"Oh."

"Yeah, I hadn't thought it through when Jeffrey said I'd be inheriting her possessions as well."

"Lorelai must really have not liked her family to not leave them a single thing." She opened the box closest to her. "So, shall we go through it all?"

"Now?"

Lucia shrugged. "Do you have something better to do?"

"No, you're right. And maybe we'll find a clue or something that will lead us to whoever killed her. There was at least one treasure, though." I showed Lucia the pendant necklace with pride.

"Wow. It's beautiful."

"I know, though I'm confused about the note that came with it." I showed her the message. "It says *our Scarlett*, plural. But *I hope to be able to give this to you* is singular."

"Hmm, good catch. Was she the only one wanting to find you, then?"

"I don't know," I said softly. "It makes me wonder if whoever my father was never wanted to look for me."

Lucia came over and hugged me. "It might not mean anything. Maybe she meant *we* but wrote *I* out of habit or something."

"Maybe."

"Do you still want to sort through the boxes?"

I nodded. "Yes, let's get started."

Lucia sifted through a few items in the box she'd opened before looking at me like she had an idea. "I think this task calls for music." She opened an app on her phone and started playing one of her favorite playlists, a mix of score music from the Marvel superhero movies, through our Bluetooth speakers. "There, that'll get us in the mood to get this done."

There was so much random stuff to go through. I left the boxes with clothing in them for later. My excuse was that I didn't think they'd hold any clues or anything, but really it felt sort of creepy to be going through a dead person's clothes. The boxes with paperwork seemed to be more promising. Maybe there was an old copy of her will or something.

"Success!" I pulled out a copy dated thirteen years ago. It had a few other Knights listed, including whoever this Isla was, but it also had a note at the bottom saying, *And give $20,000 to the child.*

Lucia read over my shoulder. "The child? What does she mean by that?"

"I think she might mean me." I read the entire paper carefully, but there wasn't anything else significant. "Maybe she didn't know my name. Jeffrey said she changed her will last week. Maybe she found out who I was then."

"Here. Let me see." Lucia read the whole thing but shook her head. "It doesn't say anything else about a child."

I dug deeper into the box. Lorelai seemed to have kept records of everything. Faded receipts dating back years ago, copies of various insurance policies from over the decades, letters addressed to her from a Viviana . . .

Whoa.

These letters were from Viviana Diaz.

Chapter Twenty-Six

"Lucia!" I yelled, despite her being only a few feet away, causing her to jump. "Look at this."

"What?" She rubbed her ear but turned toward me, knocking over one of the boxes with her elbow as she did.

"Lorelai had a whole pile of letters from Viviana. Look at them all."

Lucia grabbed some of the letters and started to flip through them. "Viviana from the thrift store?"

"Unless it's another Viviana Diaz. But look at the return address. It says Seagaze Drive, which is the street Second Chance Treasures is on. I don't know the unit number, but I bet this is it." I grabbed my phone while Lucia continued looking at the letters and opened a Google browser. I typed in *Second Chance Treasures, Oceanside, California*, and the address came up. "Yep, these letters came from Viviana's thrift store."

"Wow, some of these are kind of scary." Lucia skimmed through the pages.

"Lucia, we can't read someone else's mail."

"Technically, this is all your mail now. So yes, we can read it. Especially since they might hold the evidence we need to know who Lorelai's killer is."

"Let me see." I grabbed a letter from her, my worries about reading Lorelai's private mail forgotten. "What do you mean by scary?"

"Viviana was threatening Lorelai. She said she knew Lorelai had stolen from her and was going to the police if she didn't pay the cash value of the items stolen."

"Why didn't Viviana ask for the items back instead?"

Lucia started reading another letter. "I bet it was a scam. I bet Lorelai never stole anything and Viviana was out for a quick buck."

"Would she actually be the one to kill Lorelai over that, though?"

"These letters are pretty angry. Sounds like Lorelai didn't fall for the trick, which made Viviana even angrier. She says things like *Better watch your back* and *You'll be a goner if you ever step foot in Oceanside again.*"

I shivered. "That is terrifying."

"Viviana sounds completely nutty."

I thought of something else from my conversation with Viviana the other day. "I asked her if she ever followed up with Lorelai and the missing items, but she said she didn't. That she let it go."

Lucia barked out a laugh. "She clearly didn't let anything go."

"So she lied to me."

"And that means she could be lying about a whole bunch of things. Who knows what's going on in her mind?"

We read the rest of the letters in silence. Nothing written eased my anxiousness about Viviana. There were some pretty dark things. But one reference—Viviana saying she knew Lorelai had stolen her personal brand-new Discman—made me think of something.

"When was the most recent letter written?" I started sorting through my pile of letters, checking the tiny date marked at the top of each page.

"Hmm?" she asked, without looking up from the letter she was reading. "These letters read like the plot of a horror movie. Sorry, what did you ask?"

"When was the last letter written? The latest one I have is dated ten years ago."

Lucia started to sort through hers. "I have nine years ago."

"So did Viviana give up on her threats, or did she change her mind or something?"

"I don't know. Does it matter?"

"Maybe she's not the killer if she doesn't care anymore. These are old threats, and she seems so nice now."

Lucia shrugged. "Either way, we should still look into this."

"Do you want to go to her shop sometime together and ask a few questions?"

"Good idea."

"Should we bring the letters?" I asked.

"I'll think about it. She might not react well to seeing them again." Lucia stood and stretched. "I'm going to order takeout for dinner, and then we can keep looking through these boxes. There might be something else interesting in them."

I agreed and opened the next box while Lucia ordered from a Thai place down the street. The box was heavy and contained a bunch of books. I smiled as I pulled out a few Jane Austen novels along with other classic stories. So coming to Palm Trees and Page Turners to buy a book hadn't been only a guise to meet me. Lorelai really had been a literature lover. I smiled at the thought that I had that in common with my potential birth mother.

Lucia came back into the living room. "Food will be here in about twenty minutes. Find anything else exciting?"

"Not really. Just some books." I opened the next box. "Toiletries?" I groaned. "Seriously, Jeffrey? Did he have to pack absolutely everything?"

Lucia came over to peek into the box and made a face. "That's not her toothbrush, is it?"

I peered in closer. "Looks that way."

We both looked at each other and burst out laughing.

"This is so crazy!" I lifted my glasses to wipe a tear from my eye. "I can't believe this is my life now. Sorting through a dead, rich woman's old toothbrushes."

"I'm sure her underwear is in one of these boxes somewhere. Just wait until you have to sort through that."

"Me? What if you have the pleasure of opening that box?"

Lucia shook her head. "Oh no. Your inheritance, your underwear."

Our laughter started to die down, and Lucia pulled out a hairbrush from the toiletries box. "Hey, how positive are you that this woman was your birth mother?"

I shrugged. "I don't see who else she could be."

"Do you want to find out for sure?"

"Yes, of course. But how can we? I don't think she did a DNA test to find me, at least not according to my ancestry account, and it's not like we can get a blood or saliva sample now."

"No." Lucia waved the hairbrush in my face. "But there are other ways to get someone's DNA."

"Her hair?" I raised an eyebrow.

Lucia nodded. "As long as there's a strand that still has part of the root attached, we can get it tested. I have a friend at a genetics lab who might be able to help. He owes me a favor from some legal guidance I helped him out with a while ago." She inspected the hair-brush closely. "This strand looks like it may work."

"You actually think this could be possible?" I was doubtful. This sounded way too much like something out of *CSI* or some other crime show.

"It doesn't hurt to try. I'll call my friend tomorrow to see if he has time. It might take a while, depending on how busy the lab is, so it's better if we get started right away."

I slowly nodded, feeling a bit dazed. So this was it. I might finally find out who my birth mother was.

*   *   *

After spending the morning of my day off curled up on the couch with a contemporary romance novel and a bowl of sliced watermelon, I worked on the job posting for the bookshop's website, because, once again, I hadn't gotten around to it the evening before. Lucia and I had been too busy going through all the boxes, though nothing else of interest had come up.

Once the job posting was on the site, I made myself a tall glass of iced tea and sat down in the living room to reread Viviana's letters. I couldn't believe the same lady who owned a charming thrift shop and made cute bracelets would write such dramatic, diabolic threats: *I'll take you to court if you don't give me back the cash value of what you stole* and *You've completely ruined my business by not showing up to work. I'll never recover!* I realized an odd conversation here and there with Viviana at Second Chance Treasures didn't mean I knew her at all.

My phone lit up with a text message from Lucia.

Can we move our investigating to 1?

It was almost twelve thirty. I'd have to hurry, but I could make it to Lucia's firm by one. We'd agreed to do a little bit of snooping around her law firm today to see if we could find out anything more about Martin.

Sure, see you soon.

Thanks! Big last min meeting was added for later this afternoon.

I rushed into the shower and quickly got ready, throwing on my favorite pink sundress and a small amount of makeup before heading out the door.

I ended up parking in the grocery store lot again once I got downtown and hurried toward the law firm. It was only three minutes until one.

"Good morning, Scarlett," a voice said from behind me along the main street.

I stopped in my tracks and turned to find Viviana walking a cute, fluffy dog. I gulped, hoping it hadn't been audible, like in a cartoon, but I wasn't ready to talk to a potential murderer by myself yet. I needed Lucia by my side to face something like this.

"Um, hi, Viviana. Your dog is cute."

The little floof gave a playful wiggle of his tail in return, as if he was showing off how cute he could be.

Viviana beamed. "Thank you. His name is His Royal Highness Prince Henry."

I started to laugh and choked it back when I realized she was serious. I'd always thought Viviana was over-the-top, but I'd never noticed just how strange she could be. "Uh, that's nice. Do you call him Henry for short?"

"Of course not. Isn't that right, *Prince* Henry?" She looked down at the dog, who gave an arrogant flip of the chin in response. I had no idea how you could train a dog to be a complete snob, but it seemed as if that was exactly what Viviana had done. "So, how are things at your bookstore going? Are people buying anything despite the rumor it was the scene of a murder?"

Okay, that was uncalled for. My blood started to boil. Maybe I would confront her now, without Lucia. "You know the murder happened down by the pier and not at my shop, right?"

She shrugged. "I may know that, and the locals may know that. But the tourists don't seem to. Almost everyone who comes into my store mentions the Murderous Bookshop."

My face heated in anger. "I hope you correct them."

"I try my best." Her expression looked genuine.

"Speaking of Lorelai's murder, I had a chance to look through a bunch of her things yesterday, and turns out she was quite the pack rat."

Viviana raised an eyebrow. "Oh?"

"Yes, she kept everything. From old clothes to receipts, tax forms, letters from various people."

Viviana's eyes narrowed.

"And there were even a couple from you."

"I have no idea what you're talking about." Her gaze darted down to Prince Henry and then back to me. "I never sent her any letters."

"I think you know exactly what I'm talking about."

Her expression remained blank.

Luckily, I'd stuffed the letters into a folder this morning and stuck it in my purse before heading downtown. I slowly pulled out the folder and took out a letter. "*Dear Lorelai, this is your final **final** warning.*"

Viviana pursed her lips. "Oh, right, those silly things. I didn't mean anything by them. It was a joke."

"Threats are a joke? Those were pretty scary things you said. Plus you lied to me about not having any more contact with Lorelai."

"I didn't—ugh—I just—" Viviana seemed flustered, and I waited for her to gather her thoughts. "I was embarrassed, okay?"

"Embarrassed? About what?" We moved to the side as a couple walked past us down the sidewalk.

She sighed deeply. "You're right. I did send those letters, and yes, they did contain threats, but I would never act on them. I promise. I was angry, and I felt better after saying those things to her. I needed to vent."

"But what were you embarrassed about?"

"That I sent those letters in the first place. That's why I didn't tell you about them. I realized how ridiculous it was to send those empty threats year after year to an employee when all she'd done was leave me in the lurch. It was petty." She hung her head, clearly as embarrassed about the whole thing as she claimed.

"Leave you and steal from you, right?"

"Well, to tell you the truth, I was never certain it was her that stole from me. I don't have security tags on any of my clothes or anything, since they're all used, so anyone could have taken them. It just happened to be around the same time as Lorelai left," she said quietly. "And I was a little short on cash at the time. Being desperate can make you go a little nutty."

"Oh. What about the Discman?"

"I made that up. Yeah, pretty sad, isn't it? But I've moved on, I swear." She looked up at me, her eyes fierce. "I've pulled myself together and honestly haven't had any contact with Lorelai in years."

I knew there was some truth to that, based on the dates of the letters, but there was still one thing she could be lying about. "What about the night Martin Russell died?"

Viviana looked genuinely confused. "What about it?"

"Someone saw you running toward the direction of my home, where Martin had been killed, that night."

Viviana's eyebrows drew together. "What night was the murder again? And I couldn't be heading to your house, because I don't even know where you live."

"The murder was Monday night. So where were you going then?"

"On my loop."

"Um . . ." I shrugged. "What loop?"

"My jogging loop. I've gotten back into running and am training for a half-marathon in the fall. It's too hot to run in the heat of the day, so I wait until the sun goes down. I got a later-than-usual start that night because I was doing inventory at Second Chance."

"Does your jogging loop go down Mira Pacific Drive?" I asked, naming my street.

Viviana shook her head. "Not down that street, no. But in the Mira Costa neighborhood, yes. I live there as well. Who saw me, by the way?"

"Evelyn Maxwell."

"Oh, yes. I did run into her. I don't know why she thought I was so suspicious, though. I was wearing jogging clothes. That's kind of funny, because I remember thinking she was the one acting a little strange."

"She was?"

"Yes, she kept making it a point that she was on her way back from the movie theater, but she wasn't coming from that direction at all. It was almost like she was trying to cover her tracks or something. Said she saw a rom-com."

"Was she by herself?"

Viviana nodded, and His Royal Highness Prince Henry started to whine. "Well, I should get going. I closed my shop for lunch today and need to head back soon. But first, this little prince loves to go to the pet supplies shop down the street for free treats."

"Sure thing. Thanks for saying hi."

Viviana turned to leave but then stopped and looked back. "Hey, one more thing?"

"Yes?"

"I swear to you I didn't kill Lorelai or Martin. Please say you believe me. I don't want a rumor starting that it was me."

I nodded. "I believe you, but please correct your customers who still refer to my shop as the Murderous Bookshop. I don't need any more rumors either."

"I promise I'll correct any rumor I hear. I think we small-business owners should stick together."

Chapter Twenty-Seven

Lucia was waiting in the lobby when I arrived at the law firm. "You're late. We don't have much time now before I need to prepare for this afternoon's meeting." She started walking back toward the offices, indicating I should follow.

"I have a good reason, though," I said quietly. "I ran into Viviana outside and got her to confess."

Lucia spun around, and I smacked into her.

"Ow." I rubbed my shoulder.

"What do you mean, you got her to confess? She confessed to killing Lorelai? What are you doing here, then? Come on. We gotta get to the police." She quickly brushed past me and started to head back into the lobby.

I grabbed her arm. "No, wait. That came out wrong." I laughed. "I meant she confessed to writing the letters."

Lucia blew out a breath and rolled her eyes. "But we already knew she wrote the letters, because her name was on them."

"Yes, but she confirmed it. And I got more information about why she wrote them," I said, an edge to my voice. I was proud of what I'd accomplished during my chat with Viviana, and I didn't want Lucia to take that away from me.

"All right. Let's talk about it in my office."

We sat across from each other at her desk, and I filled Lucia in on what Viviana had said about being embarrassed over sending the empty threats.

"So where does that leave her on our suspect list?" Lucia asked, after I'd finished.

I shrugged. "Still on it, but not at the top, I guess."

"Who is?"

I thought for a moment. "Well, Viviana said she thought Evelyn was acting oddly on Monday night right before Martin was murdered."

"Right. You said Connor also mentioned she's been acting strange."

"So did Autumn."

Lucia looked puzzled. "Who's Autumn?"

"Oh, she's a customer from Palm and Page. She mentioned Evelyn had asked her weird questions the other day."

Lucia gave me a sympathetic smile. "So, are we putting Evelyn at the top of the list?"

The thought sickened me. "I hate the idea of it, but I guess so. She makes the most sense right now. Well, her or Connor."

"Right. There's also Connor, but he wasn't around the weekend Lorelai was murdered."

"True." I blew out a breath. "I don't know what to think about him, then. But do you still have time to look around today?"

Lucia looked at her watch. "I only have about ten minutes. But we can take a quick look in Martin's office."

Martin's office looked exactly the same as it had when I'd seen it last week. It was almost eerie, like it expected its occupant to walk right back in any minute. Lucia headed straight to the filing cabinet and yanked at the top drawer.

"It's locked. All the drawers are locked. Though all the paper-work has probably gone to Jessica anyway."

"I'll try the desk drawers, just in case." The three drawers were unlocked, and I started rifling through the contents. It was all basic office supplies: pens, blank legal pads, paper clips, a stapler. "There's nothing much here."

"Hmm." Lucia walked over and turned on his computer. "This is probably—yep, password protected. That won't do us any good." She typed something onto the keyboard and smirked when *Incorrect Password* popped up on the screen.

"What did you try?"

"*I am the best lawyer ever.*"

"Well, obviously, it's *I am a better lawyer than Lucia.*"

"Ha-ha." She glanced at the clock on the wall. "I gotta go, though. A cute new paralegal was hired, and he's helping me prepare for this afternoon's meeting. I'm supposed to meet up with him now. Sorry, this was a bust."

"Yeah, too bad." As we headed out the doorway, I noticed a day planner on a side table. "Hold on a moment."

Lucia leaned over my shoulder as I flipped it open to this week. On Monday evening, Martin had written *Isla Knight, seven p.m.*

"So he met with Isla a few hours before he was murdered. I wish it said where or what the meeting was about."

"Is there anything written on the day Lorelai was murdered?" Lucia asked.

I flipped back one week. "Nope, both Sunday and Monday are blank."

"Okay, go back one more week."

I did as Lucia asked, not sure what she was getting at.

She slammed her finger down on the page. "There. Look at what's written on Friday morning."

"*JFK ten a.m.*," I read out loud. "Another confirmation that Martin did fly back early and not on Monday like he'd said."

"Exactly. We need to get to the casino as soon as possible to see if he was there that weekend."

* * *

Friday afternoon meant another children's story time at Palm Trees and Page Turners, and we had a better turnout than the week before. Not by much, but still. Two families were better than one. I read three picture books to the kids and then handed out the coloring sheets while their parents browsed the store. All the while I kept an eye on Evelyn.

According to Viviana, Evelyn hadn't been with friends Monday night, and it didn't sound like she'd actually been at the movie theater either. What had she been up to, then? It would be just my luck to have unknowingly hired a killer to work in my bookshop.

"Hey, Evelyn?" I asked, between helping customers. "What movie did you see on Monday night?"

"Oh, that cute new Pixar movie. It's always fun to feel like a kid again."

Evelyn hadn't hesitated a beat, but Viviana had mentioned that Evelyn said she saw a rom-com. I had no idea if there was a new rom-com or a new Pixar movie out, but that was an easy thing to check: just ask Google . . . or Lucia. Either way, it was most likely a lie.

"How many of you went?"

This question got an odd look from Evelyn. "There were four of us. My friends Mary, Sally, and Anne came."

It totally sounded as if she'd pulled three names out of the air. "How long have you been friends with Mary, Sally, and Anne?"

"Since we moved to Oceanside." She turned to the nearest customer, abruptly ending our conversation. "May I help you find something?"

* * *

Lucia came running into our house that evening, excitement written all over her face. "You'll never guess what I found out today!"

"What?" I looked up from my laptop, where I'd been creeping Evelyn on social media. She loved posting cute animal videos and links to her book reviews, but that was about it. No killer confessions.

"Some more info about Isla Knight."

"You did? That's great. How?"

Lucia plopped her messenger bag down and pulled out her laptop to place on the kitchen table next to mine. "We checked Google searches and social media pages, but it occurred to me in the middle of a meeting to check criminal records."

I sucked in a breath. "She's a criminal?"

Lucia nodded. "She has a record, at least. All minor things, nothing to warrant a story in the paper or news; that's probably why our Google search came up with nothing."

"Do you have a photo?"

Lucia clicked a few buttons and then showed me a black-and-white mug shot. The woman looked a little familiar, but I thought that was because she looked like Lorelai. Both had the same wavy, light-colored hair, though Isla's was a complete mess in this photo. Her face was scrunched up in a scowl, eyes narrow behind large glasses, and the photo was grainy, making it hard to get a good look at her facial features.

"I don't think I've seen her around."

Lucia seemed disappointed. "I didn't recognize her either, so I was hoping you did."

"Any other information?"

"Just a list of crimes. Mostly shoplifting. Considering she comes from a rich family, it was probably for the thrill rather than actually wanting or needing the items. She chalks up to a stereotypical spoiled, rich brat."

"Do you really think she was the one to murder Lorelai?"

Lucia shrugged. "No idea. All we know is she was the one to hire Martin."

"Isla Knight." I said the name slowly out loud, hoping it would trigger something. But nothing popped into my head. "Do you think we can find her now with this info?"

Lucia shrugged. "I can keep trying, but I don't know. There was a phone number for her with a Los Angeles area code, and I tried calling it today. The number is out of service."

"What about an address?"

She shook her head. "It was blocked out except for the city."

"Let me guess. Los Angeles?"

"Yep."

"Only the second-largest city in the country. Shouldn't be too hard to find her, then." I rolled my eyes. "Let's start knocking on doors."

Lucia grinned. "Yeah, you do that. Let me know how it goes."

I buried my head in my hands and let out a groan. "She has to be connected somehow. Why can't we find her?"

"I have some other news for you. This might cheer you up."

I looked up. "What is it?"

"I was able to get the DNA samples sent off to the lab today. We're in luck. My friend has a lull in his work right now and will get the results for you in a few days."

"Oh, that's great. I think. I honestly don't know what I hope the answer will be."

"Well, I'll support you no matter what the results are." Lucia reached over and squeezed my arm.

"Thanks, Lucia." I chuckled. "You had no idea what you were getting yourself into when we became roommates, did you?"

She laughed. "It's been an adventure I wasn't expecting."

"Speaking of adventures, are you ready for another one to the Five Palms Resort this evening?"

"You bet I am."

This time we headed straight to the casino after arriving at the resort with a picture of Martin saved on my phone.

"Pardon me," I asked a casino worker near the front entrance. "Do you recognize this man?"

The gentleman peered closely at the screen before breaking out into a big smile. "Hey, that's Big M. Everyone knows him around here."

"Big M?" I tilted the screen back toward myself and blinked at it. Out of the corner of my eye, I saw Lucia attempt to hide a grin behind her hand.

"Don't remember what the M stands for, to be honest. We've been calling him Big M for so long." The man chuckled. "He's one of our most loyal regulars. In here almost every evening and weekend."

"Was he here the weekend before last?"

"Don't know. I had that weekend off. Let me go ask someone else." The man left, and Lucia and I exchanged glances.

"Sounds like Martin was almost living a double life," Lucia said. "He had one personality at work and then another here. I can't imagine anyone getting away with calling him Big M at the firm."

"If he was here that weekend, then we can cross him off the killing-Lorelai list, though. I guess being shady doesn't automatically make him a murderer."

The worker appeared with a woman wearing a matching uniform at his side.

"I hear you're asking about Big M?" she asked, a touch of a southern drawl to her words.

I hid my smile. "Yes. We were wondering if he was here the weekend before last?"

"Of course, of course. He was here with a lovely young lady on his arm. Called her his good-luck charm. And it seemed to be true. Big M definitely had a winning streak that weekend."

"Now that I think about it, though, haven't seen him much lately," the man said.

"Didn't you hear?" Lucia asked. "Big M was found murdered the other day."

Both casino workers gasped.

"That's awful." The woman shook her head.

"Man. He'll be missed," her coworker said.

"Are you two looking into his death?"

"Something like that," I replied.

Chapter
Twenty-Eight

Another day at Palm Trees and Page Turners. And another day of living in suspense over unsolved murders around Oceanside.

But I was determined to set that aside and concentrate on my work. After finally getting the job posting up on our website, I'd briefly checked my email this morning before leaving home to find there were already three applications, including the one from Autumn. Reading through those applications and setting up interviews would need to be a priority.

My determination to focus on my work and not the case didn't last long. As I rounded the corner from the parking lot, I stopped dead in my tracks in front of the bookshop.

Spray-painted in big, angry red letters across the front window of Palm and Page was written: *Give up the inheritance! It's not yours!!*

Hot tears rushed to my eyes. I couldn't believe someone would vandalize my cute bookshop like this.

A person brushed up behind me, and a gentle voice said, "Oh, dear. How awful."

I turned around and was enclosed in a great big hug by Evelyn.

"I'm going to call Steve right away. Let's get inside in case who-ever did this is still around."

I let Evelyn unlock the front door, unable to keep my eyes off the nasty message, and she ushered me inside. I slumped against a book-shelf while she called her husband's cell phone. He picked up right away, and I could hear her side of the conversation as she explained what we'd found and asked him to come over ASAP.

"Don't worry, Scarlett. Steve will find who did this. I have com-plete faith in him. And we'll get it cleaned up as soon as possible before people see."

I was still in too much shock to say much, but I knew she was being optimistic. Our customers would start showing up any min-ute, and all it would take was one photo to start circulating before all of Oceanside knew.

Evelyn continued, "Do you want me to put a sign on the door saying we'll be closed for the morning?"

I slowly nodded. We couldn't open with the police on their way to investigate. Palm and Page was already known as the Murderous Bookshop among the tourists. This would only add to their rumors. "We should post something on our social media pages as well. I'll do that while you make the sign."

"All right." Evelyn headed to the back, and I pulled out my phone. I'd finished typing out a quick post about being closed for a few hours—*I'll update when we open; sorry for any inconvenience*—when I saw Detective Maxwell and another officer standing outside. The detective stared at the message with a frown while the other officer took pictures of the window.

"Evelyn, the police are here."

She hurried out of the back with a piece of white printer paper in one hand and a roll of tape in the other. She threw open the door and rushed outside.

"Oh, Steve. Isn't this terrible?" She fell into her husband's arms. "Someone's after poor Scarlett."

He glanced at me over the top of Evelyn's head as I came outside. "It would appear that way."

Evelyn taped the sign to the front door. I thought it was hard to see, being overshadowed by the large red letters and all, but it was the best we could do.

"Any idea who wrote this?" Detective Maxwell asked.

I shook my head. "No. I was shocked to find it this morning when I arrived a few minutes ago."

"No paint or brushes or anything left behind?"

I shook my head again. "Not that I've found, but I haven't specifically looked around."

He nodded and turned to the police officer to ask him to do so. "Anything else you can tell me about this?"

Images flashed through my head. Isla Knight's grainy mug shot, Viviana desperately trying to plead her innocence, Connor showing up drunk at Martin's murder scene, Lorelai's hairbrush that could hold all the answers of my past.

"This proves someone else is desperate for the inheritance. You can't possibly still think I was the one to murder Lorelai after seeing this."

"Nothing has been determined," he said with a straight face, disguising any emotion he might have. He turned to his wife. "Do you feel safe staying here for the rest of the day, sweetie? I'm sure Scarlett would understand if you went home." His tone made it clear I had no say in the matter.

"It'll be fine, with you looking out for us," Evelyn said. "Besides, I don't want Scarlett to stay by herself."

"I'll make sure a patrol car drives by at least every hour, then. Just in case."

"Thanks, honey." Evelyn gave her husband a great big smile. He was clearly her personal hero.

I felt awkward interrupting them, but there was something I needed to know. "When can we wash off the paint?" A few cars had already gathered in the parking lot; I needed as few customers as possible to witness this.

"It won't be too long," Detective Maxwell said. "We have good photos of it."

I headed back inside Palm and Page to wait while the police finished up their work. I couldn't bear to see the customers' faces when they showed up and saw the message. I knew it'd be a mixture of horror and intrigue, and I didn't need either right now.

I went to the back and started up the desktop computer to go over my emails as a distraction.

A piece of paper that looked to have been torn from a small notebook had been left on the floor beside the desk. I recognized Evelyn's handwriting; she must have dropped it when she'd made the *Sorry. Closed* sign. I reached down to pick it up and blinked in surprise at what was written on it. *Connor Walker. Surf Side Inn. Room 211.* I remembered back to the night Martin had been murdered and Connor saying he was staying at this Surf Side Inn, but how did Evelyn know that? He'd left before she'd arrived. And more importantly, why did she care?

I wanted to ask her about it but not while Detective Maxwell was still here. It would probably not go over well with him if I was interrogating his wife. I stuffed the paper in my pocket to deal with later.

Another application had come in that morning, so now I had four to read. I briefly glanced at them, and they all sounded like strong candidates. Each was a college student looking for a summer job, which was exactly what I'd been wanting. One was even a literature major. That sounded promising.

By the time I'd looked at all four, a fifth application had come in. My heart gave a little joyful leap at how successful the employee search was going. I'd had no idea if anyone would want to work here after hearing the rumors about it being the Murderous Bookshop, but that didn't seem to be the case. I opened up the fifth application to read, and—

"Ugh! Criminology major! Seriously, buddy?" Was it a coincidence, or was he hoping to get some on-the-job experience working someplace that'd been a supposed crime scene?

My eyes narrowed when I came to the section on his reasons for wanting to work at Palm Trees and Page Turners. Yep, it sounded like he wanted to tell his fellow classmates he'd had a summer job at a Murderous Bookshop. No thank you.

But I still had four solid applicants, and the job had been posted for only about forty-eight hours, so there was hope.

"Scarlett? Are you back here?" It was Evelyn.

"Yes. I'm on the computer."

Evelyn came over. "The police are gone now. Steve says we can start washing the window whenever we're ready."

I stood from the desk. "Oh, I'm definitely ready now." But then I remembered the note I'd found. Better get this over with. I slowly drew it out of my pocket. "Actually, I was wondering if we'd be able to talk about this first."

"What is it?" Evelyn reached out to grab the crumpled piece of paper.

"It's a note with Connor's motel room number on it. I found it on the floor and figured it was yours, since it's not mine and, you know, no one else goes back here."

Evelyn's face turned red as she unrumpled the paper. "Yes, this is mine," she said quietly.

"Why do you have this? You barely even know Connor." Had Evelyn and Connor been teaming up this entire time?

"It's difficult for me to admit . . . ," Evelyn started.

It had been her! Evelyn was about to confess to me she was a murderer. I stood perfectly still, not knowing what to do, but my mind was running a mile a minute. What did one do when someone confessed to murder? Should I call the police? But her husband was the police. What if Detective Maxwell was in on it as well?

My mind was screaming, panicking. I was dead. She was going to get me before I even had the chance to make a decision. I was sure of it.

"But I've been doing my own investigation," Evelyn finished.

"Nooo, please don't kill me too—wait, what?" I could not have heard that correctly.

Evelyn's eyes grew wide. "What do you mean, kill you? And kill you *too*?" She started to cry. "I haven't killed anyone. How could you think that of me?"

"I . . . uh." I scratched my head. "You mean you weren't the one to kill Lorelai?"

This made Evelyn cry even harder. "No. I didn't kill her."

At that moment, I knew in my very soul she told the truth. "All right, it's okay. I believe you. How about we start at the beginning? What do you mean, you've been investigating?"

Evelyn sniffled and reached for a tissue from the box on the desk. "I'm so worried about Steve's job. He needs to solve this and soon, or else he might be transferred again. I thought maybe if I did my own investigating on the side, I could help him out."

Everything started to make sense now. "So that's why you were out late the night Martin was murdered. You hadn't been at the movies. You were looking around for clues."

She nodded. "And I certainly didn't murder Martin either, if that's what you were thinking."

I shook my head. "I wasn't. I promise. But what about all the comments about taking over the store?"

Evelyn stopped wiping away her tears. "What comments?"

"You keep saying if anything were to happen to me, you would look after the store. It sounds like you want to take over."

"I—no. I don't want to take over. I want to help out. I'm sorry if it comes across as anything more than that. I know you're under a lot of stress, and I want to help out as much as possible."

My face heated. Her reasoning was so innocent, and I'd let my imagination run wild. I completely blamed Connor for all this. "I'm the one who's sorry, Evelyn. I can't believe I thought that of you. It didn't even make any sense. Connor said you were asking him weird questions, and then he got all in my head."

"Well, sometimes my children call me a Smother Mother and say I put my nose where it doesn't belong. I miss them so much now that they've moved out of the house, and I may have projected that on you. I know I can step on too many toes."

I shook my head. "No. I want to hear your opinions, and I want you to take on as much responsibility as you want. From now on, there will always be an open door between us."

Evelyn nodded and smiled. "Yes, of course."

"So, tell me, have you been able to find anything while you've been out searching?"

"You've been investigating too, haven't you?" She didn't say this in an accusatory manner but out of curiosity.

"I have. Can you blame me, though? The police thought I'd murdered Lorelai, so I needed to do something to clear my name before they tossed me in jail for good."

"I'm sorry Steve scared you like that. He does like you. He just needs to do his job."

"Yeah. It still sucks, though."

Evelyn reached over and squeezed my arm. "How about we team up and finish this? I'm sure between the two of us, we can figure this all out soon."

"The police aren't close yet?"

"Not that I know of, but Steve keeps most of his work stuff to himself. I do have one major clue I haven't told him about yet. I wanted to see if something would come out of it first."

I nodded. "Okay, what is it?"

She held up the piece of paper. "I think it might have been Connor who killed Lorelai. See, he didn't arrive in Oceanside that day he came in here. He arrived a few days prior, the day before Lorelai was killed, actually."

"Really?" This wasn't looking good for Connor. "How did you find out?"

"I went down to the station on Thursday to meet Steve on his lunch break, and I saw Connor there talking to a police officer. It looked casual, not like he was a suspected criminal or anything."

I nodded. "I know Connor has a friend on the force. Maybe that was him."

"Probably. Anyway, I overheard them talking about where they wanted to go for lunch, and the cop suggested the Sunshine Café, and Connor said, 'Oh, that was the place we went the other weekend, right?'"

"And Connor told me he wasn't around that weekend because he'd gotten into town the day he came into Palm and Page." I picked up what Evelyn was getting at.

"Exactly. Then Connor said something about needing to swing by the Surf Side Inn first, so afterward I called the motel and pretended to be Connor's mother"—she looked mildly disgusted at admitting she was old enough to be so—"and asked when he'd checked in, which was the day before Lorelai was murdered."

I nodded, feeling a bit of relief that we were close to finishing this crazy investigation but also a little sick that it'd been Connor, a guy I'd once planned on sharing the rest of my life with. "I'd suspected it was him as well, because he was so motivated by my inheritance, but I wasn't sure what to think, since he hadn't been in Oceanside when the murder happened. Now we know he was."

Evelyn nodded grimly. "I'm sorry, Scarlett. I know he was special to you once."

I scoffed. "Yeah, once. But I've moved on. Do you have a plan on what to do next?"

"No, sorry. Maybe we can brainstorm something together."

"All right. Let's get that window cleaned up first so we can open. I'll think about what to do next while we work."

All we had to work with at Palm and Page was a mop bucket, but it'd have to do. I filled it with warm, soapy water and grabbed two cleaning rags before heading outside. As I'd predicted, some people did have the nerve to take photos of the red letters.

"Pardon me, please." I made my way through the small crowd. "The bookshop is closed until further notice, so we'd appreciate it if everyone went home for now."

No one argued, but no one left either. The crowd formed a semi-circle around the front window to watch us work.

Ugh, this was so embarrassing.

"Ignore them," Evelyn whispered. "They're bored tourists who need a little excitement. They'll forget about it by this afternoon."

"Yeah, but their pictures won't forget," I said as another flash went off. "Seriously? It's broad daylight. Why do they even think they need a flash?"

Evelyn chuckled. We finished cleaning the window as quickly as possible, though it was difficult, as the paint had already baked on in some spots from the late-morning sun shining directly on it. I'd have to find something with an edge to scrape the rest off later, but at least enough was gone that it was now impossible to tell what had been written. It was only a bunch of random red squiggles.

"All right. This is good enough for now," I said as we stepped back to check our work. "Time to open the store." My usual love for my job had been completely zapped. I was sweaty and gross from cleaning the window in the hot sun and depressed that my bookshop couldn't seem to attract any actual interest lately. Just those wanting to check out a supposed crime scene.

The day dragged on. After the store opened, only two people from the crowd bothered to come inside. And they bought one sci-fi paperback between the two of them. But with business being slow, Evelyn and I were able to bounce ideas off each other on what to do about Connor, though we weren't able to come up with a solid plan, aside from wanting to figure out a way to snoop in his motel room.

"I'll talk to Lucia and see if she has any ideas, and maybe my sister as well," I said.

"Is your sister also a lawyer?"

I laughed. "Nope. An architect. She's just strangely good at coming up with ideas on how to go about investigating a murder."

Chapter
Twenty-Nine

I hadn't been able to chat with either Lucia or Olivia yesterday evening. Lucia had gone out for drinks with her office friends to celebrate another win in the courtroom, and Olivia hadn't answered any of my messages. Probably deep in Olivia-on-a-deadline land. It was as if she didn't even need air when she was that focused, much less a break for food and rest.

Sunday was as busy as predicted for it being a long weekend, though nothing out of the ordinary happened. No threatening notes, and—a huge bonus—our sales started to pick up. I hoped the Murderous Bookshop rumor would be a thing of the past and tourists were once again comfortable shopping here.

"So, do you want to check out the Surf Side Inn tonight?" I asked Evelyn between helping customers.

"Did you figure out a plan?"

I shook my head. "I have no idea how to check out Connor's room, but I thought at the very least we could ask the staff if they've noticed anything weird about him."

"Good idea," Evelyn said. "I'm up for it."

"Great." We made plans to head over to the Surf Side Inn together after work, hoping Connor would be out to dinner then.

The motel was a few miles up the coast in an area with beachy-themed fast-food restaurants and an actual surf shop right beside the Surf Side Inn. When we first met, Connor had totally been the type to spend his vacation or free time surfing. Now he seemed so business focused. I was surprised he'd chosen the Surf Side Inn to stay at and not a more upscale hotel closer to downtown. The cracked pink stucco and mint-green railings around the building definitely gave the place a dated look—a far cry from the elegance of the Five Palms Resort. Maybe he really was desperate for cash.

"Which room number is he in again?" I pulled into the parking lot and parked behind a large red pickup truck, hoping it would hide us from view in case Connor was still around.

Evelyn pulled the piece of notebook paper I'd found yesterday out of her purse. "Two-eleven."

Twilight was setting in, and I squinted at the room numbers on the second floor, trying to find which direction 211 might be.

"There." I pointed to the last room on the left, the one beside a vending machine. "The lights are off, so I doubt he's in."

Evelyn unbuckled her seat belt. "All right. Let's go."

My pulse picked up as we headed toward the small check-in lobby. Hopefully, this would go well.

Inside, I rang the silver call bell, and a moment later a young woman stepped out from the back and nodded at us in acknowledgment.

"Are you here to check in?" she asked.

I shook my head, wishing Evelyn and I had come up with some sort of cover story that afternoon during work, but there hadn't been time with the busy crowd. "I'm here to see my friend, Connor Walker. He's staying in room two-eleven, but he doesn't seem to be answering his cell phone. Do you mind calling his room?"

"Sure."

I tried to keep my cool as I waited for the front-desk clerk to call Connor's room. The gentle nudge from Evelyn to stop my foot tapping told me I wasn't being successful. Maybe I wasn't as good of an actor as I liked to think I was, but I was getting more and more nervous the longer we were here. What if Connor walked in right now? I quietly let out a breath and looked up to meet the clerk's hazel eyes as she hung up the phone.

"Sorry, there was no answer in Mr. Walker's room."

"Do you happen to know where he went?"

"No, I have no idea." The clerk sounded a little annoyed now. Obviously, it wasn't her job to know exactly where all the guests were at every moment. I needed to switch tactics.

"Connor has something of mine, something important. Would you be able to let us into his room for a moment so I can quickly get it?" I opened my eyes as wide as possible, going for an innocent expression. "We'll be fast. I promise."

The front-desk clerk gave me a *You've got to be kidding me* look. "No, miss. That's against our policy. Only the occupant with a form of ID is allowed in their room."

"Yes, we understand. Sorry about that." Evelyn flashed me a warning smile.

I knew what she meant. Abort! Abort!

The clerk made an annoyed *hum* sound and then asked, "Would you like to leave a message for Mr. Walker?"

"Oh, no," I said, way too loudly. "I mean, I'll send another text. Thank you."

Before the clerk became any more suspicious of us than she already was, I hurried out of the lobby with Evelyn quick on my heels.

"Well, that was a disaster," Evelyn said.

"Argh!" I slapped a palm to my forehead. "I totally froze up in there and had no idea what to ask."

Evelyn chuckled. "I could tell."

"There's no way we can try to sneak into his room now without raising any more alarms. She's already onto us."

"We could look around the outside of his room. Maybe he dropped something outside the door."

"It couldn't hurt, I guess. As long as we're quick."

I followed Evelyn up the stairs to the second floor. It was completely dark by now, and I felt very stealthy sneaking around in the shadows. Very *Mission: Impossible*, as Lucia would say. We walked the route we figured Connor would have taken from his room to the stairs, but there was nothing on the ground.

"The curtains are open slightly." I peered in through the window but didn't see much in the dark room. An outline of the unmade bed and the glow from the alarm clock was about it.

"Well, I'm still sure he's the killer. Even without any proof," Evelyn said. "But don't worry. We'll keep looking."

I opened my mouth to agree but quickly closed it when I heard a voice from the parking lot, followed by two car door slams.

"Thanks for helping me with this, Jake. That money is rightfully mine. I deserve it."

"That's Connor." I chanced a quick look over the railing and saw Connor and his buddy Jake chatting in the parking lot directly below. Their conversation floated up to us.

"No problem. I'll do whatever I can," Jake said.

"I need that money, and I'll fight to get it." Connor let out a breath like he was stressed out. "Anyway, thanks again for picking up the tab. I'll need to remember my wallet next time."

Footsteps started heading toward the stairs we'd walked up.

"We gotta get out of here!"

"Hurry. Let's take the elevator down instead." Evelyn led the way toward the elevator, which was four rooms down from Connor's.

We both slammed the button at the same time.

"Hurry, hurry, hurry," I pleaded with the elevator. There was a creaky rumble, and the doors opened. We stumbled into our shelter.

"Do you think he saw us?" Evelyn asked as we slowly descended to the first floor in the old elevator.

"I sure hope not."

When the doors opened, I half expected Connor to be waiting outside with his arms crossed like he'd caught us, but there was no one. Thankfully, the pickup truck hadn't moved, so we were able to slip into my car and drive away without being noticed.

All we'd learned was how desperate Connor was to get a hold of my money.

Chapter Thirty

Monday was busy at Palm Trees and Page Turners, as it was Memorial Day, so Evelyn and I didn't get a chance to talk about our disastrous attempt at sleuthing the evening before. Maybe that was a good thing, since I was still embarrassed about how I'd handled chatting with the front-desk clerk. I'd have to take some improv acting classes or something to work on my thinking-on-my-feet skills. Maybe Evelyn would want to sign up as well. She hadn't been much better.

Though what I actually wished for was that the case would wrap itself up soon before I needed to invest any more time in it.

Around lunchtime, Hiroki came into the bookshop. I was busy helping a customer and gave him a quick wave from across the shop before he went to browse the shelves in the sci-fi section.

When I had a moment, I walked over. "How's it going? It's good to see you."

"Hey, Scarlett. I wanted to stop in and see how you were doing. With Connor still being in town and all." He put the book he'd been looking at back on the shelf and turned fully toward me.

"I haven't seen him since he was drunk outside my house the night Martin was murdered." I crinkled my nose in disgust. *Aside from snooping around his motel in the dark last night, that is.*

226

"Wow, he was drunk?"

I nodded. "I think it was another sad attempt to plead his case for my inheritance."

"Wow," Hiroki said again. "Connor's not who I thought he was. He pulls off the nice-guy act well, but that's not his true nature, apparently."

"Tell me about it." I rolled my eyes. "How did you know he was still in town? Have you seen him around?"

"Yes. He came into the restaurant last night for dinner with a buddy of his. I didn't talk to him, since I was in the kitchen. I thought maybe he'd left by now, but I guess not."

I gave a harsh laugh. "He's like a bad penny." I felt a tap on my shoulder and turned around to find an impatient-looking man holding up three paperbacks.

"I'd like to pay for these." His frown grew deeper. "And I'm in a hurry."

I plastered on my brightest smile. "Sure thing." Apparently, this customer was not on vacation time yet. I noticed Evelyn near a back shelf reaching to grab a book for a woman a few inches shorter than her. "See you later, Hiroki. Thanks for stopping by."

"No problem. Though I'm also here to pick out a few books for myself, so I'll see you at the cash register in a minute."

After I rang Grumpy Guy up, Hiroki was ready with two books he'd found. We weren't able to chat much, as a line started to form again. Evelyn was still helping customer after customer around the store, and it wasn't until almost two thirty that we were able to take our lunch breaks.

* * *

Tuesday was just as busy. The summer crowds were coming in hot now, and I flopped on the couch the moment I got home, too tired to make any decisions about dinner or what to do with my evening.

Lucia was out with her work friends again, so I turned on the TV and found a police procedural show to watch and called it "homework" for the case.

The detective on the show was finishing up explaining how he'd solved the case, an overly dramatic jewel theft, to his partner when our front door flung open, slamming the wall behind it. I turned off the TV, knowing that much force meant Lucia had something big to share.

"Hey, guess what?" Her shoes smacked against the wall as she kicked them off.

"That cute new paralegal asked you out on a date?"

"Ohhh, I wish. That'd be wonderful." Lucia sighed dreamily as she came into the living room. "But no. Not yet. Guess again!"

I sighed and rubbed my forehead. "I have no idea, Lucia. You finally got the recipe for those cookies that were in the break room?"

She snorted. "No. That recipe is going to the grave."

"All right, tell me."

"Your DNA results came back."

I sat up straight on the sectional couch. "That was fast! What does it say?"

"I don't know. They're sealed in an envelope." She pulled a manila envelope out of her bag. "I wanted you to open them."

"Ahh, okay." Mixed emotions coursed through me. "I don't know if I'm ready."

Lucia placed the sealed envelope on the coffee table. "Well, it's here when you're ready." She sat down on the couch across from me. "And so am I."

I stared at it for a solid five minutes, twirling the short ends of my hair as I weighed how I'd react whatever the results were. It wouldn't change anything either way. If Lorelai was my mother, she was gone now, and we'd never have a chance at a relationship.

Murder by the Seashore

If she wasn't, well, then there would still be a large chunk of my mystery unsolved. Why would a complete stranger leave me her inheritance? That made absolutely no sense. The more I thought about it, the more I realized Lorelai had to be my mother. There was no other option.

Having a sure feeling of what to expect gave me the courage to pick up the envelope.

I nodded from across the couch. "Okay. Let's do this. Let's find out who I am." I ripped open the envelope and found a single piece of white paper inside. It contained mostly a bunch of medical jargon I didn't understand as I skimmed over it, but there at the bottom, in bold letters, read:

There is a zero percent chance Scarlett J. Gardner is related to Lorelai A. Knight.

Chapter
Thirty-One

My chest ached. I blinked back tears as the words blurred on the page, unable to breathe. I hadn't realized how much I'd been convinced that Lorelai had been my birth mother.

Lucia scooted closer to me on the couch. "Hey, let me see." She gently took the paper from my shaking hands and hummed as she read the letter, taking in more detail from the top paragraphs than I had. Finally, she looked up and grabbed my hand, squeezing it. "I'm sorry, Scarlett. I don't even know what else to say. I was positive she was your mom."

I nodded, continuing to keep my tears at bay. "It's okay. This is probably for the best. I wouldn't have had a chance to know her anyway, and I didn't want Olivia to be jealous. Don't worry about me. I'll be fine. Honest. I will." I stood from the couch.

"Are you sure? Because you're rambling. You tend to do that when you're upset."

"I'm sure. I think I'm going to go take a quick nap. I'll see you later. I can cook dinner tonight, if you don't mind eating late. What would you like? Maybe some . . ." I trailed off, realizing Lucia had been right and I'd indeed been rambling. Did I really do that when

I was upset? I shook my head as if to clear it. I would psychoanalyze myself later. Nap first.

I crawled into bed and pulled the comforter up to my chin, focusing on my breathing. In for four deep counts, out for six. And repeat. My disoriented thoughts were already starting to calm down.

But now that I wasn't focused on the genetic test results, I realized this meant we still had no idea who she was. And it was even more of a mystery now. Why would she have left me, a complete stranger, her inheritance?

These thoughts kept me from being able to fall asleep, though admittedly, a nap had mostly been an excuse to have time to myself to process what little I knew about the mystery of Lorelai.

Finding Isla Knight might be my only way of getting answers, and I was positive she and Connor were working together somehow. So that meant talking to Connor would be my next priority, considering we had no idea who or where Isla was. Connor would be the easier target, and I could learn what he knew, including where to find Isla.

*   *   *

"I was up half the night trying to figure out what to do, and I think I have a plan," I said to Evelyn the next morning as soon as she got to work.

"What is it?" She clapped her hands together twice. "It's time we finally found some answers."

Beckoning her closer out of my own irrational fear that my plan would somehow be overheard in the empty bookshop, I whispered what I'd come up with.

"That could work," Evelyn said when I was finished, her eyes lighting up with excitement. "But I have one condition."

"What's that?"

"I don't want to contact the police until we know for sure it was Connor who was involved with the murders. If we're wrong—and now don't give me that look; I'm not saying I think we are—*but* if we are, this could reflect badly on Steve. I can't have that."

I gave it some thought before agreeing. Evelyn was right, not just about Detective Maxwell's reputation but about mine. I was sure it wouldn't look good if I cried wolf, since I was still under the police's radar. "All right. I agree. I'm sure I can get Connor to confess, though."

Evelyn smiled at me. "I trust you. When are you going to invite him?"

"Now?" My voice came out with a squeak. Maybe I wasn't as confident as I thought I was. "I'll ask him to come before the store opens."

She took a deep breath. "Sure. But only if you're sure."

I nodded. "Yes." I tried again to sound as confident as possible. "I honestly think it might be now or never. Who knows what Connor will be up to next?"

"I agree."

I pulled out my phone and sent a quick text. There, it was done. Now all we had to do was wait.

And we waited. There was no response by the time we needed to open Palm and Page, so I shrugged at Evelyn and went to unlock the front door. Almost a dozen customers wandered into the shop, and I busied myself helping them find their perfect beach read. Summer was in full swing now, and flip-flops tracked sand across the oak-colored laminate floors. I looked over at Evelyn to see if she'd be able to grab a broom, but she was busy ringing up a customer with a long line behind him.

It was another ten minutes before I was able to break away and grab a broom. I used the opportunity to check my phone in the back. There was still no text from Connor.

Murder by the Seashore

He had to be up to something sinister this morning, I knew it.

The thought was at the back of my mind for the rest of the morning as the traffic in the shop increased. I tried to remind myself this was a good thing after the loss of business over the past two weeks, but I was stressed out trying both to concentrate on my customers and figure out what Connor could possibly be up to.

I hoped with all my heart it wasn't another murder.

Finally, on my lunch break, my phone buzzed with an incoming message.

Scar! So glad u asked me to come over. I've been working on something for u all day! I can be there right now.

Great. I sighed loudly. Now he was able to come. I couldn't have this confrontation when the store was open. **Could you come after closing instead of now?**

Sure! C u tonite ;)

I stared at that ominous winking-face emoji at the end of his message, my heart racing as my thoughts spiraled.

Whatever Connor was up to, it was too late to stop it now.

Chapter Thirty-Two

I counted down the minutes to six o'clock. No lingering customers during the last hour of the workday made me thankful no innocent bystanders would be caught up in this mess but also anxious, since there wasn't anything to distract myself with until Connor got here.

My palms were sweaty as I straightened the random pens around the cash register after we'd closed. One slipped out of my hand, and I groaned as I bent to pick it up.

"Hey, it's going to be fine," Evelyn said. "We've got this."

"You're right. We're just talking." I moved toward the front of the store to peek out the window. "He's here. Game time."

I watched Connor, his arms full of random objects, stroll through the parking lot as Evelyn quickly took her hiding place behind a bookshelf near the back of the store, keeping as quiet as a church mouse.

I greeted Connor at the door with a wide smile, trying to act like I was truly happy to see him. I did a quick look around the bookshop to see if I'd missed any customers still browsing and then locked the door, leaving only myself, Connor, and a hidden Evelyn inside.

"Hey. Thanks for coming."

"I knew you'd change your mind, Scar. It was a mistake for us to break up. I'm so glad you want to get back together." Connor walked over to the counter and dumped everything he carried onto it. There was a large bouquet of flowers, a dripping cup of some sort of drink, and I recognized one of Viviana's signature bracelets with a palm tree charm. Turquoise beads, my favorite color.

"What's all this?"

"It's for you." Connor turned back and gave me a lopsided grin. "I told you I spent the day working on something for you. I planned on showering you with gifts to convince you we should get back together, but then you texted me like you'd read my mind. I'm glad we're on the same page. It saved me a couple of extra stops to find more items."

I blinked at him. "So you didn't get everything you planned on getting?"

"Nope. Figured there was no need now."

Wow, just wow. Connor was something else. *Cheap* would be the politest way to put it.

"But since I already had the flowers, the bracelet, and the iced chai latte, your favorite"—he said this like I should be incredibly impressed and grateful—"I brought them anyway. Again, I'm so excited you want to get back together."

I gave a small laugh. "I honestly thought you'd be more excited to be back in business at Palm and Page." I gave the iced latte a side-glance. The crushed ice had melted and didn't seem very appetizing, having traveled around with Connor all day.

He gave me a sly grin. "Well, there is that added bonus as well. So, when can I start?" He rubbed his hands together. "I can begin today if you'd like. Right now. Help you with the closing tasks."

"Sure, why don't you stay around a bit? I'd like to chat about some things."

Connor nodded enthusiastically. "Okay, yeah. Great. Whatever you need, Scar. I'm all yours."

I turned around to pretend to look at the bookshelves and rolled my eyes. He was suddenly Mr. Nice Guy who'd do anything for me. Yeah, right.

"Do you want to help me with budgeting problems I've been having?" I glanced back at him, trying not to tip him off that this was a setup.

Connor smirked. "You never were that great with money, Scar. Hey, speaking of which, you'll probably also be wanting help when it comes to budgeting that big inheritance you're getting, right?"

Bingo! He'd walked right into my trap. "I don't know yet."

"Any more details on when you'll be receiving it? And how much exactly did it amount to, anyway?"

"Why are you still so interested in my inheritance?"

He shrugged like he was trying, though failing, to appear casual. "Just am. It's not every day my girlfriend is given a large sum of money unexpectedly."

"Ex—er, never mind." I took a deep breath. Okay, this was it. "I'm not entirely sure it was unexpected."

Connor blinked. "What do you mean? You're saying you did know who Lorelai was before she died?"

I shook my head. "No. I didn't. But I think someone else did."

"Who?"

"You, Connor."

A look of complete shock and then confusion mixed with outrage flashed across his face. "I have no idea what you're talking about, but I don't like where this is heading."

"Are you saying you didn't kill Lorelai so I'd receive her inheritance and you could mooch off me for money?"

"No. Of course not, Scar. How could you think I'd be capable of killing someone?" Connor's voice rose, his anger now outweighing his confusion.

"I overheard you talking about how desperate you are for the money. How you've somehow roped your buddy Jake into helping you get it. Did Jake help you murder Lorelai? Is he a dirty cop?"

"Have you lost it, Scar? What are you talking about? When did you overhear this?"

"I was at the Surf Side Inn that night you were talking to him."

"What—why?" Connor threw his hands up. "Whatever. I wasn't talking about your money. I was talking about money I'd invested in the start-up that I lost. I want it back. Jake's not dirty. He's helping me find a legal loophole."

"Okay, well, I know you actually arrived in Oceanside the weekend before you said you got here. And so you *were* around when Lorelai was killed. You lied to me, so you could be lying about all sorts of things."

His eyes flashed. "You've been following me around and investigating me? You had no right to do so, Scarlett."

"You had no right to kill an innocent person, Connor. How did you even find out about her? Are you working with Isla Knight?"

He flinched back and gave me a blank look. "Who?"

"Isla Knight," I repeated slowly. I vaguely heard the sound of knocking on the door but ignored it. Whoever it was could read we were closed. I was so close to getting a confession out of Connor; I couldn't back down now. "I know she's in on this too."

"I've never heard of her. I have no idea what you're talking about."

"I think you do. Just admit it, and this will all go a lot easier. You teamed up with Isla to murder Lorelai and probably Martin Russell as well. I just don't understand how you know her."

The sound of the knocking turned into pounding. The annoying desperation of the customer was getting on my nerves, distracting me from my big moment.

"Just hold on a sec."

"But I don't even know who this Isla is."

"Hold on!"

I was surprised to find Autumn banging on the door. Something about her intense expression made me think she wasn't here about the job application. Unlocking it, I poked my head outside. "What's wrong? What are you doing here?"

"I don't know who this Isla Knight is!" Connor yelled again.

Argh. He made everything about him. So infuriating. I ignored him.

"I was hoping you'd be alone," Autumn said. "I came after closing so I could deal with you without interference. Why are you talking about Isla Knight?"

The edge in Autumn's voice made my blood freeze. Her face was crumpled in a scowl, an oddly familiar one I'd seen before. Faces from the last two weeks flashed through my mind. It took me a second to place where I'd seen that same scowl before, as a photo I'd glanced at a few days ago merged with the face in front of me now.

Before I had the chance to say anything, Autumn shoved her way inside, grabbed a large book off a nearby shelf, and slammed it down on Connor's head. With a groan, he slumped to the floor.

Chapter
Thirty-Three

A utumn stood behind Connor, panting, the large hardcover book still in her hands. She stared at Connor on the ground for a moment before slowly looking up, glaring at me with intense hatred in her blue eyes.

"What did you do?" I started to crouch next to Connor to check if he was breathing.

"Stay away from him!"

I straightened. "You." I held her gaze, though my voice shook with a mix of fear and anger. "You're Isla Knight. You killed Lorelai."

Isla Knight and Autumn, whom I'd thought of as one of my nicest customers, were one and the same.

Autumn was Isla. Isla was Autumn.

Autumn smirked. "Don't tell me you miss our precious aunt. You never even met her. I was the one who had to endure all those family dinners with her over the years. The ones where she did nothing but complain about how she'd no idea where you were, and yet you were the one who ended up being rewarded. Everyone was sick of hearing her complain. I was just the only one with the guts to do something about it."

"Aunt?" I tried to sort through everything Autumn, or I guess Isla, said. "But the DNA test said we weren't related."

Isla raised her eyebrows at me. "Why are you surprised? Don't tell me you never figured it out. Who did you think Lorelai was? Your birth mother?"

My face fell, and Isla started laughing. "That is what you thought. Oh, you poor dear. You have it all mixed up, don't you?"

"I guess so." I crossed my arms, still looking down. I could see Connor's chest rise and fall slightly, bringing me a small sense of relief. "You mean she was my aunt through marriage, then? Not blood related?"

Isla sighed and started tapping the book in her hand. "Your mother, my mother, and Lorelai's husband were all siblings. After your mother and our dear old uncle died and Lorelai found out she could never have children of her own, she became obsessed with finding you. Desperate for you to be a part of our family again."

"My mother is dead?" A pang of sadness washed over me. "Do you know who my father is?"

Isla shrugged like it didn't matter. "Never knew either of them. Your mother died right after you were born, and she never mentioned who your father was to my mom or Lorelai."

My soul was crushed. I almost didn't want to know, but yet— "How did she die?"

"Sickness? Broken heart? I don't know. I'm not here to give you your family history lesson, Cousin Scarlett." She let out an exaggerated sigh. "I'm here for my inheritance. That money shouldn't even have been Lorelai's to begin with. She wasn't a descendant of my grandparents, just their daughter-in-law. But they worshipped her. Thought she was the most wonderful person. None of them liked me very much."

"I'm assuming your criminal record had something to do with that."

She gave a bitter laugh. "Apparently, being thrown in juvie when you're sixteen gets you written out of the family will, and being arrested for shoplifting and stolen credit cards at twenty doesn't get you a second chance. I could never live up to their high-and-mighty standards. But you, you were like a blank slate to Lorelai. Both the niece and daughter she'd never had. Oh, but that money definitely doesn't belong to you. You didn't know you were a Knight until now."

"You're right. I didn't know I was a Knight." I tried to keep my cool, hoping Isla would do the same. "Do you know how Lorelai found me in Oceanside?"

"Obviously—through that little ancestry registry you did. She tried reaching out initially, but I guess you weren't too interested in connecting with her, since you never responded. Another reason you don't deserve the money." Isla punctuated each word with a tap of the book. "And then it was easy to track you from there. Your name and photo are on your bookstore's website. Lorelai couldn't stop talking about how much you look like your mother." She rolled her eyes.

"I'm assuming you weren't actually interested in working here, then."

Isla laughed. "I was, if only to get closer to you for an opportunity like this. And I'm definitely not going to school or anything in the fall. Once I've finally gotten a hold of my fortune, I'll never have to work again." She tossed the book aside with a thud and dug into her purse. "Anyway, enough talking." She pulled out a gun.

Well, this had escalated.

I screamed and stumbled backward, bumping my back into the counter. I snuck a quick glance behind me and saw Evelyn still hiding in the shadows behind the bookshelves. I could see the light from her phone recording Isla's confession. "The police are already on their way, Isla, and anyone could walk by. They'll hear the gun go off, and you'll be the only one here. You'll be caught in the act."

Isla let out a dark laugh. She took a step over Connor's still unconscious body. "You think I'm that stupid? I'm going to set this whole thing up to look like an accident. Now, go stand by that bookshelf." She pointed to the one Evelyn happened to be hiding behind.

"No." I shook my head furiously, figuring out her plan and deciding to call her on her bluff. "If you're trying to set this up to look like an accident, then you won't shoot me."

The safety clicked.

I gulped.

Isla raised an eyebrow. "I will if it's in self-defense. And you won't be around to share your side of the story."

Evelyn sprang out from her hiding spot and waved her phone around. "Yes, she will. I got everything you said on record. And I texted my husband, a police detective," she added smugly, "to hurry his butt down here."

Isla's face turned bright red with anger. "Anyone else hiding?" She dramatically glanced around. "No? I'll kill you as well before the police get here, then. That doesn't change my plan." She started waving the gun wildly around in the air. "Both of you, now, stand by the bookshelf."

We listened, though I walked as slowly as I could, buying the police as much time as possible. Isla quickly locked the door of the bookshop. Once we'd reached the bookshelf, Isla pointed her gun directly at Evelyn.

The thought of losing Evelyn after all we'd been through was more pain than I could bear. With a cry of desperation, I launched myself at Isla and tried to knock the gun out of her hand. Isla had been caught off guard only for a second and was quick to defend herself. After a few moments of struggle, she grabbed me from behind, and I was surprised at how strong she was. I rocked side to side, trying to break out of her grasp, but her arms wouldn't budge.

"Lean forward!"

"What?" My head snapped up at Evelyn.

"Lean forward to shift your weight, and then throw your elbows into her." She demonstrated.

Isla started to tense up behind me, as if preparing for my upcoming attack. I acted quickly, following Evelyn's instructions, and Isla slammed back into the cash register counter, the gun flying out of her hand.

I winced, waiting for it to randomly go off like in the movies, but all was silent.

All except Evelyn storming forward to join the fight. Between the two of us, we were able to get a tight hold on Isla, and with a free hand, I picked up the gun, holding it tight.

"That's enough!" I tried to yell, but my voice was dry, and my words came out as a croak. I tried again. "It's over, Isla."

Evelyn now had Isla's arms pinned behind her back, and I kept the gun aimed at her with both hands.

"Whoa." I stared at my sweet, middle-aged employee. "Where did you learn all these self-defense moves?"

Isla was crying now as she squirmed and tried to break free of Evelyn's strong hold.

"Steve taught me some things when he was in the police academy. He said he could learn better by teaching it to someone else." She grinned. "And I enjoyed learning."

"That's amaz—"

I was interrupted by the earsplitting sound of glass shattering. Detective Maxwell plus six police officers stormed into Palm Trees and Page Turners through the broken front window, all shouting with their guns drawn.

Chapter
Thirty-Four

Detective Maxwell rushed over to Evelyn and Isla, snatching a pair of handcuffs off his belt as he reached the counter. I slumped against a nearby bookshelf for support as I watched the detective slap the cuffs on Isla's wrists and ask his wife if she was okay. Evelyn nodded enthusiastically, looking to be on an adrenaline high.

"Sir?" An officer interrupted Detective Maxwell and Evelyn. "There's an unconscious man over here."

Connor! I'd completely forgotten about him. He was still lying on the ground, now with another police officer kneeling next to him. I was thankful to see he was still breathing.

"His pulse is strong, and he's not bleeding from the wound on the back of his head. I think he'll be okay." The officer gave his quick assessment. "Probably will have a major headache when he wakes up, and he should be checked out by a doctor just to make sure."

Connor let out a loud groan and blinked his eyes open. He flinched at having a couple of police officers staring down at him and struggled to sit up. "What—what happened? Where am I?" His gaze searched the bookshop and came to a rest on me. "Scar! What's going on?"

The police officers and Detective Maxwell all looked at me expectantly, and I took that as my cue to start explaining what had taken place over the last half hour or so. "You were knocked out, Connor."

He tenderly touched the back of his head and let out another groan when his fingers came in contact with the sore spot. "With what? A mallet?"

"No, a book."

Connor blushed. "Oh."

I took pity on him and said, "It was a really big, thick book, though," to make it seem less pathetic and gave a small smile of encouragement.

"What all happened here, Scarlett?" Detective Maxwell interrupted our civil moment.

My eyes followed Isla as she was led outside the bookshop and toward a waiting police car pulled right up to the door, red and blue lights flashing. "That's Isla Knight, a niece of Lorelai. She's the one who murdered her."

Detective Maxwell narrowed his eyes. "Are you sure?"

"Yes." I nodded eagerly. "And we have her confession recorded."

Evelyn waved her cell phone. "That nasty girl admitted to everything. And she's the one who hit Connor on the back of the head. We got it all, honey."

Instead of looking pleased like I'd been expecting, Detective Maxwell looked furious. "You did what? Miss Gardner, what did you get my wife involved in? You're very lucky Connor was the one to get hit on the head and knocked unconscious and not Evelyn."

"Hey!" Connor rubbed the back of his head. "It wasn't lucky for me."

"I was getting desperate, Detective. I needed to clear my own name out of fear of being tossed in jail again—"

"It was a holding cell!" the detective said through clenched teeth.

"And I knew I needed to act fast to get a confession. There was no time to get the police involved." I kept Evelyn's concern about her husband finding out and us being wrong to myself. Along with the fact that we'd been totally off about who the murderer was and that it was just our luck Isla had walked in during our attempt at getting a confession out of Connor.

"That still doesn't give you license to do what you did." Detective Maxwell practically had steam coming out of his ears. "I should arrest you."

"That won't be necessary," said a breathless voice from behind me. Lucia patted me on the arm like she was tagging in and said quietly to me, "I came after work to see if you wanted to hang out at the beach again this evening. Only to find your parking lot full of police cars!" Her eyes went wide before looking back over to Detective Maxwell. "My client was well within her rights to—"

"Actually, Lucia, I've got this." I smiled at her as a surge of confidence washed over me. Lucia was my best friend, but I didn't need her to fight my battles anymore. It was time I started standing up for myself. "Detective Maxwell, I'm not going to feel sorry for what I did. I cleared my name as a murder suspect, and I got a murderer off the streets. Yes, Connor did get hurt"—I turned to him—"and I'm sorry about that."

Connor shrugged. "Will you make it up to me by sharing your inheritance?"

"No," I said, before continuing what I needed to say to the detective. "But it all worked out in the end. I'm very proud of Evelyn and myself, and I think you should be as well."

Detective Maxwell didn't look convinced or like he agreed with my statement, but he did appear to be calmer.

Evelyn stepped over to him. "Steve, you can take all the credit for this arrest. Think of how it will help your career."

I knew that was all Evelyn had really wanted, and though I didn't know the logistics of Detective Maxwell being able to take the credit, I knew Evelyn was proud of us as well.

Detective Maxwell looked like he was trying to stay cool for his wife's sake and then waved another officer over. "Simmons, take Miss Gardner's statement." He walked away to talk privately with Evelyn.

"I'm impressed, Scar," Lucia said before the officer came over to start asking me questions. "You were awesome. You're sure you're all right, though?"

"Yes, yes. I'm fine. I'll fill you in on all the details later."

"Well, I'll still stick around. Just in case you need me." She stared down the approaching officer as she said this last part.

I smiled to myself. I could start standing up for myself, but I doubted Lucia would ever not be protective of those she cared for. It was part of what made her a good lawyer.

Chapter
Thirty-Five

"Cheers!" Cups clinked around the table at Miku Miso: Sushi and Grill before we each took a celebratory sip of the restaurant's finest sake, compliments of Hiroki.

"Man, I wished I'd been there to see it all go down." Hiroki poured himself more of the sake. "I'm going to need to hear that story again."

I laughed. Evelyn and I had finished telling our tale to Hiroki, Jules, and Lucia. I'd suggested a celebration dinner that night to go over everything, and we'd invited Evelyn and Jules along. We'd invited Detective Maxwell as well, but Evelyn said he was still swamped in paperwork at the police station. I hoped it wasn't an excuse and that he wasn't avoiding me. I might no longer be a murder suspect, but I knew I still wasn't the detective's favorite person in Oceanside after what Evelyn had gone through. He blamed me entirely for her involvement.

Hiroki had been finishing a shift when we arrived, but after seating us, he pulled up a chair to join the group.

"I'm still trying to wrap my head around everything that happened. I can't believe I'd been so convinced Connor was a murderer."

I shook my head and grabbed another California sushi roll from the center platter to put on my own plate. "I know he's a little nutty, but it was ridiculous to go that far."

Lucia let out a snort like she disagreed but kept quiet otherwise.

"It wasn't only you who thought that," Evelyn said. "I was convinced as well."

"Yeah, so how did you get involved in all this?" Jules asked Evelyn. "I want to know everything!"

Evelyn hesitated for a moment, and I had a feeling it was because she didn't want to reveal her true reasons for investigating, since it involved the private matter of her husband's career. "I needed to see justice brought to our community. And I knew there was no chance our sweet Scarlett would ever murder someone." She leaned over and patted my arm.

Everyone made small murmurs of agreement, and I smiled sheepishly, embarrassed by the memory of how I'd once thought her capable of murder.

"You just didn't want to lose your job if the store went out of business due to the owner being in jail."

Evelyn laughed. "Well, that was an added benefit. I started looking around for answers, and then when Scarlett and I both discovered we were doing the same thing, we teamed up."

"So, that Autumn girl you were with at the Sunshine Café the other day is this crazy murderer person?" Jules asked.

"Yep," I said. "Real name is Isla Knight, and she's Lorelai's niece. She met up with Lorelai on the pier, poisoned her water bottle, and pushed her into the ocean." Evelyn had filled me in on Isla's confession and the rest of the details of the case, which she'd heard from Detective Maxwell.

"That's some messed-up family vibes," Lucia said.

"Turns out she was the black sheep of the family and was cut off from the inheritance after being arrested the first time. Lorelai was in control of the family fortune after her in-laws passed away. She put a clause in the will that no one with a criminal record could inherit the money. That was part of the reason Isla was trying to frame me for murder by putting the poison bottle near Palm and Page."

"No other family members were after the money?" Lucia asked.

"Everyone else was apparently apathetic about it. They had their own money and had gone their separate ways from Lorelai years ago. Her obsession with finding me had divided them. Isla was the only one who felt entitled to Lorelai's inheritance."

"And Lorelai was your aunt as well?" Hiroki asked, his expression gentle, as if he was unsure about asking about a potentially sensitive subject.

I smiled at him. "Seems that way. Sounds like Lorelai was my mother's and Isla's mother's sister-in-law, and my mother passed away a long time ago. My father was never around. I was adopted right after instead of staying with the Knight family. I'm not exactly sure why, but Lorelai had been looking for me ever since to connect, and she wanted to leave me part of her inheritance. That piece got larger and larger as Isla was cut off and other family members went their own ways."

"So, what are you going to do with all that money?" Lucia asked.

I shrugged. "I'm thinking of expanding Palm and Page. Maybe even adding a little café with an outdoor eating and reading area."

"That sounds lovely," Evelyn said. "We have such a great view of the ocean; we should be taking advantage of it."

"Agreed." Jules's eyes gleamed. "And if you need someone to help run the café . . ."

"Oh my gosh, yes! Why didn't I think of that sooner? You'd be perfect to run it. They won't miss you at the Sunshine Café?"

"Ha! They don't know what they've got. I'm so underappreciated. Besides, I'd much rather work for you."

"This is going to be awesome." The blueprints for adding a café and the delicious menus I could create with Jules's help were already coming together in my mind.

* * *

My phone happily dinged with an incoming video chat notification.

"Hey, Liv! How's it going?"

"How's it going with me?" My sister gave a mock look of surprise. "Um, no. How's it going with you is more like it. How come I needed to hear from Mom and Dad instead of you that you tossed a murderer in jail?"

"Because I literally got off the phone with them five minutes ago." I'd finally given my parents the full version of events that morning before work, now that Isla had been arrested and I was no longer living in fear of being either murdered or arrested myself. "I was going to tell you too, but I wanted to grab breakfast first." I held up my toasted bagel as proof. "I can't believe you already know."

"Whatever. So, tell me everything."

Since Olivia apparently already knew most of what had happened from my parents, I filled in some details between bites.

"You have one crazy cousin there, sis."

"I know. It makes me so glad I have you and Mom and Dad."

Olivia chuckled. "We're pretty normal. So Lorelai had tried contacting you before all this?"

"Apparently. I had my notifications turned off on that ancestry website. I just got, I don't know, nervous, I guess. I wanted to check any potential messages on my own time but hadn't gotten around to it for a few weeks." I sighed. "I should have left them on."

"Hey, don't beat yourself up. You did what you thought was best."

"There was only one message when I signed in. Lorelai just said she wanted to connect, but she didn't say who exactly she was. I think she pieced together who I was from knowing my first name, my account profile saying I'd moved back to SoCal, and then my name and photo on Palm and Page's website. Apparently, I look a lot like my birth mother."

"Well, now maybe you can connect with other Knight relatives. Just not this Isla."

"She's definitely not invited to any of my family dinners."

"Did she kill Martin as well?"

I nodded. "He figured out what Isla was up to, including that she'd been the one to kill Lorelai, and realized he was in way over his head with her as a client. I think he was on his way to warn me she might try something crazy when she killed him on our front porch. I guess he was an okay guy in the end."

"Yikes."

"Little did he know she'd already done something crazy by pushing me off the pier the night before."

"I'm so glad you're all right. You really do need me as your spirit guide sister with all the trouble you've gotten yourself into."

I held up my hands in defense. "No more trouble. I swear."

* * *

Now that I was an ace detective—okay, maybe I was being a little smug, but I was still so proud of what I'd accomplished; not everyone could say they'd solved two murders—I finally felt like I should have the confidence to successfully run Palm Trees and Page Turners. No more of this psyching myself up to take on each day. I would just do it.

Easier said than done, though.

I unlocked the front door of the bookshop, ready to greet our customers and whatever else the new day had in store for me, but my newfound determination vanished as our first customer walked through the doorway.

"What are you doing here, Connor?" I asked in a low voice, so the other customers coming in wouldn't pick up on my irritable attitude.

"Okay, hear me out one more time, Scar."

I opened my mouth to protest.

"You owe me, you know. For the whole getting my head smashed in at your store. Due to you tricking me to come here, I'll add."

I sighed. He did have a point. "Fine."

"We made a good team. The perfect team for running a bookshop, with your love of reading and my love of business and numbers. You have to admit that, at least." He paused like he was waiting for me to smother him with praise for being right.

Well, I did have to admit Connor was partly right. On paper, we were the perfect team. But as I'd found out the hard way, in practice, we were a disaster.

I crossed my arms and waited for him to continue.

"Um, well, you see." He seemed thrown off by my lack of response. "I think I deserve to be part of the team again. I can bring great things to this place, especially now that you're rich."

"Seriously, Connor? It's always back to the money with you."

"Scar, think about it. You have some serious dough now. I can help you invest it and make more, and help you turn this place around."

That did it. I threw open the front door and held it for Connor to let himself out. "This place doesn't need to be turned around. It's perfect as is, and any plans for expansion won't involve you. Goodbye, Connor, and please do us both a favor and never return. You'll never be part of Palm Trees and Page Turners again."

Evelyn came up behind me. "See ya, Connor," she said loudly and cheerfully before he had time to protest. She then started waving her hands toward him like she was sweeping him out of the store.

Mouth hung open, Connor headed out the doorway, and I yanked the door shut behind him before turning around to high-five Evelyn.

Epilogue

Six months later

"Delivery for Scarlett Gardner!" A man in a courier uniform stood at the front of Palm Trees and Page Turners. A large rectangular box was perched on a dolly beside him.

"Oh, yay! It came." I bounded over and signed the delivery notice. "Do you mind bringing this into the back?"

"No problem."

I led the way, giving Evelyn a thumbs-up as I passed her helping a customer.

Winter had brought a slower pace to my little bookshop, but it worked in my favor, as it allowed time for building the café addition without making me feel too overwhelmed. Only a few weeks until our grand opening, and Jules, Evelyn, and I were planning a big party for it. Plenty of food from the café, and everyone in attendance would receive a Blind Date With a Book.

"Right here." I patted the lunch break table, and the courier lifted the box onto it.

With a quick "See you," he left.

I rubbed my hands together in anticipation before grabbing a nearby box cutter and tearing into the package.

For the last three weeks, Palm and Page had been without the beautifully painted sign out front, replaced with a temporary reader board. The local artist who'd originally created the sign had been updating it to read *Palm Trees and Page Turners Bookshop and Café*.

And it was perfect. I gasped as I pushed the tissue paper away, running my fingers over the carved letters. I couldn't wait to put it back up outside.

My bookshop was already starting to thrive, and I looked forward to seeing where this next adventure would bring me.

Acknowledgments

Thank you to the incredible team at Crooked Lane Books, especially Rebecca Nelson, Madeline Rathle, and my wonderful editor Tara Gavin. Thank you to the cover team for the beautiful and colorful cover; I'm in love with it!

Thank you to my agent, Dawn Dowdle, for believing in me and in this book. I can still hear you saying "I love it!" when I first pitched it, making me so excited to write Scarlett's story.

Thank you to my beta readers: Rose Kerr, J. C. Kenney, Elia Seely, Lisa Bergen, and Caitlin McCaughey. Your feedback meant the world to me, and many thanks for making this book the absolute best it could be. Thank you to the Vernon Critique Group for all your support and encouragement.

Thank you to my friends and family. Thank you to my parents for telling everyone they know about this book. Thank you to my brother and sister-in-law for excitedly being the first to preorder it. Thank you to my in-laws for your enthusiasm for my writing. Thank you to my husband for supporting me every day, and thank you to my son for being the most adorable toddler ever (that has nothing to do with this book; I just wanted to tell the world).